DOLL PARTS

WAYNE SIMMONS

snowbooks

Proudly Published by Snowbooks in 2012

Copyright © 2012 Wayne Simmons

Snowbooks Ltd.
Tel: 0207 837 6482
email: info@snowbooks.com

www.snowbooks.com

British Library Cataloguing in Publication Data

A catalogue record for this book is available from the British Library.

ISBN 978-1-907777-53-0

*'You will with the Banshee chat,
and find her good at heart.'*
WB Yeats

PROLOGUE

The blonde nurse stood in front of Benny, sizing him up.

Benny couldn't move. He was frozen to the spot.

She lunged, locking her jaws around his arm.

Benny cried out. Reached for her hair, ripped his arm free and rammed his right knee into her kisser. He followed through with a boot to the head. Then another. A wretched feeling of guilt accompanied each clash against her teeth.

She pulled away, checked her mouth. Looked up at him, surprised.

Golden locks tumbled across her face.

Blood dripped through her fingers.

Her eyes started changing, and Benny could hear those sounds: the slippery-when-wet flapping, the fleshy squelching. He'd heard *those sounds* before, right before *her kind* had attacked *his kind*. They were the sounds of rage, of raw anger, of skin stretching across skin. Benny had really pissed this bitch off, and now she wanted payback.

She came for him a second time.

Benny was a big lad, had done a bit of boxing in his day. He stood his ground as she lunged, then dipped to his left and caught her with an uppercut on his way back round. He followed through with a classic 1-2-3 combo, getting his range with the jab, then throwing out the straight right, all the while shifting in to land the left hook to the side of Blondie's face.

She stumbled back, dazed.

"Fuck," Benny cried.

Bitch has a gob on her like fucking steel.

Benny worked his knuckles, massaging them, blowing some air on the ragged skin. He might have broken something.

She held back for a while, gathering her senses. Again, the eyes started turning. Louder, faster. The sound drilled into Benny's gut, making him heave.

He needed to get away from there.

What was I thinking, sizing up to one of these things? That wasn't part of the drill!

Five minutes ago, Benny had been standing by the hospital entrance with Frank, looking out, eyes fixed on the parked ambulance across the way. Old Frank held the keys, jingling them nervously in his hand. He looked at Benny and nodded. Sprinted across that tarmac like a man half his age, leaving Benny standing like a lemon before chasing after him

Not that it had done Frank much good.

Benny could see him now, slopped half-in-half-out of the ambulance's back doors, face torn, mouth agape like a wide-open zipper, two of those creatures chewing on his intestines.

He gagged, looked away.

Focus, Benny boy. Focus.

The bitch he'd been hammering was back on her feet.

She looked more pissed than ever. A banshee-like shriek erupted from her mouth, causing Benny to wince. Her lips were still bleeding. She wiped them with her hand, blood spreading across her face like cheap lipstick.

The two who were chewing on Frank's guts looked up. They weren't happy: Benny had disturbed their meal. Their eyes flipped colours, rolling back in their skulls to find a deep, angry red.

Benny swore under his breath.

This is it, lad.

It was then that he heard a voice calling from the hospital.

...

Red stood at the side entrance to Whiteabbey Hospital's main building, holding the door open. He could see Benny standing by the ambulance, three of those things on his case.

What the hell is he doing?

"Benny!" Red cried. "Get your ass back in here!"

Benny didn't argue, leaving the ambulance and sprinting towards the hospital.

The creatures gave chase. They were closing fast. The blonde made a grab for Benny's jacket, catching hold of the hood, dragging him back.

Red swore loudly. Left the doors swinging and pelted across the tarmac.

He grabbed Benny's outstretched arm, desperately tried to pull him free. But the creatures held tight, hissing like hellcats, their eyes spinning even faster.

The blonde suddenly started clawing at the other two, desperate to have Benny all to herself.

"Lose the coat!" Red yelled.

Benny shuffled out of one sleeve, then the other, wincing as the jacket peeled from the fresh wound on his arm, taking some of his skin with it. He cried in pain, cursing like a sailor. But he was free, the three bitches falling in his wake.

"Move it," Red said, lifting Benny by the collar, and pushing him on.

The two men sprinted towards the hospital.

The creatures pulled themselves together, then bolted after them.

Once in, the two survivors fought to seal the doors behind them, struggling as the pursuing creatures heaved against the closing gap.

The blonde nurse managed to squeeze her head through the opening, straining against the door, growling at the two survivors. Red pressed his shoulder against the wood, careful to keep his face away from her snapping teeth.

"Hold her still!" came a cry from nearby.

Looking up, Red found Cecil rolling into position further down the hospital corridor. The older man slammed the brake on his wheelchair, then produced a sawn-off shotgun from under his blanket. Raised the double barrel, pulled back the hammer, veiny hands shaking as he took aim.

"Holy sh– " was all Red could manage before Cecil let rip with the first cartridge, bursting through the blonde head and showering Red and Benny with blood, brain and chipped wall plaster. The wheelchair rocked back with the recoil. It overturned, sending Cecil to the floor.

The pressure against the door weakened.

Red kicked the remains of the creature back outside, then slammed the doors closed.

Benny wedged a brush shaft between the doors' handles, and it held.

The two men fell against a nearby wall in relief.

"Jesus…" breathed Benny.

Red eased a shaking hand through his ginger mop of hair. "Look, I told you what would happen," he scowled. "But you wouldn't fucking listen, would you?"

Benny didn't argue. His eyes remained fixed on the door. "W-what the fuck are they?" he asked.

"How the fuck would I know what they are?" Red fired back. "They make no fucking sense. None at all."

Benny raised his hands, looked at them in turn. "I was punching her, Red. It felt wrong. Like beating on your wife or…" His voice paled, hands clenching into fists. "They got Frank," he said in a small voice, and then he started to weep.

Red dipped his head. He wasn't fond of blubbering, wasn't fond of any expression of emotion. Yet tears had flowed constantly amongst the hospital survivors since that Sunday in June, when most of the world had fallen dead around them. And with this latest turn of events, eyes wouldn't be getting any dryer.

Red looked up, noticed Benny's arm. "You hurt?"

The younger man didn't reply, still upset.

"Here, let me see that." Red unravelled the torn sleeve of Benny's shirt. Gently touched the skin, searching for any breaks.

Benny winced.

Red's brow furrowed in surprise – and surprise wasn't something he thought he could feel anymore. But the doctor in him knew there was something not quite right with Benny's wound. It wasn't just the look of the lacerations - sinewy threads of flesh, severed veins protruding like little dead worms - it was the blood as well: it seemed to congeal when it should be flowing.

"What's wrong with it?" Benny asked, worried by the look on the doctor's face.

"Not a thing, mate," Red said. "You're okay. Nothing to worry about." All lies, of course. Benny's arm looked *fucking weird*. And *fucking weird* in the medical world was rarely good.

Red retrieved a bandage from his lab coat pocket, carefully wrapped the wound. It would need to be cleaned properly, treated to stop infection. He'd get a chance to examine it more closely later, but for now he just wanted to cover it.

A noise came from across the corridor, causing the doctor to jump, his heart so close to his mouth he could almost taste it. His eyes found Cecil's wheelchair. It was still on the floor, one of the wheels spinning. The old man's head poked out from under the chair's tartan blanket.

"One of you ladies wanna help me up?" he complained.

PART ONE
THE BUS

ONE

Barry Rogan was fucked.

Sweat peppered his brow, a raging fever burning through his body. Blood and piss soaked the blue denim of his jeans. His gouged-out eyes were bandaged. He clawed at the dressing with his fingers.

Caz could feel the heat radiating from his face.

They were on a bus: Barry's head lay upon her lap, his lean frame stretched across the disabled seats at the front, near the driver's cabin. He was dreaming, shaking; drool blubbered from his lips as he muttered something that didn't make any sense.

"Shhhh," Caz soothed. "You need to rest."

It was only a few hours ago that those creatures had swarmed their Land Rover, close to Belfast's city centre. They'd pulled Barry through the window, ripped him apart as Caz watched on, too frightened to help.

And now Barry was dying.

In her hand, Caz held a little silver crucifix, gripping it so tightly that it was cutting into her skin. It was a symbol of hope, but inside the teenager felt hopeless. Her heart continued to beat, but the blood ran cold. A single tear rolled down her cheek unchecked.

The bus continued its journey up the M2 Motorway, the noise of its engine coarse and angry. The woman behind the wheel was called Star. Ink covered her skin, the colours providing a stark contrast to the grey mood.

Star flicked the catch on her gas lighter, sparked up a cigarette.

She noticed Caz in the rear-view mirror and said, "Y' alright, doll?"

Caz wiped her face. "It's Barry," she said. "He'll die unless we get him some help. I've done what I can, but there's blood and… God knows what else… seeping through his bandages."

Star dragged on her smoke, glanced in the rear-view again.

Caz could have sworn there was a look of pity in her eyes, were she to believe that any emotion at all stirred beneath the tattooed woman's cold exterior.

"You're right. He don't look too good," she said, then dragged on the cigarette again. "Ain't much more we can do for him, is there?"

"We could take him to a hospital," Caz offered.

Star laughed humourlessly. "You're joking, right?"

"No, I'm not joking. We might find something that can help him. Painkillers, fresh dressing. Anything to give him a fighting chance. He'll die if we just leave him like this."

"We should keep moving," came another voice. It belonged to Professor Herbert Matthews. He sat in a nearby seat, hands gripping the safety bar for dear life. "Those creatures could come back at any moment. The longer we stay on the road, the more dangerous – "

"Listen, Prof," Star interrupted, "Barry's one of us. That outweighs any bullshit you feed us about what we *need* to do."

The old man glared at her with faintly-masked disdain. "We agreed to go directly to the airport. That's what the plan was."

Close to the professor, a few survivors huddled fearfully in their seats. Herb had spotted them on the outskirts of Belfast's city centre, after the first attack of the creatures, and he had insisted that Star pick them up. The old man no doubt reckoned he'd done his bit already; Barry's welfare was irrelevant, given the bigger picture.

Star didn't agree: "Fuck your plan," she sneered.

"We don't have time to stop!" Herb protested, his face purple. It was weird, Caz thought, to see him so agitated. In his dressing gown and pyjamas, he looked like something off children's TV; a doting grandfather; the mad professor in one of those films they'd play on Sundays. Yet, as Caz was beginning to realise, another part of Herb Matthews commanded authority.

She remembered his speech, before they'd left Belfast. Talking about his plan: how a group of survivors from an airport in Manchester had contacted him on his old radio, about their hope for Herb to set up base at Belfast's main airport and establish some sort of communication network with other survivors around the world.

It made sense.

But Star had other ideas.

The tattooist sank her foot on the brake, spinning the steering wheel in a precarious 180 degree turn. The bus swung sideways, the screeching of its wheels echoing out into an otherwise silent dawn.

Several survivors were thrown from their seats. They cowered on the floor, hands wrapped around their heads as the bus continued to slide. Caz held

Barry; Herb gripped the safety rail even tighter, clinging on for dear life.

The bus skidded to a halt. Remained perfectly still on the motorway, the engine dead.

For a moment, no one spoke.

Through the vehicle's windows, miles of tarmac could be seen sprawling back towards the north. The mango light of sunrise spilled across an empty field. Several houses dotted the horizon, the bodies of their residents no doubt still rotting in bed.

Star took a final drag on her cigarette, then threw it to the floor. "Whiteabbey Hospital," she announced. "We passed a sign for it back down the motorway. We'll go there, get Barry what he needs. Any complaints?"

Herb said nothing. One hand grasped his chest. His breathing came heavy and fast. He looked like he was going to puke.

"Good," Star said. She shifted the gear into first, fired up the ignition.

Caz looked down at the wounded Barry, still wrapped in her arms. She pressed an ear to his chest, listened to his breathing. It came in shallow gasps, paling with every second.

His hands reached to his face, tearing more dressing away to scratch at his hollowed-out eyes.

Blood rolled down his cheeks like tears.

TWO

The red–haired girl with the flapping eyes stared at him.

A poorly ironed t-shirt clung to her chest. The words FORGET ME NOT were scrawled across the front of the t-shirt in child's writing. Her skirt swayed gently in the morning breeze.

She smiled at Barry Rogan.

He was terrified of her. Wanted her to go away, to leave him alone.

He clawed at his missing eyes, hoping to erase her image from his mind. His sight was non-existent – Barry knew that. Even in this drugged-up hallucination he found himself in, Barry could still recall what those monsters had done: how they had swarmed him, slicing his genitals with long fingernails, then feasted on his torn flesh. He remembered looking on in horror as blood spat through the decapitated shaft of his penis, before the redhead's fingers had dug into his wide-open eyes and torn them from his head.

Yet, Barry could still see. And not like seeing in your sleep: that green-tinged, old movie effect. No, this was different. Barry was somewhat conscious: he could hear himself crying, could hear Caz talking, trying to soothe him, and he could see.

He could see FORGET ME NOT.

She was smiling. It was a knowing smile, a smile of piety. One of those *I-know-something-that-you-don't-know* smiles. Or even worse, an *I-know-something-that-you-don't-know-but-I'm-not-going-to-fucking-tell-you-what-it-fucking-is* kind of smile.

A blank canvas stretched behind the creature. A wall of air, pure and white.

Barry was floating. Or his seat was floating. Or maybe the whole fucking bus was floating.

He kicked his legs, trying to find some sort of footing. He didn't want to go to hell *just* yet, and that's where he would end up, no matter how far north he floated.

Sure, he *deserved* to go to hell. He deserved torture at the hands of those bitches. He deserved each and every scar that was smarting, every last surge of pain that was screaming from inside of him. Barry deserved all of it and more. He was a fucking disgrace to humanity. No one needed to tell him that.

Christ, what I did to her…

The redhead looked at him, and Barry remembered her face like it was yesterday. Lying on the bed. Doped out and limp. Her FORGET ME NOT t-shirt rolled up, exposing her breasts. Vacant eyes staring at him as he loosened his belt.

Barry had raped her.

He'd raped all three of the girls that had attacked him.

That had happened. That had *actually* happened.

And now he was floating. A blind, cockless man floating in a fucking white mist.

FORGET ME NOT continued to stare at him. Her eyes stopped flapping, turning from red to a serene shade of green. Watching through hollow eye sockets, Barry saw her lips move to speak.

Yet he couldn't make her out.

The only sounds Barry could hear were the muffled noise of the bus engine and Caroline Donaldson's concerned voice. He tried to shush Caz, reached for her mouth, but she grabbed his hands, forced them down. In the state he was in, she was easily stronger than him.

FORGET ME NOT continued to speak, still trying to get his attention. It was the same word she was saying over and over again. He could almost read it from her lips. Something with three syllables. Something important, something that he *knew* was vital to his very survival…

Yet still lost to him.

THREE

Aida Hussein woke to find shards of glass on her lap.

She checked her face, finding blood. As her vision sharpened, she realised that the front of her car had burrowed its way through the window of an electrical shop in Belfast's city centre.

Her head was buzzing, her memory hazy.

She remembered travelling up the M1 motorway from Lisburn to Belfast. She'd been staying at a school for some time, sheltering from whatever it was that caused the world around her to suddenly break down and die. Something terrible had happened at the school … something she couldn't quite remember… and she'd been forced to flee.

There was someone in the car with her. A woman… Kirsty! That was her name, wasn't it?

They had met at the school, Aida remembered that much. *Something* had been wrong with Kirsty; maybe she was hurt or sick or... something. Aida remembered having to take shelter for the night, hiding from some kind of threat. Waiting until dawn before helping Kirsty into one of the cars parked by the school and then setting off.

But Kirsty wasn't in the car with her now. Aida looked to the street but couldn't see her there either.

She remembered crashing. Someone – or something – had stepped onto the road in front of her car, forcing Aida to swerve.

She quickly undid her seatbelt, clambered out of the car.

Glass from the shop window littered the front bonnet. A television and DVD player lay busted on the pavement nearby; iPods from the window display surrounded the vehicle. She'd made quite the mess, yet when Aida checked herself up and down, brushing her body for cuts or breaks, she found little to be concerned about. Apart from the graze on her cheek and a fat lip, she seemed pretty much unharmed.

The buzzing in her head paled, giving way to the sound of the car alarm. The harsh wail of the alarm made her wince. She rubbed at her temples, suddenly remembering more from before, more of what had happened at the school; in her mind, she could picture people screaming, running, dying all around her.

Her heartbeat quickened.

Aida suddenly felt exposed. Vulnerable. The early morning sun leered at her. She hurried up the deserted main street, looked for somewhere to hide, somewhere to gather her thoughts.

She found Tesco's supermarket.

Spat on the front window, then furiously rubbed with the cuffs of her sleeves to remove the dust and grime. Peered through the cleared glass.

The supermarket seemed empty. No sign of anyone or anything.

Aida pushed against the door, wincing as it creaked open.

It was quieter inside. The noise of the car alarm faded as the door closed behind her, giving way to the faint buzz of insect wings.

A smell of decay drifted towards her.

Aida took a few more steps. The sound of her shoes on the floor echoed throughout the store. The light was poor. There were shadows everywhere.

A sudden noise.

"Kirsty?"

A rat scurried out of the shadows, startling Aida. She pressed one hand against her heart.

Looked around, eyes more alert now, adjusting to the shade.

Kirsty was nowhere to be seen.

Neither was the thing from earlier, whatever it was she'd swerved to avoid.

Even the horrific images from the school seemed muted.

As her head cleared, Aida wondered if she'd imagined everything that had happened, if it had been part of some hallucination brought on by exhaustion and stress or that gash on her head.

But then she saw the bodies.

Early-bird shoppers from that fateful Sunday all those weeks ago were strewn throughout the store. Their skin looked raw, the flesh rotting, plagued by flies. A putrid smell wafted up the aisles.

Aida placed a hand over her nose.

She was just about to turn back and leave the supermarket when her eyes fell upon the lines of food and drink. Her survival instinct kicked in; she didn't feel so good now, what with the flies and the smell and the nausea, but she'd need to eat sometime. There were plenty of non-perishable goods around, tinned fruit and meat. She could grab some things here. It would only take a few minutes…

Aida reached instinctively for one of the store's wire shopping baskets. Realising how little use it would be, she replaced it, choosing instead a sports bag from the nearby end display. She pulled the tags off the bag, dropped them to the floor. She'd fill it with enough provisions to last her a couple of days then get moving again, see if she could find Kirsty or someone else who could explain to her exactly what was happening.

She moved deeper into the store.

Found more bodies. Walked past them as if they were mannequins made of plastic, rather than flesh and bone. They couldn't shock her. Aida wished that they could, but they couldn't.

She reached the frozen section at the back of the store. Water pooled around the freezers, their contents soaked through and spoiled beyond use.

Aida moved on.

It felt too quiet all of a sudden.

Supermarkets had been chaotic places, filled with life and noise: children squealing at their parents, young couples laughing and carrying on, the constant hum of freezers and bland piped music. But all these sounds were gone. Only the drunken buzz of bloated flies and the sharp beat of Aida's heel remained.

She kept walking.

Filled her bag with canned goods and bottled water. Added a pack of chocolate bars, some biscuits – anything non-perishable, anything the flies didn't want.

A shadow fell upon her.

Aida gasped, a chilled sweat running down her spine.

But it was nothing.

Trick of the light?

She needed to calm down, relax. Only bodies in here. And they couldn't hurt her.

The deeper she went into the store, the staler the air became. Mouldy bread and rotting meat had been locked in here for weeks, along with the dead. There were more flies. They drifted towards her, suddenly interested. Aida swatted them away, hurried on.

As she turned another corner, Aida felt like she was being watched.

An eerie presence permeated the supermarket.

Maybe she'd been wrong: maybe there *was* something here to be frightened of. The dead didn't bother her anymore, but their spirits were another matter entirely, and it suddenly felt like this place was full of ghosts. Aida could hear them all around her, whispering in the shadows, grieving and angry, looking for answers that she couldn't give.

Grabbing a last tin of fruit, Aida made for the exit.

A sudden scream left her lips.

There was someone in front of her.

Not a body.

Not a ghost.

Someone alive.

A middle-aged man wearing a grey shirt and Homer Simpson tie looked up from his camp bed. His eyes were wide and alert. His clothes were stained, a thick beard framing his long face. A half-drunk bottle of Coke was in his hands. Vodka sat on the floor beside him. Bad vibes radiated off him like heat.

Aida apologised nervously to the man, dropped her sports bag and hurried on past.

The man yelled something. Got up, stumbled after her. Tried to call her again, to tell her something, but everything that came out of his mouth sounded like 'gah' to Aida.

She kept walking. The sound of her heels was faster now, echoing throughout the store. She heard shuffling noises behind her, to her left and her right. Rambling speech seemed to surround her.

GahGahGahGah

Homer-Tie was still in pursuit.

Aida turned another corner.

She didn't run, somehow thinking that running might cause the strange (and clearly insane) man to lunge for her. She didn't look behind or to the side, wishing she could close her eyes until she was outside again. But still the noises continued, seeming to swell, the man's footsteps apparently everywhere.

For an awful instant, Aida thought that there could be a whole pack of men in the store,

GAHGAHGAHGAH

everyone of them wide-eyed and panicked. All with unkempt beards, straggled hair and Homer Simpson ties.

She turned into another identical aisle. Allowed herself a quick glance over the shoulder, confident that she was going to make it to the light, back to the reassuring emptiness of outside.

She slammed into Homer-Tie.

Stared into his eyes. Couldn't look away.

A reek of booze filled the space between them. His shirt was dense with sweat, soaked in fear. He was the very definition of putrid to her.

Then he touched her.

It was too much. Aida yelped pathetically and then tripped, falling against a display of canned soup. The cans went everywhere, the noise of metal hitting floor ringing throughout the store.

Homer-Tie jumped with her, screaming in time with Aida. He seemed demented, slapping at his own face, pulling his hair and beard. Tears leaked out of his eyes, more babbling from his lips.

Aida tried to get away from him, edging backwards on the slippery floor.

Homer-Tie produced a knife. Looked to Aida, tears still damp on his face. Moved towards her.

He was going to kill her, Aida was sure of it.

A shrill cry rang suddenly throughout the shop, announcing the presence of what appeared to be ten to twelve young women. They were beautiful: that's what first struck Aida. Some of them were naked. One wore pyjamas while another was dressed in a leather skirt and black lace bra. A single shoe hung off Leather Skirt's foot, somehow still strapped to her leg.

At first they ignored Aida, stepping out from adjacent aisles to completely surround the man with the Homer tie and kitchen knife. They seemed to study him, pacing like a pack of wolves.

And then it started.

With a grace and speed equal to that of any wild predator, the women pounced on Homer-Tie, tearing into him before Aida's very eyes. Their scratching nails ripped across his skin with abandonment, hands dipping between the tears, scooping lumps of his flesh into their mouths, feasting hungrily.

Aida struggled to get back on her feet, desperate to flee.

Homer Tie's blood pooled out towards her. The creatures were fighting over his scraps like street dogs.

Aida's movements unsettled them; one of the pack turned from its meal, a heavy smear of blood drawn across its face like jam.

As it looked at Aida, its eyes began to slide into the back of its head, changing colour…

FOUR

The bus travelled through the gates of Whiteabbey Hospital, then stopped dead.

Star rubbed condensation from the window of the driver's cabin and peered out.

A group of women surrounded the front entrance. A single ambulance sat near the steps of the nearest building, back doors hanging open in useless anticipation.

"Fuck it. We're too late," she said. "Let's get out of here." She glanced in the side mirror, shifted into reverse gear. Eased her foot on the accelerator, turning the wheel as she went.

"But Barry – " protested Caz.

"Will be as dead as the rest of us if we try getting in there."

"Wait!" Herb ordered.

Star hit the brakes. "What?"

Herb pressed his hand against the glass and looked out at the creatures. They were lined up neatly along the hospital car park like soldiers. Only their hair moved, gently caressed by the breeze. They *must* have heard the engine of the bus, yet not a single damned one of them had as much as turned to look. It seemed like they were waiting for something (or someone) from inside the hospital.

The old man shuffled in his seat, eyes narrowing. "The doors at the front are boarded up from the *inside*."

Star followed Herb's gaze.

She could see what he meant: wooden planks had been nailed behind the smashed glass panes of the doors. And not only that, but some of the windows in the main building were boarded, also from the *inside*. Star was reminded of the housing estate where she grew up. How some of the houses, used and abused by their tenants, became so run down as to be deemed uninhabitable. Cheap wood would have been nailed to their window frames – from the inside, if the windows were broken – achieving the same vibe she looked upon now. Only the wall murals and graffiti were missing.

"So it's boarded up," she said. "What does that tell us?"

"It tells us there are people there," said Caz. "Trapped inside."

Star shrugged. Looked again but still couldn't see anyone.

Her eyes shifted to the car park. There must have been twenty bitches out there. She remembered what had seemed like a hundred times that many at the bus station the previous night. Star had survived her first encounter with them but wasn't keen on facing them again.

"Fuck it. I don't see no one."

She reached again for the gear stick, jammed one foot on the clutch, the other revving the accelerator.

"Wait, I said!" came the professor's voice again. His eyes remained fixed on the building. The lines on his face were rigid; Star could almost see a thought bubble hovering above his head.

He reached slowly for something under his seat, produced a pair of binoculars.

Removed his glasses. Picked out his target and raised the binoculars to his tired, puffed-up eyes.

"I can see them now," he said. "First floor window." He dropped the binoculars, still staring intently at a window on the first floor. "And Caroline's right: they are indeed trapped."

FIVE

Red sidled up to Benny, both men looking from the first floor window to the parked bus.

"Still there?"

Benny nodded in response.

The doctor went to turn, but Benny grabbed him. "I recognise some of them," he said.

"What, the people on the bus?"

Benny dropped his voice. "Not the people on the bus, you idiot! *The women* – I recognise some of the women!" He looked around, leaned in closer. "When I was out there, it was all a blur. But from here, when I take my time, look them up and down, there's some of them bitches I know."

Red peered down at the line of creatures waiting by the doors. They all looked the same to him: pretty, perfectly formed, demonic.

He pointed at his temple, twirled his finger. "This shit plays with your head," he said to Benny, then patted him on the back.

He turned from the window, looked at the small band of pyjama-clad patients gathered in the ward. "Alright, we're going to have to make a run for that bus," he said. "If it leaves, so does our best hope of making it out of here alive. Those bitches have us hemmed in, and there's fuck all we can do about it."

He hooked a thumb at Benny. "Nurse Benjamin here has doled out your meds for the day. So I want no whining out of anyone. We're all going to make it, hear?"

"Not me, Doc," came a voice. Slumped back on his wheelchair, old Cecil shook his head. "I'm finished. I'll only slow you down and get someone killed."

"Bullshit," Red countered. "You're going first. So load up your shotgun and let rip at any fucking thing that stands in your way, mate."

"Jesus," muttered Benny, on hearing the full extent of Red's plan, "This is insane. Let's hope those guys on the bus have got something better up their sleeves, or we're all fucked."

Red shot an acid glance at his friend. "Just get them lined up and ready."

Benny's eyes narrowed. "Me? Why? Where are *you* going?"

Red didn't reply.

He moved past the gathered crowd, into the first floor ward. Found a little space, and grabbed a moment to himself.

Fumbling in his pocket, Red retrieved his phone and switched it on. He usually kept it turned off, trying to save the battery. Flicking through his address book, he found an entry titled DADDY'S LITTLE GIRL. Red pressed SELECT, uselessly attempting yet another call on a phone with no service provider to a young woman who…

No. Not giving up, he thought. *Not yet.*

Dead tone.

Sighing, Red switched the phone off, shoved it back into his pocket.

He suddenly thought of what Benny was saying, about how he recognised some of those things out there. If that were true, then what were they?

Vampires? Zombies?

Red was a medical man; he couldn't believe that. And God knew, with his little girl still out there somewhere in this all-new Big Bad World, he sure as fuck didn't *want* to believe it.

He put the thought out of his head.

Ran a hand through his hair, looked across the ward.

Each bed held a dead body. The bodies were wrapped in blankets. Some of the blankets were stained with blood. All of them were doused in ethanol.

Red fumbled in his lab coat pocket, found a box of matches. They'd been given to him by Benny only yesterday. He smiled at the message scrawled across the front of the packet, a playful insult. Benny was a right dick sometimes.

But he was right. Red's plan *was* insane.

He pulled out a match and with shaking hands lit up a cigarette, drawing on it deeply. He smoked quickly and then threw the still burning stub to the nearest bed.

The body lit up like a pig on a spit.

Red left the ward.

Benny and the others were waiting for him, lined up by the stairs.

"Okay, let's roll!" Red ordered.

…

Terry would be waiting. God knew what he'd think when Herb failed to make contact at the arranged time. This wasn't part of the plan; it could mess everything up, get him killed, get everyone –

No.

That was the old Herb thinking, telling him to do the wrong thing.

He could hear Muriel's voice in his head, telling him to do the *right* thing, the *brave* thing. He'd lost his dear wife in body, but he thanked God that her spirit lived on within him.

The old Herb was a creature of habit, a slave to routine. Deviation troubled him; he didn't like surprises, having spent the last ten years doing a damned sight less than his fair share, hiding in his study like some kind of biblical leper, afraid of what lay beyond his door. When Muriel had passed, he'd been left in turmoil, not knowing what to do with himself.

But those days were gone.

Herb was a new man.

The old Herb had died when he'd stepped across the doorway of his home, venturing out into the big bad world for the first time in years. The new Herb had braved the country roads, travelling to Belfast, where he emerged a stronger, better man. A man with resolve, direction. A man that could gather a busload of survivors together and make something of them. Those survivors in the hospital had a chance *because of him,* no matter how the very audacity of such made Herb feel.

His heart was thumping.

He rubbed his eyes, tried to steady himself. He couldn't afford a panic attack. Not now. He needed to be strong, confident, dynamic. Those were the qualities required of a leader.

The bus was moving into position, ready for a quick exit from the hospital grounds.

Herb looked out at the creatures, still standing by the doors of the hospital, fixated only on the survivors inside.

Not since the heyday of his academia had Herb been intrigued by *anything* like he was intrigued by these women. The way they moved. Their absolute, flawless beauty. Those marvellous, flapping eyes.

But they terrified him.

Everything about them was unique and profoundly disturbing. Like science fiction become fact. Horror become –

"You know this isn't going to work." It was the voice of Star.

"O-of course it is." Herb countered, hoping to God he sounded like he was in control.

"And your confidence comes from…?"

"From *you*, dear girl." He smiled nervously, handed the tattooist one of two handheld radios. "Press then talk," he instructed.

Star grabbed the radio from him. Climbed out of the driver's cabin, shoved the radio into the side pocket of her bloodstained combats. Found a cigarette, jammed it between her lips.

"I'll be talking, alright," she complained. "It'll be, like, 'Fuck you, arsehole,' once I get to that ambulance. I ain't hanging around to see whether those bitches rip my fucking head off, that's for sure."

Herb ignored her ranting, handed her a gun. "I'm no expert, but I believe there's no trick to this model. It's point and shoot. No safety to worry about or anything like that."

Star snapped the gun from him, grunted.

Herb rubbed at his temples, looked to the door of the bus. It looked back at him like the doorway to hell itself.

"Okay, here's the plan," he said, turning to address the survivors. "Star, you, my dear, are to head for the ambulance…"

The tattooist lit her cigarette, exhaled in Herb's direction.

"Once there," Herb continued, wafting the smoke away, "climb aboard, wait for my signal, then start the engine and make as much noise as possible. Christ knows, that shouldn't be too hard for you."

"But – "

"But don't – drive – off," he ordered, spelling the words out as if Star were a child. "Not until I give the signal – " he pointed at the radio " – through *this*."

Star went to protest again, but Herb fended her off with a dismissive wave of his hand.

He turned to Caz. "Caroline, I want you out on the steps, helping anyone frail or wounded onto the bus." He looked at the other volunteers gathered by the door. "Everyone else should be waiting by the doors to help settle the newcomers. Star's distraction should buy us *some* time, but not much. We'll all have to work quickly to – "

Herb stopped for a moment. Looked around at the survivors. He could see fear written across their faces. *These people aren't soldiers,* he mused. *They aren't warriors or strategists…*

He adjusted his glasses, continued a little less militantly: "Look, it's imperative that we remain calm when dealing with these monsters. I'm convinced they're drawn by strong emotions: fear, anger, guilt, grief. The longer we can hide our feelings, the more chance we have."

Star laughed. "And where will *you* be, Prof, while we're out there trying to find our inner fucking peace?"

"On the bus. I'm the getaway driver."

"I'll do that. You can run to the fucking ambulance."

"I'm old. I don't run."

"Fuck you," Star scorned, but the professor sensed a little give in her attitude.

"Fuck you too," Herb said. "With bloody great bells – "

He was interrupted when the first floor window of the main building blew out.

"Good Lord," he breathed.

His heart seemed to freeze in his chest. He became Old Herb again, his cowering, petrified self that hid in the study.

The curtains inside caught fire. The blaze would spread quickly throughout the main building.

Herb's eyes found the creatures. The flames didn't seem to scare them, but smoke was spilling out in thick plumes. Soon, it would fill the car park, obscuring everyone's vision.

He turned to find Star glaring at him.

"What now?" she demanded.

SIX

The creatures swarmed Aida.

She tried to escape. Crawling away from them, desperately trying to find her feet. But there were too many arms reaching for her, fingernails digging, teeth snapping. At first, they could only get enough purchase on Aida's blood-slicked, wriggling body to tear skin, but the blood loss itself was weakening her. And the weaker *she* became, the stronger *their* grip became.

One of them, poodle permed with the left eye shadowed and the right *au naturel*, gripped Aida's hair, tearing a clump away. A layer of scalp followed, the hopelessly overpowered young Egyptian shrieking in both shame and torment.

Another gnawed at Aida's knee bone, trying to get her teeth around the cap to separate it from the rest of the leg.

They were ripping her apart.

Fighting over her meat like dogs, clawing at each other as much as they clawed at Aida.

But then…

At first, Aida didn't recognise her. She was but another pretty head amongst all the others. Yet as the newcomer's face drew closer, it dawned on Aida who it was: the blonde highlights, the full lips, the sad, ever-grieving expression…

Kirsty?

Aida felt herself being wrestled from the crowd and crudely flung across the supermarket's floor to slam against yet another display of tinned goods.

A banshee-like cry left the newcomer's lips, leading to what could only be described as a stand-off: Kirsty on one side, twenty or so of the creatures on the other.

Blood pooled in the gap in between.

Kirsty dipped her foot in the blood, slathered it across the floor.

Here's the line, she was saying. *Don't cross it.*

The other creatures sneered at her, jaws snapping in defiance. But the line wasn't crossed.

Aida felt herself fading, the heavy loss of blood she had sustained stealing her from consciousness. Several cans fell from the shelf above her, striking her patchy head, their feeble weight enough to send the young survivor into limbo.

SEVEN

Star made her way across the hospital car park, towards the stalled ambulance. She could only pray that the keys were in the ignition. Otherwise she would be hotwiring the fucking thing, and she hadn't tried that little mischief in quite a few years.

She stole a glance at the women (or whatever the fuck they were). They hadn't moved a muscle, eyes still fixed on the entrance to the hospital.

A quick look to the first-floor windows confirmed the blaze was spreading. Its heat was strong. Star still couldn't see anyone inside the hospital, wondering once again if she were doing all this shit for nothing.

She moved past the first of the creatures, careful not to make any sudden or jerky movements.

Closer now, only a few yards from the ambulance.

She noticed that the rear doors were open. From her approach, Star could make out the body of a man hanging out the back, intestines slopped like bloody sausage meat from his severed gut.

She swallowed hard.

Her pace quickened.

She made for the driver's side of the ambulance, found the door locked. Peered through its glass, couldn't see any keys in the ignition.

Star swore.

A slight cough tickled the back of her throat, but she fought against it.

Her eyes rolled desperately to the right, casting another glance towards the women. Most remained focused on the flames, but one of the pack, a small girl with messy pigtails, was staring right at Star. A liquid sound could be heard over the flames as the eyes turned in her pretty little head.

Less than ten hours ago, Star had been surrounded by hundreds of whores like Messy Pigtails. At first, they hadn't been interested in the tattooist, seeking out other prey: that of a child, ripping her tiny body to shreds, the child's blood sprinkling over their faces like rain. But Star wrought revenge, attacking them with venom, spilling *their* blood.

She didn't remember a lot after that. They had rushed her – she remembered that much – but Star had stood hard and fast against their fury, her blade slicing into every bitch within reach.

Perspiration broke across her brow as she recalled the brutal encounter.

She left the driver's door, edged around the side of the ambulance towards the rear.

Found the body again.

Poor bastard had been savaged. What remained of his skin and clothes was coated with blood, making it difficult to tell what age he was. His coat was mostly intact. Star bent down to search its pockets, hoping to find the keys to the ambulance's ignition.

The heat from the flames was in her face. Heavy grey plumes escaped the building, filling the hospital car park.

Some of the smoke caught in Star's throat, causing her to splutter again. Her splutter soon gave way to a full-blown smoker's cough, her bark ringing out across the car park.

Star bit into the side of her wrist, tried to steady herself.

She couldn't breathe.

Struggled to remain composed.

But the coughing got worse; she bent double over the bumper of the ambulance as it shook her entire body.

Two more women stared in her direction. Their eyes started to flicker..

Star's coughing continued, stealing her very breath, leaving her beetroot-faced with exertion.

She felt the ground sway.

Several more women looked in her direction. The fleshy sound of their eyes grew louder.

Star fumbled clumsily for the gun in her pocket. She was finished. She knew it. Those whores weren't going to let her get away twice, but she would take a few of them down with her.

The sun shifted slightly in the sky, throwing a sliver of light across the tarmac. Star's eyes were drawn to a glint of metal next to the ambulance's back wheel.

The key.

A bunch of the mother-fuckers, actually. She wasted no time in snatching them up, shoving the handgun back into her baggy combats.

Star rushed for the driver's door. She was finding it hard to focus, the smoke even thicker now, her eyes watering. She wiped her face, fumbled a random key in the lock.

"COME ON!"

Nope, not that one.

Tried another one.

Wrong again.

Tears were streaming down her face, the smoke blinding her.

From behind, she heard commotion. It was *them*. God knew how many of the bitches. She didn't dare look.

Stabbed the lock with a third key.

Click.

She was in.

Star ripped the key out of the door, pulled it open.

They were on her.

She slammed the door on one creature's hand. Pulled her gun, aimed it squarely in another's face, firing. A thick-soled DM boot kicked at a third, allowing room to close the door.

Star locked it tight.

Glancing in the wing mirror, she noticed the clinical white paint of the vehicle splashed with blood. The creature she'd fired upon struggled on the nearby tarmac. Several others were trying to clamber through the back doors.

A ferocious noise drew her attention front and centre: five pairs of fists beat upon the glass of the windscreen, angry red eyes staring in.

"Fuck this."

Star rammed the ignition key into place. Scowling, she kicked the engine into gear and sped out of the hospital car park, several women tumbling from the rear of the ambulance along with the body they'd mutilated.

More of enraged creatures raced after her, vying to get a grip on the swinging rear door.

EIGHT

"Wait, for God's sake, you obnoxious young…"

Herb threw his walkie-talkie to the floor in disgust.

His plan was going to hell before his very eyes. The pack by the hospital had split, spreading out across the car park. It would be impossible for the hospital survivors to negotiate their way through now.

Caz rolled her eyes. She had never expected Star to play ball.

Barry Rogan called out in pain. More wounds reopened, probably by his own hand. Blood flowed freely, dripping from his seat, pooling on the floor.

"There!" shouted Herb. "Don't you see it?"

He pointed to the hospital's side doors, close to where the ambulance had been parked.

Caz spotted an occupied wheelchair sneaking out, steered by a man wearing a white lab coat. Several other people, some wearing pyjamas, one or two in hospital uniform, followed. They were moving towards the bus.

"No, you fools, " Herb muttered, "Stay indoors until…"

Until what? Caz wondered. *Until they burn? Until those things break in?*

She bit nervously on her bottom lip.

Reached into her pocket, where the little crucifix resided.

Gripped it in her hand, then said, "We have to help them."

...

There was dancing. Cheerleaders dancing, to be precise. Beautiful, young, (defenceless? drunk? DRUGGED?) cheerleaders kicking their feet and swinging their blood-stained pom-poms.

Barry Rogan watched them.

Five girls lined up in a row, each with a different letter of his first name branded onto their foreheads. Blood pumped freely from the pom-poms. The girls were singing; their lips moved in time with the music, but it was a song that Barry couldn't hear.

The picture sharpened as if tuned in better to some TV that only he had access to. The song became clearer. A melodic and catchy number, repeating its chorus line over and over again.

One word, three syllables.

Blah-Blaah-Blah .

The middle syllable was drawn out slightly. Barry strained to listen, but he still couldn't catch it.

Still the girls danced, singing that chorus line over and over again.

Blah-Blaah-Blah.

It got louder, more pronounced...

BLAH-BLAAH-BLAH.

And then, as the music swelled, FORGET ME NOT marched into the picture, shaking her pert little ass in time with the beat. She stood in the middle of the dancers, facing Barry, her t-shirt drenched by the blood-spitting pom-poms, its slogan blurring.

The song reached a climatic finish, legs, arms, pleated white skirts and bloody red pom-poms swinging. As the final bar rang out, each dancer slid into her final position.

FORGET-ME NOT strolled provocatively up to Barry. Leaned in to kiss him, then pulled away. A wide grin spread across her lips.

Everything within Barry screamed.

NINE

It didn't take long for Star to lose her tail. Those things were fast, but not fast enough to keep up with an ambulance doing 90mph down the M2.

She knocked the speed back to 60, relaxed in her seat. Fumbled in her pockets for cigarettes. Sparked up, took a long drag. Exhaling, Star checked the fuel gauge: there was enough juice to keep her ticking over for a while.

Sweet.

Star reached for the radio's dial, had nearly pressed it before catching herself. She rolled her eyes. Not much chance of Real FM being on air today.

Or any other day, for that fucking matter.

Her mind scanned over the last few weeks since The Great Whatever. Fuck knew, it had been one hell of a ride. The sudden fall of humankind. That gothy chick nose-diving the floor as Star was tattooing her. Meeting people like Caz and Herb and Sean and –

Tim. Don't forget Tim.

Star recalled finding Tim's body by the bandstand over at Belfast's Victoria Square shopping centre. Those whores had done a number on him, ripped him to shreds.

She remembered the little crucifix lying near his corpse. It had been a gift from Caz. Star had lifted the cross, cleaned it of the lad's blood, then took it to Caz and pressed it into her hand.

Star dragged heavy on the last embers of her ciggie before winding down the window to flick it out. The engine of the ambulance continued to hum. The sudden noise of a bird pierced the quiet air.

She caught a glimpse of herself in the side mirror and was disturbed by how she looked. Her dreads were a mess, like dead cacti sprouting from her head. There was probably shit living in there now, a whole family of fucking bugs feeding off her scalp. Purple rings circled her eyes, partly from make-up, but mostly due to lack of sleep.

Heroin chic, eat your fucking heart out.

The tattoo on her neck was hardly visible, caked by blood and God knew what else. It was a Medusa head: pretty face with snakes hanging out.

Kinda fitting, when you think about it.

Star remembered the day she'd got the tattoo. An American artist called Tyler had done it at the London convention a few years back. It was a nice piece. Good clean line work. Solid colours.

Meant the fucking world to her.

She'd got it to celebrate her first five years as a tattoo artist. Tattooing was the only thing she'd ever felt comfortable doing, and she wanted something to mark that, a coming of age sort of tattoo. Medusa meant a lot of things to a lot of people. For Star, the old girl was about identity; after years of disenfranchisement, of feeling like a square peg in a round fucking hole, Star had finally found her place in life, her niche.

There was power in her ink.

Sometimes, Star could feel it flowing through the needle. Something dark, otherworldly. Something that made her hands tingle and her heart swell.

Maybe it was this force or power that those bitches felt last night, during their first encounter.

Does it frighten them, the way it sometimes frightens me?

She reached to wind the window up again.

A hand suddenly grabbed for her. Its chill seeped through the tattooist's skin.

Shocked, Star sank her boot on the breaks, spinning the ambulance in an immediate series of circles.

It slammed against the lane divide.

The creature that had clung to the vehicle's exterior screamed out in pain, caught between the side of the ambulance and the barrier.

The side window gave.

The creature scrambled through. Its clothes were missing from the waist up, breasts dangling as she moved. Both legs had been mangled in the impact. Blood flowed like ink as the creature trailed itself through the driver's cabin.

Star kicked back against the bitch, aiming both boots at its goddamned face.

The creature slipped against the blood-slicked dashboard, flicking a switch. The ambulance's siren kicked in, its sharp bleat whirring across the empty motorway.

Still it came, long-fingered hands swiping.

Star backed away, into the passenger's seat, cursing loudly. One hand scrambled for the handgun, now lying in the foot well.

The creature pulled itself forwards, jaws drawing closer to the tattooist's face, seeking purchase. Star struggled to push it away, to find some way of escaping, but it was no good: she was hopelessly trapped in the constrained space of the driver's cabin.

The creature's hand swung again, nails raking across the tattooist's cheek, tearing the skin.

Star cried out in pain. Swore. Spat in the bitch's face.

Pulled her gun hand back, reached into the pocket of her combats, where she found her Zippo and pulled it free. Flicking the catch, Star shoved the Zippo's full flame right into the bitch's eyes.

The creature screamed out in pain, shutting both eyes quickly as it retreated from the flame.

Star reached into the foot well of the ambulance and retrieved her handgun.

The creature lunged at her again, but Star was ready, pushing the gun into its face, pulling the trigger with determination. The shot rang out, nearly deafening the tattooist. A putrid mix of brain matter and blood showered her face as the bullet tore through the creature's head. The damn thing flailed wildly before falling dead in the ambulance's driving seat.

Star dropped the gun, slumped back into the passenger seat. She lay there for a moment, blood and gore still thick on her face.

She fumbled for her cigarettes, using the same lighter that had saved her skin to spark up. She drew deeply on the cigarette then exhaled.

The siren continued to scream. Star jammed the cigarette between her lips, then reached to switch it off. The noise died, but its echo was still ringing in the tattooist's ears.

Star wiped her eyes. The wounds the creature had inflicted were smarting, and she grimaced against the pain.

Fucking lucky, she told herself. *Could have been a lot worse.*

She'd been careless, allowed herself to relax. She wouldn't make that mistake again.

Star opened the door, kicked the dead creature's body from the cabin.

She settled herself in the gore-filled driver's seat, still toking on the cigarette.

She turned the ignition key, swearing as it failed to catch.

Outside, thirty creatures moved towards the wafting grey of her tobacco...

TEN

A pony-tailed girl bit into the arm of the nurse. The nurse tried to shake her off but failed.

To Herb's right, a wheelchair swerved to avoid the lunging hands of another creature, this one tall, lanky, and dressed like a Sunday school teacher. The old man in the chair pulled a sawn-off shotgun from under his blanket and blasted the woman's left breast across the tarmac.

Herbert Matthews watched the carnage unfold. Against the horizon, the hospital continued to burn, smoke pouring out onto the car park. Yet Herb felt powerless to do anything. He was frozen to the spot, consumed by fear.

Sixteen-year-old Caroline Donaldson pushed the professor aside.

She climbed down from the bus. Fought her way through the smoke, across the car park. Went to grab hold of the nurse's free arm.

The incoming wheelchair collided with her, sending her sprawling across the unforgiving gravel.

Caz rolled quickly away from the advances of another creature. The damn thing grabbed hold of her, but she kicked violently, crying out with every slam of her shoe against the creature's snapping jaws.

Her cry was enough to snap Herb out of his daze.

He took aim with the shotgun, blew her attacker's leg off.

Caz scrambled to her feet.

Herb looked next to the nurse struggling against the pig-tailed girl. His hands were shaking too much to take a shot.

Another survivor intervened, hacking at the bitch with what looked to be a golf club.

Caz ran to help.

The wheelchair rolled up to the bus, the eyes of both its occupant and driver begging for access. Herb stepped further back into the bus.

The driver, a red haired man who looked like a doctor, protested: "Help me get this poor critter out of his chair, for God's sake!"

Herb didn't move. "B-bad back," he muttered. "Can't bear weight."

It wasn't the whole truth: Herb was feeling decidedly faint, as if too much air from The Great Outdoors had travelled to his head. The noise had reached an unbearable max, and his old hands could hardly hold the shotgun, never mind a wheelchair. His pulse was racing, and Herb knew what that meant… he was about to have that panic attack he'd been desperately fighting off.

"Fucking hell, man. I need your help here," the doctor pressed.

The wheelchaired man shook his head. Loaded the shotgun with two fresh shells, then slammed it closed. He looked up at the bus, and for an ugly minute, Herb wondered if one of those shells was for him. Instead, he spun in his wheelchair, pointed the barrel at an approaching woman, and fired.

The recoil shook the chair as much as Herb's nerves.

The old man's aim was wide, but the buckshot offset the creature that hung onto the nurse's arm.

Several other creatures approached, leaving the wheelchair-bound man to choose which deserved his second shell most.

"COME ON!" yelled the doctor. To Herb, his voice sounded like a siren going off, the bellow of an old air-raid warning.

He could hear Barry Rogan behind him, screaming in unison.

Through the thickening smoke, he watched in horror as the creatures butchered the fleeing survivors. It was all too much. His nerves were truly shot: as the doctor continued to bay for his attention, Herb fell back against the driver's cabin of the bus.

Muriel! Where are you?

He needed his wife more than ever.

He watched helplessly as Caz kicked against another of the creatures. Herb could hear her screams as she grabbed the damn thing by the hair, swinging her fist wildly into its face. She was just a child. Her violence was unnerving.

Herb felt a stinging pain break across his chest. He reached one hand to his heart. Tried to call out for help, but the doctor was busy lifting the disabled man out of the wheelchair all on his own.

The two nurses from before made it to the bus.

One of them worked with the doctor to get the disabled survivor and his wheelchair onto the bus.

The other nurse covered them, raising a golf club. "Come on!" he goaded, brandishing the club as several women padded towards him.

One of the women made a move, but the nurse swung admirably, connecting with the creature's mouth, sending a couple of teeth into the glimmering, sunlit sky. The others withdrew a little, allowing all four men to scramble onto the bus, wheelchair in tow.

One of the nurses jumped into the driver's cabin, firing up the engine.

"W-wait!" Herb called.

Caz was still out there.

A few more survivors were littered amongst the creatures, some fighting, others running for the bus.

Herb pulled himself to his feet, reloaded quickly. In a last stab at glory, he raised the shotgun and fired both barrels into the pack. His hands were still shaking, his aim wide. But the noise alone was enough to distract the creatures, allowing room for another couple of survivors to board.

Finally, Caz scrambled on.

Behind her, a middle-aged man was dragged to his knees by a woman in a dirty nightdress. The poor bastard cried out for help, the sound of his voice dampened as Herb grabbed the nearby lever, slamming the folding doors of the bus firmly shut.

Several pairs of hands slapped against the glass, patting uselessly as all eight wheels of the vehicle skidded on the tarmac, then sped away.

As they pulled onto the main road, the screams of those left behind faded.

ELEVEN

She awoke with the taste of blood in her mouth.

Aida jolted up. Puked. Started to cough.

She wiped her hand across her mouth, ventured a look around.

She was in a room. A pinprick of light made its way through a gap somewhere above her. She could make out a little of the floor, some kind of tiling effect giving way to the crude, dirty blanket she lay upon. Save for a wall to her immediate left, Aida couldn't see much more of her surroundings.

Flashes of memory teased her mind. The supermarket. The man with the Homer tie. The creatures.

The pain was unbearable. It rushed through her body in waves.

More nausea.

Again, Aida gagged, but this time nothing came up.

She fell back upon the blanket, her mouth dry and scorched, limbs on fire. Tears spilled from her eyes, stinging her scarred cheeks.

Sudden movement.

A scuttling from the other side of the room. A whimper or growl. The sound of paper flapping against the wind.

Aida felt her body tense.

One of the creatures was in the room with her.

She sat up again, reached both hands across the floor, feeling for something that she could use to defend herself.

The sounds drew closer.

She could see it now, edging towards her.

And then the creature was on her. It placed its hands upon her chest, pushing her back onto the makeshift bed.

Aida was powerless to resist.

The creature tugged at her clothes, ripping them open, exposing her breasts. Slathered something over her skin.

Aida fought to cover herself up, placing both hands over her breasts. They felt wet. A thick, sticky substance coated them, warm and yet cold all at once, stinging yet also soothing. Aida had never felt anything like this before and it terrified her.

A shift from the clouds outside offered more light.

Her eyes adjusted. Aida realised she was covered in blood. But not her own: this was the creature's blood. Darker, more viscous than her own blood. It spread across her skin, seeping into her mouth and nose. Aida sputtered again, tried to clear the blood from her throat. She couldn't breathe, fought to clear her airways.

The creature's face drew closer. The lipstick was smeared, eyeliner pooling around its eyes. Blonde highlights ran through its hair.

Kirsty?

Kirsty's hands were in the air, cupped as if holding something. Aida watched in terror as more blood poured down from Kirsty's hands, then slathered onto her tanned skin. The blood settled then seeped into Aida's wounds, bubbling and frothing as it went. Her eyes widened, yet she still couldn't scream.

TWELVE

Caz sat curled up in the back of the bus, blood on her baggy t-shirt. Her breathing came heavy and quick. She was scared, more scared than she could ever remember feeling. More scared even than yesterday, when those bastards had taken her and –

"So what's your name, pet?" asked the doctor.

Caz didn't reply. *Couldn't* reply.

"What age are you?"

As he spoke to her, the doctor treated the arm of a twenty-something student type. Other survivors groaned for his attention.

"Sixteen," Caz said, still trying to catch her breath. "Why do you ask?" The softness of her voice sharply contrasted that of the doctor. Red was a Dublin man with the dulcet tones to prove it.

"No reason," he said, "Just checking you're still with us."

"Look," Caz said. "I have a friend dying over there." She pointed down the aisle towards Barry Rogan. "He's the one you should be worried about."

"Give me a minute, would you? There's a lot of people to worry about on this bus." He patted Twenty-Something's shoulder, moved on to the next in line.

Caz rolled her eyes and pulled herself up using a handrail. She'd damaged something on her left side, and it was hurting. Wincing, she filed past the other survivors, the bus now almost full. The doctor was right: there was blood everywhere and a lot of messed up people, some barely conscious.

She gripped a nearby seat as the driver cut another sharp corner. A quick peek out the window told her they were sliding back onto the motorway, retracing their steps towards the International Airport in Templepatrick.

Herb stood by the driver's cabin, both hands clutching the safety rail. He looked pale. This whole episode had taken a lot out of them all, but for someone of his age (*What is he? Seventy? Seventy-five?*), it must have been particularly heinous.

A few more steps and Caz reached Barry, the badly injured survivor still secured across the disabled seats at the front of the bus.

Geez, he looked bad.

His crotch was black with God knew what. Blood crusted on his hands where he'd been scratching at the dressing. His exposed eye sockets made him look like some kind of horror puppet. The newly arrived survivors were avoiding him like he had something they might catch.

Caz felt guilty. It seemed that anyone who got close to her ended up dead or dying.

It was only yesterday when Barry had convinced her that a cruise through Belfast's death-riddled streets was a good idea. And he had been right: Caz had enjoyed the drive, the wind through her hair, the sunshine bathing her, the scenery – all of it had been wonderful.

Until those bastards at the petrol station had taken her, that was. Snatching her while Barry was in the shop. Dragging her away, kicking and screaming.

To that house.

To do those things.

If it hadn't been for Barry coming after her, she wouldn't be alive.

She tried to think who else would have made the effort, put their own life on the line. Would Star have bothered? Not likely. The morose tattooist had barely spoken two words to Caz in the whole time they'd known each other. What about Sean, the DJ? Too busy drinking himself into a coma every night.

Nope, only Barry cared enough.

And Tim – my poor, lost Tim.

And look where that had got them. Both attacked brutally by those things. Tim dead, Barry ripped apart as Caz watched on, helpless.

She heard a sudden whistling from behind. Doctor bloody Ginger. "Woooh-heee," he exclaimed through pursed lips, looking at Barry.

"Look, can you help him?" Caz pressed. "Redo the bandaging? Give him blood or – "

"*Give him blood?* Are you taking the piss, love? I can't do anything like that in the back of a fucking – "

"JUST," Caz cut in, her voice rising in irritation before being checked, "Do something for him. Anything. As long as you make him comfortable."

She turned to move back down the bus, visibly upset.

"Hey," the doctor called after her.

Caz stopped, sighed. Looked back.

"What is this guy to you, anyway? Brother? Boyfriend?"

She felt for the cross in her pocket, gripped it tightly. Her eyes moistened, and Caz worried for a moment that she was going to break down and cry.

"He's nothing to me," she said, quickly. "But he gave up *everything*."

She looked once more at the pathetic mess that was Barry Rogan, jittering and pissing blood on the floor.

A tear rolled down her cheek.

The doctor nodded. He seemed to understand.

Silently, he leaned in to give Barry Rogan the care he needed and, perhaps, deserved.

Caz turned back and made her way through the small crowd clogging the bus's aisle.

THIRTEEN

Aida was awake.

Her eyes were open; the darkness had receded.

She felt… fine. Great, in fact. And that worried her. Because, God knew she'd felt far from fine the last time her eyes were open.

She looked around, adjusting to her new surroundings. She was in the middle of a large lawn, maybe a park. It was warm, despite the breeze. Dead bodies festered in the bright sunshine.

Aida wondered if maybe she was dead too. At one with Allah, enjoying the solace of heaven.

She remembered, back in the supermarket, being attacked by the creatures. How they'd ripped at her flesh, dipping their teeth in between the skin to tear her insides out. Blood had filled the space where she lay, Aida fading in and out of darkness.

She looked at her hands now, noticing how perfect they seemed. Blood had hardened on her torn clothes, but when she studied the flesh underneath, Aida found nothing but healthy skin.

She had been healed somehow. She wasn't going to die.

Kirsty was sitting right across from Aida, face bowed, legs sprawled out, like a child at a picnic. Her eyes were a lush, contented green, as if mirroring the foliage surrounding her.

Aida wasn't afraid of her. She could feel something building between them, a connection of a sort, an understanding.

She remembered feeling like this back at the school in Lisburn, when she'd first encountered this creature: Kirsty bent over the grave, hands covered in soil, lips smeared with blood, the unearthed body of her husband in her arms.

Aida decided to try something. "I know your name," she said to Kirsty. "I knew your husband too. He was called Steve, and he loved you very much. You remember Steve, don't you?"

Kirsty looked up, briefly, before bowing her head again. She plucked a daisy from amongst the grass. Began rubbing its petals delicately against each finger.

"You remember being with Steve. And your son, little Nicky."

Still, Kirsty played with the daisy. The sun dipped behind a cloud, and the shadow from a nearby tree fell over her face.

Aida continued, "You remember what those people did to Steve?"

Kirsty's head rose sharply. She glared at Aida, eyes flickering, losing their green serenity, swirls of red filling each pupil as they began to turn.

"That's right," Aida continued, "you remember…"

Kirsty remembered all too well. How she'd moved through the school, hair cloaking her face, lighting upon the survivors like a fox among hens. Hunting. Killing without mercy. And then, as the blood of each kill had settled on the smoothly polished floors, digging up the grave of her husband.

To grieve.

To feast on his flesh.

Aida rose softly to her feet.

Padded across the park lawn towards her feral friend.

She bent down and held her own brown eyes on the confused, flickering eyes of Kirsty Marshall. Noticed a blood red tear running down the creature's cheek. Wiped it away.

Kirsty didn't move.

Aida could still see the small daisy in her hand, all its petals intact. Carefully, she moved her own hand over the daisy, reaching for its petals. Aida began to pluck the petals, gently caressing Kirsty's hair with her other hand, whispering softly into the creature's ear.

"He loved you," she said, rhyming the words as she tore each petal away, "Loved you. Loved *you*." As the last petal was plucked from the daisy, more tears escaped. "Steve loved *you*, Kirsty," Aida said, drawing the creature to her breast and comforting her. "He couldn't live without you."

Kirsty's eyes watered freely, the bloody stream soaking Aida's clothes. The tears felt hot, stinging her skin, yet the young Egyptian woman made no protest. She smiled, soothing her friend as they continued to embrace.

The click of a gun's safety interrupted them.

FOURTEEN

Caz left Barry in the care of the doctor.

She realised that she hadn't asked for the doctor's name, nor had he asked for hers. *Even manners are failing us*, she mused. The one thing a girl of her breeding thought would never go.

She padded across the floor, grabbing the railing as they ran over a bump in the road.

Herbert Matthews stood by the driver's cabin.

Behind the wheel sat a young and not altogether unattractive male nurse from the hospital.

Caz looked to the road in front. The sun was beaming now, and she squinted against its glare. This wasn't a part of the world that she knew too well. Sure, her parents had taken her on many a holiday when she was a child, but she had generally slept through the journey to the airport. Slept or daydreamed – that old decadence of hers.

"Won't be long now," Herb announced, turning to her. "Another ten minutes, max. Sooner, if this maniac keeps up the speed he's doing."

Caz managed a smile. This whole airport thing was his big plan. She knew how much was riding on it, how much it all meant to him. And that alone might be enough to hold things together for all of them, at least for a while.

In this broken down messed-up world, *any* hope was a luxury.

Even false hope.

Caz gripped the cross in her pocket again.

"Oh God, no," Herb said. His face suddenly fell. He reached in towards the driver, forced him to slow down.

Caz looked out the bus windows, fighting against the sun's glare to see what it was that had spooked the old man.

Mere yards ahead of them, a white coloured vehicle rested by the side of the road. It was surrounded by the creatures. They seemed distracted, almost aimless in their movements. Blood was splashed across their faces and clothes, as if they had recently...

Fed?!

A heavy silence fell throughout the bus. The stalled vehicle was an ambulance, almost certainly from Whiteabbey Hospital. Almost certainly the one that Star had driven off in. Each and every survivor looked out as they passed the scene, fully aware of what it meant: another one of their number brutally slain.

The driver looked to Herb expectantly.

"Drive on, damn it," Herb snapped. "There's nothing we can do for her now."

The bus picked up pace, drove on.

FIFTEEN

They could hear the airport before they reached it. The POC-POC-POC of gunfire filled its airspace. There was screaming.

Several cars littered the road as they passed, broken glass surrounding their jarred, open doors, savaged corpses in their seats. A pack of creatures moved throughout the wreckage, sniffing like dogs.

The noise of battle grew louder as the bus inched forwards, swerving lightly to avoid more stalled cars.

An almighty sense of dread fell upon the survivors.

Red was first to speak: "You must be fucking joking, driving us in the direction of that god-awful noise."

No one replied.

"AW, COME ON, PEOPLE! Has nobody any fucking wit around here?"

He looked to Cecil in the wheelchair, parked in the aisle just behind him, but the stupid old twat was somehow fast asleep. Benny must have gone overboard on his meds.

Red wiped his hands on his lab coat, threw the tools of his trade into a white plastic shopping bag.

He left Barry Rogan, stepped towards the driver's cabin.

This was where the main movers and shakers held court: the old man in the dressing gown, Benny at the wheel, and the pretty little tyke he'd been chatting to earlier. Red hoped to talk a bit of sense into them. He had been happy to jump on any bandwagon that got him out of his previous situation – trapped in a hospital with a bevy of crazed women on his tail – but when said bandwagon was heading towards an even greater threat, the doctor's enthusiasm waned.

"Are any of you guys listening to a word I say?" he asked.

"There were people there, all along," the old man muttered under his breath. "Why the hell didn't I know that?" He turned towards Red, a glazed look across his eyes. "They should have *told* me there were people there!"

"What are you talking about?"

"The airport!" the old man ranted. "It was supposed to be my job to set up base there, no one else's!"

"I've no idea what you're on – "

The bus ground to a sudden halt.

Benny turned from the wheel, blew some air out. "Look, I'm not being funny," he said, "but driving any closer is suicide."

Finally, Red mused, *Someone else with a bit of cop-on.*

But the old man ignored Benny, moving past the driver's cabin and pressing his face against the windscreen. Red studied the back of his head, caught a glimpse of something… an insect, maybe… bouncing around the thinning hair of his scalp.

Sighing, the old man retrieved his shotgun, started to load it.

Benny looked nervously to Red.

Outside the battle raged on, the rattle of gunfire puncturing the quiet air.

"Look mate," Benny reasoned, "we're all very grateful, you know, with the help you gave us. But, Christ almighty, it's crazy out there. You must understand – "

"Oh, I understand, alright," the old man replied. "You're a coward. You're all cowards."

"Oh, come on," Red began, but he was cut off by a single wave of the old man's hand.

"You see", continued Herbert Matthews, "If *I* had been as cowardly towards you and yours back at the hospital, we wouldn't have a bus this full, now would we?"

"You're not serious," Red barked. "Jesus Christ, man, you were hardly Che fucking Guevara back there! Spent most of the time cowering in the corner, leaving us to deal with those things on our – "

"You know what they did to cowards?" Herb broke in, his voice more aggressive, sweat breaking across his brow. "In the War, when my father was in the trenches, fighting the Nazis. You know what they did to cowards back then?"

He aimed the double barrel at Red.

"They shot them."

PART TWO
THE AIRPORT

ONE

Father Patrick Reilly drained the sink of bloody water.

He replaced the plug, loosened the cap on a second bottle, then poured again.

Reilly dipped his hands into the fresh water, noticing how the reflection distorted in the misty pink cocktail. He could get lost in this: the swirls of blood mixing with crystal clear water, the cool touch against his skin.

Very pagan, he mused.

It was also very pagan to be involved in a blood sacrifice.

Reilly's eyes found the handgun sitting on the closed lid of the disabled access toilet.

He ran a damp hand through his hair.

Jesus, what have I done?

A knock came against the cubicle door.

Reilly froze.

He glanced at his hands. His palms were completely clean, but his nails were still stained in places.

Another knock, then a heavy sniff.

Reilly knew then who was at the door. He blew some air out, relieved. "Coming now," he called.

The priest lifted the soap, scrubbed his hands one last time, paying particular attention to the fingernails.

Once done, he emptied the sink, watching as the contents swirled down the plughole.

The brilliant white of porcelain looked back at him.

No blood was left.

Not here, anyway.

Reilly reattached the white collar to his shirt, then wiped the perspiration from his brow. He felt like shit. So fucking tired. He was living on his nerves alone, right now.

He lifted the handgun, checked it, then slid it into the back of his belt.

Waited for a moment, steadying himself, then opened the cubicle door.

Jimmy's face looked up at him. Drool was building in the corner of his mouth, glistening in the artificial light. Reilly turned away, suddenly disgusted by the younger survivor. If there was a God – and Reilly was even less sure now after all that had happened – then why the fuck would he allow *Jimmy* to survive when other perfectly good, functioning human beings had…

Jimmy started to cry.

Reilly swallowed hard, corrected himself. "It's okay," he said, patting the younger man's trunk-like shoulder. "I'm sorry. It's okay."

Jimmy looked up at Reilly, shamefully presented his hands. They looked as bloodied as Reilly's had been.

"Didn't you wash them, Jimmy? I told you to wash them."

"I couldn't get it out," he said.

"Did anyone else see your hands?" Reilly probed. "Any of the others."

"Only Jeff."

"Only Jeff," Reilly repeated. "That's okay, then."

He led Jimmy to the nearby sink. Lifted another bottle from the stack on the floor, then poured the contents.

"Dip your hands in," Reilly instructed.

Jimmy did as he was told, dipping both hands in the water. He rubbed them together, still unable to get the blood out. Looked up at Reilly.

"Here, let me," Reilly said, reaching in with his own hands. He worked at Jimmy's fingers, scrubbing with the soap to remove the blood from his nails.

He noticed Jimmy staring as he worked. "What?" he asked. "What is it?"

Jimmy's voice became very serious. "I didn't like what we did at Gate 22," he said. "I didn't like it at all."

Reilly looked back to the sink, continued to work at Jimmy's hands. "You won't have to do it again," he said in a quiet voice.

"You promise?"

"I promise."

"Jimmy the Saint's a good man, right?"

"Very good," Reilly agreed. "The best."

Reilly finished up, emptied the sink.

"Come on," he said.

They made their way back towards the others.

...

Templepatrick Airport had become something of a haven to thirty-odd survivors.

Under the leadership of Reilly and his aides – among whose number tradesman Jeff Craig counted himself – the flock of survivors had enjoyed the relative safety and comfort of everything the airport offered. A powerful generator lit a well-stocked and spacious mall. They had canned food and gas cooking facilities. Transport and fuel.

But they could lose it all in a heartbeat.

Those damn creatures were back.

More of them than yesterday. Hordes of the things everywhere – two, maybe three deep at the perimeter fence. Clawing at the wire, the shrill rhythm hard on Jeff's ear.

There was no way it would hold.

Staring through the glass of the secured alloy doors of the airport's main building, Jeff recalled how the first perimeter fence had quickly been breached by the creatures. How they'd broken through and pounced upon the survivors, tearing them limb from limb, like something out of a bloody horror movie.

Now, Jeff watched and waited as the same creatures gathered, their tireless campaign of destruction still live.

His new fence would hold them for a while but after that, there would be nothing but these glass-fronted doors and a TIG weld between the creatures and the remaining survivors.

And that seemed way too close for comfort.

Jeff pulled a cloth from the front pouch of his overalls. Removed his flat cap and drew the cloth across his balding forehead.

He jumped as a hand pressed on his shoulder.

"Geez, Father," he breathed, holding his chest in relief, "you nearly gave me a heart attack!"

Patrick Reilly regarded the tradesman thinly.

Beside him stood Jimmy the Saint, a worried look written across the younger survivor's podgy face.

"More of them," sighed the priest.

"They're trying to get through," Jeff said. "We've reinforced the fence. But with limited equipment and only a handful of people able to work after what happened yesterday…" He shook his head. "I just don't think it's going to hold for very long."

Reilly drew beside the tradesman. Leaned one arm on the glass of the alloy doors, tapped his fingers in quiet contemplation.

"How long?" he asked.

Jeff surveyed the fence as he considered Reilly's question. It was a mess, pretty much incorporating anything the survivors could lay their hands on, twisted and wrapped together like something you'd see at one of those modern art galleries. He'd done his best with it, but Jeff knew the damn thing wasn't going to hold for very long.

"Half an hour? An hour?" He reckoned it would be longer, but, like every tradesman, Jeff thought it best to lean heavily on the side of pessimism when it came to estimates.

Reilly pursed his lips.

Jimmy laughed nervously.

"Is Jock back?" Reilly asked, fingers still tapping.

"Nope. Haven't seen or heard the chopper since things kicked off." Jeff sighed. "He's not coming back. You know that, and I know that."

"What about Cole?"

Jeff replaced the hanky in the front pouch of his overalls. Folded the flat cap in his hands. "You don't trust Cole, do you?"

"No, I don't. But he's pretty much the only hope we have left, isn't he?"

"He's not much against that crowd," Jeff warned. He cast another glance towards the pitiful barricade. It was weak, ineffectual, not fit for purpose. And to a man like Jeff, who took pride in his work, sloppiness was a cardinal sin. "That fence. It just isn't – "

"It's all we've got," snapped the priest. "A knackered fence and that madman, Cole."

He swore loudly, slammed his fist on the glass.

The outburst made Jimmy jump.

Tiredness was making Reilly even more irritable than usual. Before the creatures had attacked, he had been an impatient man. He'd come close to snapping with just about everyone at the airport. Thankfully, Jeff was always there to take him aside, whisper a quiet word into his ear before sending him back out to face his public. But it would take more than quiet bloody words to sort this mess out.

"Talk to Cole," Reilly said, finally. "Tell him to do whatever it is he's planning."

Jeff nodded. "What about the… *other thing*?"

"Done," Reilly said quickly. He glanced at Jimmy, then back to Jeff. "Gate 22. That's where we left them. We did the best we could to lock it up, but you might want to seal it properly, when you get a chance."

Jeff shuddered at the thought. "Where are you going now?" he asked Reilly, keen to change the subject.

"Back to the canteen," the priest replied. "Time to bullshit those poor bastards that there's a God up there who actually gives a damn about them."

Jimmy's eyes widened on hearing the priest swear.

"Well, good luck with that." Jeff said. He placed a hand on Reilly's shoulder. "Look, I just wanted to – " he began then stopped. He dropped his hand, sighed, then said, "I'll give Cole the word."

He moved towards the enclosed stairs leading onto the airport's rooftop. Stopped, still distracted, turned to Reilly whose eyes remained fixed upon him. Said, "You did what needed to be done, Father. At Gate 22, I mean…"

The priest regarded him thinly for a moment, then turned sharply to leave.

TWO

In his short journey from the airport's main entrance to the rooftop, Jeff had time to weigh things up in his mind about how they fared.

His prognosis was not good.

They were trapped in an airport that was poorly defended. Belfast International's main building was a reasonable size of place, but pretty much open-plan. Were those bitches to break through the fence (as they most surely would), there weren't a lot of doors to close on their faces. Sure, there were a few storerooms, toilets and shops. But nothing substantial and certainly nothing that could be seen as a long term option to hole down in.

Escape from the airport was an option, but with Jock and his helicopter gone, airlifts were out of the question. The majority of the survivors wouldn't be fast enough to outrun those things. And even if they could, where would they go?

It was imperative, therefore, to deal with the threat now, Jeff decided, before it escalated. But, with little weaponry and a very limited trust in the one man who claimed to have any military experience, things were looking bleak.

Jeff climbed through the hatch, onto the roof of the main building.

He found Cole, standing by the rooftop's edge, looking down upon the gathering hordes of creatures. This was a man Jeff would have found uneasy company in the old world. In the new world, however, he might just be the airport survivors' last hope.

Cole turned as Jeff padded across the roof, said, "How's it going?"

His accent said Derry, his wardrobe anything but. Cole cut a bizarre profile in daylight – six foot four with a closely shorn head, dressed in the bizarre ensemble of military fatigues and drag. His face was made-up to the nines. Finely manicured nails caressed his rifle.

"Morning," Jeff replied. "All set, then?"

"Well, I could do with Jock's help, but I'm guessing he hasn't come home yet." Cole gestured up to the sky, "No word of him there."

"We're on our own. Reilly's given the word. We're ready to go."

Cole nodded. Motioned for Jeff to join him at his vantage point, looking over the airport's grounds.

Jeff looked across the airport complex: the runways to the north and west, the neatly parked planes, the fire engines and other emergency vehicles tucked out of sight. In the Old World, thousands of passengers would have passed through this place each day.

A number of creatures gathered by a small patch of turf just past the fence near the runway. Jeff's eyes lingered on them for a while. They stood by a graveyard. The survivors had given up burning the corpses they'd found at the airport, the smell becoming too much to stomach in the still, warm air of the Northern Irish summer. With horror, Jeff realised that the earth by the graveyard had been disturbed, the creatures he watched now looking not unlike some of the bodies they'd buried…

Jeff looked quickly away.

His eyes found the control tower. Beyond the tower, more car parks, holding more vehicles. The short-stay car park, with its modest shelter, in front of that.

He looked to the fence.

From the rooftop, it looked even weaker. It was tall enough, and with the chicken wire style mesh, the creatures wouldn't be able to gain enough purchase to climb up. But it was still only wire. Those damn things could probably chew through it, given enough time.

And then what?

Jeff recalled the work done to reinforce the wire, to create some kind of second line. He'd found a 350TE arc welder in the airport's maintenance bay, hooked it to a portable genny, hoisting the whole shebang onto a luggage buggy, and wheeling it out to the perimeter fence.

Cole had been standing guard, right where he was now, looking out for the survivors as they worked below.

They'd rounded up weightier items first; the bottom part of the trolleys, stanchions from dismantled track way, bases from portable barriers - anything that was heavy and could form a good base for a barricade. They then brought looser items, such as spare tables and chairs, wheels, anything metal they could find.

Jeff recalled the sparks flying into the night as Ballymena man, Noel, one of the few among the survivors who knew anything about metal work, worked his 3.5 inch angle grinder, buffing off the coatings on the various shapes of metal, allowing Jeff purchase for both welds and return clamp.

It had been Jeff's job to weld all the shit together and link it to the fence in some way, but he'd taken a lot of shortcuts. He'd kept the output too high, for one thing, all too aware how much of the fence there was to get around. He'd been forced to slow his movement for the thicker material, the end of the rod wobbling like a bitch, but it was almost impossible to remain on target. He'd even managed to stick the rod at one stage, blowing the fuse on the welder, slowing progress down even further.

And then there was the rain.

It came on again halfway through the night. He'd asked some of the others to cover the mains cable and welding machine with brollies. He knew that too much rain would cause a short, popping the breaker on the genny. Water in the genny or the welder would have meant game over.

Thankfully, that hadn't happened.

Jeff had managed to create fairly solid tack welds across the entire perimeter fence. But those tack welds wouldn't be enough on their own, and he hadn't had time to take a second run. That was the problem: the work remained unfinished; Jeff could pick out its weaknesses from where he stood now.

He wondered if the creatures could do the same.

He watched them now as they continued their assault on the fence. His eyes lingered on one: a thickset girl with her hair cut into a bob. She wore a white blouse and tie, perhaps a school uniform. Blood stained the blouse.

They didn't make sense to Jeff, a man for whom The News and The Weather and The Shed made sense. A man for whom welders and grinders and return clamps were daily speak – not science bloody fiction. Yet here they were: four lines deep, fighting against each other to get to the front – tearing, biting, scratching at that bloody fence.

Christ, there is no way it'll hold.

Jeff sighed, removed his cap. He rubbed his head, absentmindedly. A little rash was building where he had been scratching – an outbreak of spots where his hair had thinned. The skin felt hard and dry, seeming to fold like corrugated iron across the top of his skull.

He noticed some fabrics piled up on the ground below, mostly ripped carpets and clothing from the malls. The material circled the airport building like a moat, placed halfway between Jeff's fence and the main entrance.

"What's that?" he said to Cole.

The other survivor smiled. "Ever heard the Johnny Cash song, *Ring of Fire*?"

Jeff frowned. "This isn't a joke, you know. Those things killed half of our people last night."

"I know that," snapped Cole, annoyed at Jeff's tone. "I was there. Remember?"

And he *had* been there. Seeming to enjoy the drama, the eccentric soldier had been in the thick of it, holding the creatures off as the fleeing survivors found solace in the main shopping area of the airport. Jeff had thought Cole dead until early evening, when the rain came beating upon the roof so hard that it felt like an Act of God, and he discovered Cole holed up in a toilet cubicle, a faint smile on his lips, covered in blood – either his own, the creatures' or a worrying cocktail of both.

Jeff shook his head, unsure how else to react.

Part of the fence suddenly split, a ferocious cry rising up amongst the women. A few of them were fighting to widen the gap and gain access.

Jeff looked to Cole. "Do something, for Christ's sake."

Cole retrieved a nearby milk crate, stacked with glass bottles stuffed with rags. He plucked one of the bottles, retrieved a lighter from his pocket and lit the rag. The thing flared immediately.

One of the women was through the barricade, sprinting towards the main building.

Cole hurled the Molotov, clearly aiming for the mote of fabric. He was bang on target, a whoosh of fire igniting where the bottle burst on the ground. The flames spread across the mote, each piece of fuel and av-gas-soaked fabric catching then rising up like a wall of flame.

The attacking creature shrieked as she lit up, but it didn't stop her. She kept running, heading for the entrance like a stuntman from some damn movie.

More of Jeff's fence was breaking, the crudely welded debris tearing away like silver foil. The creatures pushed from all angles. Broke through and bolted towards the airport's main building.

The flames weren't stopping them.

Cole swore loudly. Retrieved his rifle. Clipped in a fresh magazine, then aimed the muzzle in the direction of the creatures.

"Gonna get noisy around here," he warned.

And then he fired.

THREE

Father Reilly moved further inside the airport complex to meet the shell-shocked survivors.

They were congregating within the main shopping complex of the Departures lounge. Newsagents, eateries and a faux-antiquated pub made up the bulk of this area. It was the main assembly area for the survivors. They would eat here, talk. Participate in prayer or mass.

As Reilly approached, the survivors eyeballed him expectantly.

They were a sorry-looking bunch. The correct term would have been congregation, but these poor bastards were more like a herd to Father Reilly. And he was their fucking shepherd.

"Have they come back, Father?" asked a pasty-faced old coot in the corner. His accent was rural, most likely West counties. It had a stupidly melodic 'Father Ted' quality about it that may have amused Reilly, were he in the mood for comedy.

"They *have* come back…" Reilly confirmed.

An immediate draw of breath from the survivors. Nervous whispers.

"…but we've managed to secure the airport."

Cries of relief. Some people hugging each other.

"Action is being taken to repel them as we speak."
Reilly didn't want to dwell too much on said action: a half-arsed bombing campaign led by a cross-dressing mad man.

"What about the helicopter?" asked the group's chef, an Australian, and one of the few survivors to have a bit of spark about him. He leaned back in his chair, arms folded over a belly that could feed those bitches for a week. For a moment, Reilly entertained the idea of throwing the fat bastard over the top and buying the rest of them some time.

"Jock's still in the air." It might have been the truth. The *whole* truth was that no one knew where Jock was. Jeff suspected the Scotsman had done a runner on them, and Reilly tended to agree. Which was bad news, of course: Jock was the only one among them that could fly anything more useful than a kite.

"Is he coming back?" asked Chef, and then he muttered, "I fucking wouldn't," looking at the others, smiling with twisted amusement.

"Of course he's coming back," snapped Reilly.

A sudden blast followed by the distinct sound of gunfire startled the group. Voices erupted, some people getting out of their chairs and moving across the floor, ready to flee again.

Jimmy the Saint laughed. It was a nervous laugh, soon giving way to tears.

Reilly placed his hand on Jimmy's shoulder. Brought everyone together again.

"It's okay," he placated. "Those are *good* sounds, the sounds of our own people fighting the enemy back." He paused, took a breath, thinking desperately for more comforting things to say. "This whole affair has shaken us all. Of course it has. But we need to remain strong, to trust brothers Cole and Jeff to do their bit out there while we do our bit in here. Are you with me?"

He meant prayer. It was Reilly's default: *If in doubt, get the silly cunts down on their knees.*

Most of the survivors nodded enthusiastically at the idea. They were so scared they would agree to anything.

Reilly turned to Jimmy. "Are you with me, lad?"

"Yes, Father," Jimmy replied, shifting in his seat, wiping the tears away with his sleeve.

Reilly ruffled Jimmy's hair. "If we lose faith, we lose everything," he continued to the group, a stern undertone to his voice. "Prayer will provide the food that your mind and spirit needs to hold on to faith. It helps us concentrate, focus on what's important."

The sound of explosions and gunfire rattled on.

Reilly closed his eyes and started to pray.

FOUR

Aida froze.

A nervous looking man stood in front of her, his handgun pointed in her direction. His mouth was quivering, a look of desperation painted across his stubbled face. An old WWII leather pilot's cap clung to his skull, dusty looking goggles pushed up onto his forehead.

"S-say something," he stuttered. "Something fuckin' human."

"Like… what?" Aida asked.

The man went to reply, then paused. He began to laugh. His face scrunched up, tired and wrinkled eyes seeming to gain life again.

He looked back at Aida, eyeing up the figure beside her.

His face turned serious again. "What's wrong with her?" he asked, pointing the gun at the creature once called Kirsty Marshall.

Aida pulled Kirsty close, then froze. Her voice would often fail her when under pressure. She struggled to find the words she needed first in her native Arabic, then in English: "Nothing," she said. "She's just… frightened."

The pilot looked suspiciously at the pair, finally letting the gun drop to his side. "Sorry," he said. "It's just with those things around…" He let the sentence trail off, then asked, "Where are you staying?"

"Nowhere," Aida replied.

He considered that for a moment. Swore under his breath. "Look," he said. "It's not safe around here. You need to come with me."

Aida smiled weakly. This wasn't ideal, but she wasn't going to argue.

The creature seemed to understand the necessity of playing along with what was happening, keeping its eyes dipped behind its mop of hair and arm around Aida's waist.

"Kirsty," Aida said. "That's her name. And I'm Aida."

"Pleased to meet you both", the man said. "I'm Jock. Now let's get the fuck out of here."

FIVE

Bitches. Ten o'clock.

Jock had noticed them earlier, when he'd first landed the helicopter. They seemed to come out of nowhere, fading in as the night's rain faded out. Jock had dodged them, making a beeline for the trees, before moving further into the park, hoping to hide a while until they passed and he could return to the helicopter.

It was then that he'd run upon these two honeys.

One of them was tanned, not unlike the Asian girl he'd shacked up with in Tibet, around the time he was smuggling dope for the Chinese mafia. She was the chatty one. The blonde seemed a little shy on the uptake, but who could blame her in a situation like this.

"Wait," Jock whispered.

The two girls stopped, ducked behind the park wall. They waited as the bitches moved across the path in front of them. Eleven o'clock. Twelve o'clock. One o'clock, two…

Three of the creatures stopped, turned. Tipped their noses, eyes moving, a wet, papery sound cutting through the still air.

Jock reached for his revolver, gripped it tightly.

The creatures' eyes stopped flapping, settling on an almost pink shade of red. They turned to look towards the survivors' hiding place and the colour grew deeper, nearly black now.

"Fuck," Jock muttered under his breath. He turned to the other two, yelled "RUN!"

They tore across the park, heading for the clearing where the helicopter stood. Jock wasn't as fit as he used to be – too many pies and a taste for booze had slowed him in recent years. The younger girls overtook him easily, leaving him huffing and puffing behind them.

"Hey," he called. "Wait up, for fuck's sake!"

Two of the creatures were hot on Jock's heels, another striding through the trees in an attempt to cut him off. Within seconds they'd have him within grabbing range.

He had to act now.

Jock closed his eyes and then pulled a trick he hadn't tried since he was seven years old: he hit the ground, rolling himself into a ball on the grass.

The first creature collided with him hard, plummeting over the top of his curled up torso.

The second followed, also tripping.

The third slowed, wondering what was happening. It gave Jock enough time to pull himself up, reach for his revolver. She lunged for him, but he was quick, aiming for the creature's face, firing once, twice, the second bullet dropping her like a stone, her blood soaking his face in the process.

"Fuck!" he swore, spitting gore from his mouth.

He wiped his face on his sleeve.

Turned and started running again, heart pounding like a pneumatic drill.

He continued through the last stretch of trees, reaching the clearing. Reloaded the revolver, hands shaking, eyes glancing nervously around him.

More of them?

Bodies drew towards him en masse. Hands everywhere, reaching for him, tugging at his clothes.

Jock aimed the revolver again. Fired a round. Then another. A chest exploded nearby. A head to his left. It was then that Jock realised that the flesh he'd just punctured was human.

"Fuck!" he swore. "Fuck! Fuck! FUCK!"

A middle-aged man fell, blood seeping across Jock's sleeve as he fought to hold on.

The other survivors split, running off in different directions.

Jock tripped, falling to the ground with the dying man, gun tumbling once more from his grasp.

A set of hands grabbed the gun and then reached for Jock, pulling him to his feet. It was the tanned girl from earlier, Aida. She yelled in his face, "WHAT DO WE DO?"

Jock stepped away from the dead man at his feet. Pulled himself together. God knew, it wasn't the first time he'd killed a man.

He spotted the helicopter, standing regally in the centre of the clearing.

"Come on," he said, pulling Aida with him.

They ran across the clearing.

Ten or fifteen survivors moved around the chopper, their faces shadowed by the surrounding trees. Most of the crowd seemed to be survivors – Jock could almost smell their nervous sweat – but a few more ominous shapes darted in the trees around them.

"These people," Aida said, "can we take them with us?"

"No way," replied Jock. "There's no room." He couldn't see the other girl anywhere – the blonde friend. There was no time to look for her. They had to get out of the park quickly.

They pushed forward, bustling against the other survivors. Everyone was panicking, fighting to get into the helicopter, pulling someone out then clambering in to replace them, before getting bailed out by the next in line. It was a free-for-all; no one seemed to have any intention of flying the damn thing.

Aida lifted the revolver high into the air. She cocked the hammer, threatening to shoot.

Sharp movement from the trees. Someone lost their arm to a sudden ripple in foliage. Shrill screaming followed. Panic notched up a decibel as the survivors around the helicopter realised what was happening.

An angry faced man tried to fight Aida for the weapon, but she turned the barrel on him, firing at blank range, spreading his brains across the woman behind.

The crowd around the helicopter diluted.

Aida pushed forward, Jock following.

More resistance, this time from a young woman with deep blue eyes and a red, raw face from crying so hard.

Aida drew the revolver and blasted again, mercilessly. A splash of crimson spoilt Jock's t-shirt.

She aimed next at the three survivors fighting for space in the helicopter's cockpit. One shot was all she needed: the body of a young man fell, the other two leaping from the aircraft and sprinting away, allowing her to climb up.

She turned to reach for Jock.

Once in, the pilot fumbled with the controls, igniting the propellers quickly. The familiar WOOSH-WOOSH sound built to a gradual frenzy as the chopper powered up.

Aida was in the seat behind him. She still held the gun, cradling it like it was a baby. Tears glistened on her tanned skin like sugar.

Jock grabbed her shoulder. "Hey," he yelled over the noise. "It's okay. You made it."

"Not without killing," she spat.

Jock's eyes fell upon the gun.

"Where's your friend?" he asked, thinking of the blonde from earlier.

Aida pointed.

Jock swung his head around, noticing the other girl move through the dissipating group of survivors. There was something wrong with her eyes: they were shifting, changing, just like the eyes of the creatures. The pilot watched as Kirsty Marshall gutted a man, long nails raking through his flesh.

What the..?

Jock turned back to Aida, only to find the revolver pointed in his direction. "She's coming with us," she yelled over the noise of the propellers, gun mere inches from the pilot's face.

SIX

The sounds of carnage grew. They were almost certainly coming from the airport, and everyone on the bus could guess what that meant – whatever haven Herbert Matthews had promised them was now crumbling before their very eyes.

People started complaining, protesting.

All eyes fell upon Herb and his shotgun. The old man was grimacing, sweat lashing off his forehead. He looked nervous, panicked, his body shaking all over.

"Keep d-driving!" he stuttered at Benny.

"It's suicide," the nurse protested. "Come on, man. You're gonna get us all killed!"

"Just do it!" Herb scowled. He raised the shotgun to the driver.

Most of the survivors quieted down, careful not to push a man who already looked close to the edge.

But old Cecil had other ideas, pulling his shotgun from under the blanket of his wheelchair and aiming it in the professor's direction.

Herb was faster, spinning quickly to unload his first barrel, blasting a sizeable hole in Cecil's chest.

Caz caught a slap of gut in the eye. Other survivors were showered with the disabled man's blood.

Cecil's shotgun, while aimed at Herb Matthews, reeled slightly to the right on impact of the blast. His trigger finger shook, the shell leaving one barrel and tearing a chunk out of the bus driver's head.

Benny died immediately, his brain pasted across the driver seat window, his body slumping against both wheel and accelerator, launching the bus in kamikaze fashion through the front entrance to Belfast International Airport.

...

Darkness.

The whirr of the engine woke her. A nauseous feeling in her belly followed, even before her vision had fully returned.

Caz sat up, spitting and coughing into her hands. She wiped her face, vision finally clearing. She'd one clanger of a headache, but she was alive and seemingly mobile – that much was a relief.

A quick look around confirmed the worst: the bus had crashed. Several bodies were entangled within the wreckage. Flames sparkled amongst the crumpled metal of the bus.

Her hands bled freely. Ignoring the discomfort, Caz pulled herself from the floor of the vehicle.

She noticed that half of the bus – the front half – was now embedded within the front entrance of the airport. The back of the bus, however, was still exposed to the outside – the blown-out windows giving way to the bright light of day.

Caz made her way to the front seat of the bus, where she'd left the ailing Barry Rogan. Barry hadn't moved much in the carnage. He was still alive, his chest rising and falling with each breath, but his legs had got somehow trapped under the seat in the crash, meaning it was impossible to move him – even if Caz had the strength to try.

A stirring from behind startled Caz. Turning quickly, she noticed a ginger mop of hair rise from the dust and embers. It was the doctor.

Caz moved to his aid, helping him to his feet.

"Geez," Red protested. "I'm getting way too old for this shit."

"Are you hurt?" Caz asked.

"Only my feelings," he quipped. One look at his bloodstained lab coat suggested he was lying. A sudden wince confirmed this, but he steadied himself, turned to Caz and asked, "Where's Benny?"

"Who?"

"Benny. He was driving."

Caz looked to the driver's cabin, her eyes narrowing at the sight that met her. The body of a man sat rigid in the seat, his skin painted in blood and dust. There was something spread across the window beside him. It looked like puke, but Caz suspected it was the poor sod's brain.

She turned away.

Red stumbled through the debris towards his friend, cradled his head in his arms, and swore. "Anyone else make it?" he asked in a quiet voice.

Caz looked around, finding nothing but bodies and debris. "I don't know," she said. "You'll need to check. You're the doctor, right?" She felt sick just looking at this mess. "Barry's still alive," she said, "but he's trapped. I don't think we can move him."

Red released Benny, glanced briefly at Barry, and pursed his lips. It was as if the wounded survivor were a lost cause. Instead, he moved towards the back of the bus, checking each body he came across.

Caz watched him as he worked.

Some of the survivors were like Barry, not even worth checking – silently grilling within the flames, skin charred, their faces still despite the fiery heat cooking their flesh. A wheelchair wrapped around one of the seats of the bus, several survivors – including the chair's occupant – crushed together in a foul mess of skin, bone and metal.

Caz turned her head again, and this time started to retch.

The doctor continued his search, moving through the remainder of the bus, clambering through the debris. He paused before stooping, painfully, to the floor. He lifted something and threw it aside, and Caz realised it was the shotgun belonging to Herbert Matthews.

Herb's body was close by.

Caz watched as Red checked for a pulse before turning and, in a regretful tone, saying, "The old coot's still breathing."

A sudden rattle from the rear of the bus startled both survivors. They turned towards the noise, gasping as one of the creatures clambered through a blown out window.

SEVEN

"A *what*?" Reilly exclaimed.

"A bus," Jeff repeated. "It came through the front."

"Good God." The priest ran one hand through his hair. "Has it left us exposed? What about that barricade you – "

"Gone," the tradesman cut in. "The whole front entrance has been breached. We need to close up Check In, pull our defences back. That's the only way to lock this place up tight again."

"Okay, get to it." Reilly ordered.

He looked around, choosing several of the healthier survivors gathered beside him for prayer. He pointed them out, instructing them to follow Jeff. At first the men didn't move: Reilly had to reassure them that they weren't being asked to fight, but rather to strengthen the doors (he had a way with words, and he used it to his advantage at times like these).

Jeff led the men away, hurriedly.

Reilly called to the tradesman as he was leaving. "Where's Cole?" he asked.

Jeff paused before answering. "You don't want to know…"

...

He'd broken a nail. It would mean having to put a false one on, and that pissed Cole off. Unlike the other survivors, vanity wasn't something that had fallen by the wayside for him. Quite the opposite, in fact. With his satin dress and perfectly made-up face, the burly Derry man was a sight to behold.

He heard noises. High pitched squeals, scratching. The Dolls circled the bus like a pack of hyenas, waiting on him to drop.

Cole tried to focus. He needed to get this right. A wrong move now could prove fatal.

His heart beat like a drum.

The Voices babbled, clouding his head.

"You'll break more than a nail if you get too near those whores," one Voice whispered unhelpfully. It belonged to Showgirl. She was always jealous when it came to other women, but she held particular disregard for *strong* women. And they didn't come much stronger than those bitches down there.

"I know what I'm doing," Cole said. "So why don't you just shut the hell up and let me concentrate."

Rabbit whined something in his ear. Cole shushed the little toe rag without even listening. Some Voices were just never useful.

He glanced down once more from his rooftop perch. The smoke was thick around the wreckage; it would provide a little cover for him if he acted fast.

Cole took a deep breath and then dropped down onto the bus's roof. He was a big guy and landed heavily.

Several Dolls sneered at him, licked their lips.

He thought of retreating then suddenly realised it would be impossible to get back up on the roof again – a blunder that Showgirl wasn't going to let him away with: "Kinda burned your bridges, sweetheart," she said, dragging on her cigarette.

Cole shushed her again. All this excitement was clouding his judgment, and her damned nagging didn't help matters.

The Dolls drew in closer to him, pacing the bus, waiting to make their move. Cole could hear their Voices too; an almighty din threatening to drown out the other Voices in his head. He wanted to listen more closely, tune into the incoherent noise, but Showgirl was having none of it.

He could picture her in his mind.

She wore a 1950s sailor uniform, navy blue with white stripes and a miniskirt riding so high, Cole could see her panties. As the Dolls filled his head, Showgirl pulled a machine gun out and fired. The hail of bullets tore through their number, wiping them out within seconds. Showgirl winked at Cole, saluted, then gently blew on the gun's muzzle.

She hooked a thumb at the creatures clawing their way towards the entrance of the airport. "Can't do anything about that lot," she said. "Any boom-booms left? Might help thin the herd, a little."

Geez, there's a thought.

Cole reached for his backpack, carefully dropped it onto the roof of the bus. Inside, he found one last bottle. He checked his position, lit the bottle's rag, then chucked the damn thing.

Several creatures caught fire, the blaze quickly spreading through the crowd.

The windscreen popped from a nearby car as its engine blew.

Cole turned from the explosion, feeling the heat rise up his back.

"Nice work," Showgirl encouraged. "Now get your ass out of here. Those bitches are gonna be real pissed now."

But Cole ignored her, instead searching for some way into the bus.

A sunroof caught his eye, near the middle of the vehicle, seemingly unaffected by the crash. Cole slung his rifle over one shoulder, then pulled a sturdy looking crowbar from his belt. He bent down on one knee, began to work the sunroof with the crowbar, ripping it open in two attempts.

He checked his hand, noticed he'd lost another two nails, and swore once again.

He looked inside.

Saw bodies, jutting out of the wreckage like broken toys. Debris everywhere.

Something was happening at the front of the bus, but from his current vantage point, Cole couldn't see who or what it was.

"Don't you dare go in there," Showgirl warned him, sternly. She was dressed as a dominatrix now, head to toe in leather, a thin cane in her hand.

Rabbit stood beside her, ears back, those big dopey eyes of his wide and watery. "Oh my gawd," he droned in his hillbilly twang, "you're going to get us all killed…"

But Cole's *own* voice – the one that everyone else could hear – shushed both of them. He was too damn curious to stop now. He'd come this far. His blood was pumping.

Those overgrown Barbie Dolls didn't scare him.

They were back in his head now. Bouncing around with the other Voices, despite the best efforts of Showgirl. They lacked cohesion. Raw emotion and instinct were their currency. Their intensity was deafening. But their power – *their mystery* – it was tangible to Cole. He liked being near the Dolls. He didn't underestimate their ability to destroy him, but he still liked to be near them.

He dropped down into the crashed vehicle.

Noticed one Doll dead ahead, moving down the bus towards him. Several others clambered through the broken windows at the sides.

Cole slung his rifle, aimed for the first Doll then fired. The blast slammed her against the nearby seating.

He turned to the second Doll.

She swung for him, her razor sharp nails tearing through the sleeve of his dress and ripping his skin.

Cole twisted his body away from her, bringing the gun around and slapping her head with the butt. She went down hard. He followed through with a round to her head, blood, skin and brain recoiling back on his own face.

He wiped his eyes, then checked his arm. Just a scratch, nothing to worry about.

Cole looked to the driver's cabin, now buried halfway into the airport's front entrance. He squinted against the dust, spotted two figures, and raised his rifle again.

The figures retaliated, one pointing a shotgun in his direction. Cole realised they were survivors like him. Held one hand up in protest, said, "It's okay. I'm not gonna hurt you."

The male survivor lowered the shotgun.

Cole followed suit.

"You've got to help us," the male said. "There's a wounded man here. Can you help me get him out?"

Cole moved quickly to help the man. Between the two of them, they were able to lift the wounded survivor and carry him to the doors.

The other survivor, a young girl, worked on the bus's main doors, now leading to the inside of the airport. She managed to prise them open enough for everyone to squeeze through, if they moved one at a time.

The girl went first, her petite frame easily making it.

The male survivor went next.

Cole fed the wounded man through the gap into the other two's waiting arms. He pulled himself through the doors, then headed quickly with the others through the breached Check In area, away from the crashed bus.

Cole noticed a number of faces looking out at him from the glass doors directly ahead. Behind the glass was Departures. Last night they'd sealed these doors, placing a metal sheet across the join and riveting it to the alloy doorframes. But Cole could see tradesman Jeff Craig among the faces on the other side: if anyone could get them through, it was going to be Jeff.

The young girl was first to reach the doors. She beat upon the glass, petitioning for help.

A noise from behind startled Cole.

He motioned to the other survivor, requesting he take the wounded man the remainder of the way on his own.

Cole turned, cocked his rifle, squinting in the dark to find the threat.

The Voices were babbling again, and he shushed them irritably.

Behind him, the two newcomers continued to yell and bang on the glass fronted doors, desperate to get into the relative safety of the airport.

A familiar sound echoed from the bus. It was monotonous, tedious. A fleshy slapping of skin on skin.

More Dolls.

The first one crawled from the bus like an overgrown spider. All arms and legs and hair. Her eyes glared at Cole, homed in on him.

Cole aimed quickly, fired.

His first round struck the Doll in the chest, knocking her back inside the bus. Cole sensed her terror as she kicked and shrieked on the floor.

Another Doll was climbing from a window. Cole turned his attention to her, firing more confidently, splitting her head and splashing blood across the side of the bus.

More from the sides. They were spewing out like ants from a rock.

Cole moved forwards as he pumped again, then again. Each shot counted, cutting into the Dolls like hail, slicing flesh and bone. Each squeal of pain excited Cole, and he kept moving, firing off round after round, cutting an arc around the most exposed side of the bus. He had the sudden urge to climb back on board, continue his purge there.

Someone called out to him from the airport, pulling him back to his senses. They had got the door open – he could escape now.

A part of Cole was disappointed, but the Voices were babbling in his head again. And not just the Voices he recognised, there were others trying to get in again. Doll Voices…

Cole fired again, screaming to blot them out, emptying his clip as he retreated. Some of the other survivors were on him, grabbing the gun from him, then pulling him through the door into Departures.

Once through, he pulled away from them, retreating further into the complex.

Those damn things were still in his head, and he needed to get them out.

A razor lay in the sink. It was coated with blood.

Cole was in the bathrooms near Gate 10.

His pants and trousers hung around his knees, dress hiked up his arse. He'd worked that fucking razor over scars on his thighs, reopening the wounds. It was usually enough to get rid of the Voices for a while. But these bitches were different. They were still in there.

Cole stood by the mirror, eyes squeezed shut, slapping his shorn head with the palms of his hands. "Get out!" he cried. "Get out, get out, get out!"

Silence.

His eyes snapped open. He looked at his reflection. But where his own reflection should have been, Cole saw the face of a Doll. She smiled, called to him through the glass. And then there were more of them, crowding around her, looking out at him and smiling. Rambling in their incoherent language, shouting as if Cole couldn't hear them.

Need this to fucking stop!

Cole punched the mirror. Beat the glass until it broke, shards spilling onto the floor like tiny slivers of ice.

It worked.

The Dolls were gone. No longer looking at him, no longer talking to him. Spider web cracks ran throughout the remaining glass on the wall, Cole's blood gathered in messy spirals of pink.

He leaned against the bathroom wall to catch his breath, allowed himself to slip down the tiles to rest on the floor. He checked his hands, finding more blood and bruising. The scars on his legs bled freely.

In his mind, Cole could see Showgirl cowering on the ground, arms wrapped around Rabbit. She was wearing a white dress. It was ripped down the front and at the sleeves, revealing fresh wounds down her arms and across her breasts.

Tears ran down her cheeks.

"Don't you dare let those bitches in here again," she said.

EIGHT

The view from the helicopter was deceptive.

Belfast's city centre looked cleaner from the sky. It was as if the place had somehow been scrubbed; the veil of dust spreading throughout the city's glass fronted buildings and windows was now removed.

A thick plume of smoke told another story – one of life, of resistance. Revolution was still in the air, a base desire to live and breathe expressed in small pockets of rebellion. Nothing seemed organised. It was every man for himself, the madness in the park all too indicative of this. Belfast no longer existed in any tangible sense. Like every other city and town throughout Ireland – and probably the whole world – it had become a living hell for those left alive and a playground for those who were… well, something *beyond* life.

As the helicopter continued its journey north, Aida allowed herself a cautious glance at the creature beside her.

Kirsty was shivering. Her eyes flickered. Fresh blood hardened on her lips. Less than ten minutes ago, she'd fought like a demented cat, slicing her way through a crowd of survivors without mercy.

Aida had killed too, firing the gun to clear a path to the helicopter. Her body felt numb. She wanted to feel guilty, but couldn't feel *anything* right now. She'd taken life, shed blood, so why couldn't she care? What was this world doing to her?

Jock turned his head, looked at Kirsty. Even with the goggles covering his eyes, Aida could tell he was scared.

"You don't have to be frightened of her," Aida told him.

"Yeah? Try telling that to the poor bastards she ripped apart back there."

"Look, it isn't as simple as that," Aida said. "She's different from the others."

"Yeah, right," Jock laughed.

He turned back to his controls.

"Where are we going?" Aida called to him.

"I'm going to the airport at Templepatrick. But you're not coming with me." He hooked a thumb at Kirsty. "I'm not bringing *her* anywhere near the place."

Aida's heart sank. She gripped the gun tighter, showed it to Jock. "I'm not leaving her. She… she didn't leave me."

Jock clocked the gun, then looked to Aida. "If you kill me, we'll all go down."

"Maybe I don't care anymore," Aida told him. With shaking hands, she pressed the gun to his head. Pulled the hammer back.

Jock shut his eyes, waited.

Aida sighed, replaced the hammer. Allowed the gun to fall.

She tried a different approach: "Look, we could smuggle her in, pretend she's sick."

Jock laughed. "Like *that* would work…"

"It worked with *you*."

Jock shrugged. "Fair point. But I'm still not taking her there. That's final."

"Please," begged Aida. "I promise, it'll only be for a while. Look, I saved your skin back there. You owe me. You know you do."

Jock was quiet for a moment, thinking things over: Aida could almost see the cogs moving beneath his old leather cap. "No, it's madness," he decided. "Look, I'll drop you off somewhere else... somewhere safe, but not the airport."

"Please," she pressed. "You've seen what it's like down there..."

She looked to the ground, watching as a pack of women circled a stalled car on the M5.

Jock followed her gaze.

Two survivors huddled together by the car's open door. One of the creatures swooped in and Aida looked away.

"Please," she begged again.

Jock watched the scene play out, then turned, looked at Kirsty, then at Aida again. She could still see fear in his face, his eyes wide and bright behind the goggles, his mouth drawn. But there was something else there now. Pity, maybe.

"Jesus, okay!" he said, and then looked away and thought for another while. "Look, I think I know a place where we can hide you both," he added. "But you have to play by *my* rules, got it?"

"I promise," Aida said. She reached a hand through to the front, gripped Jock's shoulder. "Thank you," she said.

He looked at her hand. "I must be insane," he said.

Aida squeezed his shoulder once more.

Beside her, Kirsty Marshall's eyes were still flickering.

NINE

Caz stood at the doors to Check In, one hand pressed against the glass.

She was thinking about Barry Rogan.

A single tear ran down her cheek.

He was still on the bus. Vulnerable, alone, left to the mercy of those creatures.

Caz had been scared. It was what those things did to you, no matter who you were. There was nothing else she could have done for him, but Caz still felt guilty: they'd taken Tim – they'd even taken Star – and now she'd given them Barry.

Caz could see one of them, now. Staring in from the other side of the glass. Mapping her gaze perfectly, tracing every movement like some messed up reflection.

Behind the creature, a few more gathered. Nonchalant. Serene. Sated. As they drew in closer, Caz could almost read their minds: they were thinking about how to break through these doors.

The first creature turned away from her, studied the metal sheet stretching across the glass, holding the alloy doors together. She ran her finger along the door's join. Reached with her other hand, tried to pull the doors apart. But it was no good. There was no purchase to be gained. The metal sheet would hold.

She looked back to Caz, hissed.

Her lips were caked in fresh blood, and Caz wondered if some of it belonged to Barry.

The teenager wiped her face.

Barry was dead. She had to put him out of her mind.

...

Barry wasn't *quite* dead yet.

He lay on the bus, FORGET ME NOT standing over his body, running her fingers over the ragged stump that used to be his genitals.

She started to sing again. The same song as before. Barry still couldn't make the words out. The chorus was the same: one word with three syllables. He was sure he knew it, or maybe it reminded him of another song. The same catchy melody and toe-tapping beat.

Suddenly, she changed form. Still wearing her FORGET ME NOT t-shirt, but now cloaked in fairy wings and holding a magic wand. She rose up from the floor, waved the wand, singing that damn chorus line over and over again. One word. Three syllables.

Barry strained to listen, tried to make out the word but failed.

Glitter fell from the wand, showering his wounds.

Barry reached for her with his hands, longing to touch her, explain that he had changed, that he was sorry for what he'd done to her all those years ago, but she moved to avoid his grip. Hovered above his reaching fingers, continued to shower him with the glitter.

And then Barry got angry. Shouted at her, waved his fists. Called her a BITCH and a WHORE and a CUNT.

But none of that mattered – he was powerless, could do nothing to stop her.

The glitter continued to fall, sparkling as it settled on his body, tingling against his skin. Its energy surged through his veins. His breathing grew stronger, his heart swelling within his chest, the torn flesh knitting together before Barry's very eyes.

He looked again to FORGET ME NOT and she smiled.

She had plans for Barry Rogan.

Big plans.

TEN

They landed on the mostly disused side of the airport's roof.

Jock pulled the goggles from his face, then climbed out of the helicopter. He opened the side door, ushered his two passengers out, stepping back as the blonde exited.

He knew this was a bad idea. He knew because a man like Jock *wrote* the very definition of 'bad idea', and he'd never done anything even nearly as stupid as this.

They moved towards a hatch in the roof.

A ladder brought them down to a dingy looking corridor. "It leads to a couple of holding rooms," Jock said, fumbling in his pockets for a cigarette as he walked. "They were cleaned out a couple of weeks ago, so no one really comes down this way anymore."

He paused by a door. Lit up, glaring at the two women with his bad eye, the one that had kept him out of Fly School.

The door opened into a dusty old room with nothing but a couple of lockers and a table inside.

Jock led the two women inside.

He sneaked another peek at the blonde. She stood with her back against the wall, glaring back at him. In the poor light, she looked even more human than before.

Jock dragged on his cigarette.

What the fuck am I doing?

Sure, the bitch seemed fairly placid right now, but how long would that last? This was a wild animal he was dealing with, a killer. There was still blood on her clothes from the last time she'd gone homicidal.

Aida tended to the blonde as though she were a child, wrapping her with an old blanket she'd found in the locker. The blonde didn't put up any fight at all. She slid down the wall, dropped her head as if to rest for while.

Aida turned to Jock, smiled weakly. Her belly suddenly rumbled, and she reached for it with her hand, as if embarrassed.

"You're hungry." Jock said. He fumbled in his pockets, produced a chocolate bar. Handed it to Aida. "There's other stuff in the chopper. Some water, maybe, and more blankets. I'll bring it all down for you."

"Thanks," came the reply. It was suspicious gratitude but gratitude nonetheless. Aida still had his revolver and didn't look like she was too keen on giving it up any time soon.

Jock made his way down the corridor, up the ladder and back onto the roof.

He returned to the chopper. Retrieved some bags. They mostly contained basic provisions for his journey, a journey stalled by some half-baked sense of responsibility for those he'd left behind at the airport.

Which reminded him…

He had some explaining to do.

ELEVEN

Belfast International was Northern Ireland's largest airport. Smaller airports existed: one closer to the city centre and another in Derry, but the International had acted as the main airspace to and from the northern part of Ireland for as long as most people cared to remember. Now, of course, it was only half an airport.

The crashed bus had succeeded in writing off the main entrance and Check In desk. But before that, on that very first day, an even more dramatic crash had occurred: the formidable bulk of a Boeing 747 nose-dived its way through Arrivals.

This left only the eateries and small mall of Departures available to the survivors. It was a spacious area, containing pretty much all they needed: comfortable seating to sleep on, non-perishable snacks by the truck load and a merry swag of designer clothes, pharmaceutical and electrical goods to pillage.

There was light, power, and with a fully equipped kitchen and a storeroom full of gas cylinders, the survivors could enjoy some basic hot meals, courtesy of the airport's cigar-smoking, foul-mouthed Aussie chef.

Chemical toilets replaced the plumbed variety, the latter being mostly blocked up with concrete.

All in all, it wasn't the worst of places to call home, boasting a hell of a lot more than the shadowy streets of Belfast City.

Until now.

Red found himself at Gate 10, a room with a view of the runway and several hundred dead bitches amongst the parked Boeings.

It was his new surgery.

He'd laid the unconscious Herbert Matthews across one of the more comfortable seats, wrapping his tired old body in clean warm blankets from the mall. For the doctor, this was as basic a medical facility as you could get. With virtually no equipment (save what he'd packed hurriedly into a plastic bag) he'd only been able to stop the blood loss, then clean and dress Herb's wounds, using paper stitches for the more serious cuts. Were an IV drip available, Red could have got some fluids into him even while he was out. In the absence of such, Red could only make the old coot comfortable, hoping his own constitution would swing favourably.

"I'd wondered where you'd got to," came a voice from nearby. It was the young girl from the bus. Red had lost sight of her after the crash, but here she was. Cute as ever.

"I think they're kinda excited about having a doctor," he quipped. "There's already a priest, cook, dentist. I guess a doctor puts the cream on the cake."

Caz tried to smile but failed. Instead her eyes glassed over, and her lips tensed.

"Hey," Red said, "It's okay."

"It's not okay," Caz retorted. "It'll never be okay again."

Red could tell she wanted to cry, to let it all out, the worries and pain and heartache that a girl her age shouldn't have to deal with. She reminded him of his daughter, a few years younger, maybe, but a similar way of carrying herself. He was just about to say something, to offer some kind of comfort, when a sudden movement from Herbert Matthews' bed distracted him.

Red moved quickly to the old man, checking to see if he was conscious. "Can you hear me? Hallo?"

Caz dabbed at her eyes, composed herself, then asked, "What can I do?"

Red looked around, thinking of what he needed to keep the old man afloat. "Some water. Check the machines around here, or the bar areas. Quickly, go!"

She hurried off.

Red turned back to Herb, called his name.

He felt his hand being grabbed. A rasping, dehydrated voice spoke to him. "Muriel...?" it said.

"Only on Tuesdays," the doctor quipped. "Today I'm Red." He pulled a thermometer from his bag, eased it through the old man's cracked lips. "Suck on this, for a minute," he said.

Caz returned with a bottle of mineral water. She gave it to Red, who checked its contents. "This is fucking sparkling," he mumbled to her, irritated.

"It's all I could find!"

He shook his head, took the packet of straws she'd brought. Split the pack, drawing one out then dropping it into the opened bottle. "Here," he said, removing the thermometer from Herbert Matthews' mouth, inserting the straw instead. The old man drank, greedily, while Red pulled back. "Take your time," he warned.

With his other hand, Red checked the thermometer. He wasn't worried by the reading. Sure, Herb was cold, but it wasn't anything life-threatening. A few more blankets and some fluids should sort him out. That was Red's diagnosis, and he was sticking with it.

"Did... did we make it... home?" mumbled the old man.

He wasn't making sense, perhaps still in shock. But the words weighed heavily on Red's mind. He'd spent most of his pre-bitch post-apocalyptic time doing the rounds at Whiteabbey's hospital, trying to keep a few survivors above flatline. Now, he found himself as resident doc of a refurbished airport tending to this bloody fool.

Neither situation felt very homely.

Once upon a time, Red had lived a simple life in the country, away from everyone else. He'd enjoyed his home comforts, familiarities that made a place live and breathe: an open fire and beer fridge; the shitty sofa that was just too damn comfy to replace; an overgrown garden – all things lost to him forever.

Herb Matthews pointed to the windows. "The rain," he said. "They don't like the... rain."

"Who doesn't like the rain?"

"The creatures!" he cried. "Those *beautiful* creatures!"

"Shhhh, try not to talk," Red said. "You're safe now; there's nothing to worry about."

Don't like the rain?

The doctor rolled his eyes, not quite sure what the old fool meant. Nobody liked the rain. Damp, dreary days were all too common in Ireland, especially in the countryside where he had lived. But now there might be something to love about it, because as Red turned to the windows, watching those little beads beat upon the glass, he could see that what Herbert Matthews was saying was true...

There were no creatures.

Only moments ago, before the first pitter-patter, their numbers had stretched right across the runway.

Now, he couldn't spot a single one.

TWELVE

Chef's beady eyes surveyed the length and breadth of the airport kitchen area.

The place was a fucking mess.

A bottle of Coke lay broken across the tiled floor. Drawers were hanging open, their contents strewn everywhere. A single frying pan, still containing the remnants of breakfast, lay half-in-half-out of the sink, unwashed.

Most of this shit was the result of looting, someone having done the place over just before everything went Pete Tong. But the unwashed pan was just pure laziness.

Chef's staff scurried around, picking everything up, tossing the good stuff into plywood banana boxes, bagging the rest. An older woman stacked the boxes in the corner, later to be sorted then placed back in the drawers and cupboards. A few others carried the stuffed bags away for storing until they could dispose of them.

Chef felt increasingly angry as he watched the staff clean around him. He'd worked bloody hard on this kitchen, made it his own. Only for someone to come and tear it all apart for a few measly scraps.

Thieving bastard!

The cunt that did it was probably dead now. Ripped into slices like the preserved ham he'd stolen. This consoled Chef a little. It was just reward for their fucking sins.

"Still can't believe it," he lamented to the man beside them. "Have they no fucking gratitude?"

The man beside him was called Archie, and he agreed wholeheartedly. He agreed with everything Chef said. That was Archie's main purpose in life: to laugh whenever Chef laughed, to tut whenever Chef tutted. He was like the Aussie's shadow, albeit a smaller, skinnier, less verbose shadow.

Chef sighed, exasperated by the whole affair.

He looked out across the canteen. The tables were packed with pretty much anyone who still walked upright. They gathered around Father Patrick Reilly, hanging on his every word, like he was The Good Lord himself. Chef didn't care much for Reilly. He found the man's pious and fluffy charms nauseating and terminally fucking boring. Chef was not a religious man, nor had he ever been. Chef was nothing. Chef was simply Chef.

His eyes swept to the left, catching a tall, nervous-looking man ease his way through the canteen, and he smiled. "I don't fucking believe it…" he muttered to himself.

Chef pushed his way through the kitchen, eyes fixated on the newcomer. "Jock!" he called, "Hey, Jock!"

Some of the others turned at his bark. Jock stopped, looking to see who was calling him. Waited when he saw that it was Chef.

"Where were you?" Chef asked him.

"What do you mean?" Jock said. "I-I took the chopper out for some recon and – "

"Bullshit," laughed Chef. "Recon my ass! You took off, didn't you?"

"No, I didn't fucking take off. Wise up, would you?"

Chef shook his head, still smiling. He wondered why Jock was getting so worked up. It wasn't like he cared if the Scottish cunt had been on the fly. Chef would have done the same, were he a fucking pilot. "Look, Jock, I'm only messin' with ye. So calm yourself down, or – "

He felt a hand on his shoulder.

Ushering him gently to the side, Father 'Prick' Reilly stepped up to interject. "Welcome back," the priest said, offering his hand.

Jock shook it sheepishly. "Look, I wasn't running," he said.

"I know that. Everyone knows that." Reilly looked to Chef challengingly. "Isn't that right?"

Chef shrugged.

"We were worried, that's all," Reilly continued. "It got so… confusing back there. Very confusing. I'm sure no one blames you for being scared."

Chef laughed, mumbling something about piss stains and pants, but he was heartily ignored.

"It's not just here," Jock said in a low voice, pulling Reilly to the side. "Those things were *everywhere*."

"How far did you go?"

"Circled the city centre. Some of the outskirts, too."

"And you saw them everywhere you went."

"Pretty much, yes."

"Well they're gone now," Reilly said. "Since the rain came, it seems.

He thought for a moment, then looked Jock sternly in the eye and asked, "Did you see any survivors when you were out there?"

Jock blinked, played with the leather cap in his hands. "Not a one, mate."

Reilly studied Jock's face for a moment, then smiled. He placed one hand on the pilot's shoulder, as if to congratulate him for a job well done. "Good to have you back with us."

He went to walk away when Chef spoke: "Yeah, for how long?"

Reilly stopped, turned to him. "Sorry?"

"Those creatures. You say they're gone, but for how long?"

"You know I can't answer that. Now if you'll excuse me…" Once again, Reilly went to take his leave.

"I guarantee you they'll be back," Chef called after him. "And that's when we should hit them with everything we fucking have! That'll keep them the hell away, you mark my words!"

Archie agreed. But he was probably the only one. None of the other survivors seemed up for a fight.

"Well, good luck with that, guys," Jock quipped, spirits lifting now the priest had gone. "Meanwhile, I'm starving. So, what have you boys got on the boil?"

Chef looked at the man, incredulously. "Are you fucking joking me? How the hell do you think I've had the time or inclination to work today? Never mind the fact that some bastard stole a load of stock last night!"

Archie mumbled agreement.

"You must have something left. I'm fucking famished!" Jock pressed, mouth agape as if to show Chef just *how* hungry.

"You cheeky bastard!" Chef laughed. "Listen, best I can do for you is a bag of crisps. There's not much left in there, you know. And what's there needs sorted."

He clicked his fingers.

Archie ran off, then returned with a six-pack of crisps, gave it to Chef.

Chef split the pack, threw a couple of bags to Jock. "You owe me," he said, pressing his finger to the pilot's chest. "So, next time you decide to take off, save a seat for me. Okay?"

Jock smiled thinly.

THIRTEEN

Caz woke.

It was night-time. The moonlight bathed her skin.

She rubbed her eyes. Looked around.

She was still in the lounge of Gate 10. Across the way, she heard the snores of the doctor she had met only hours ago. Nearby, Herbert Matthews was breathing heavily. From outside, she could hear the rain, comforting with its pitter-patter against the windows and roof of the airport structure. Lulling with its hypnotic song.

But there was something else.

A dull echo resonated deep in her ears. She couldn't work out whether it was real or just in her head.

She looked again over at the other two survivors. Neither had stirred.

There. A banging sound. Barely audible over the downpour.

Caz rose from the airport seating, threw aside the sheets. She quietly slipped into her shoes, still listening for the sound.

There it was. Just like before. Three bangs.

She made her way over to the sprawling glass windows, hazarding a glance outside. She almost expected to see the women. There had been hundreds of them earlier before the rain started.

Another three bangs.

Caz felt her heart skip.

She reached into her pocket for the crucifix. It was a reflex action. A pine for comfort. Like grasping the hand of a lover.

Caz slowly made her way across the tiled floor of the lounge, back into the main mall area of the airport.

She passed some of the other gates, also populated with dozing survivors, dog-tired into sleep, despite their fear. One of them, an old man she had noticed talking to the priest earlier, suddenly bolted upright. He looked straight at Caz, the moonlight catching his eyes. Then, he simply lay back down again.

The banging grew louder the further she walked through the airport.

She moved beyond the Departure gates and back through the main shopping mall.

She passed several shops. A designer clothes store, somewhat pecked over by the survivors. A pharmacy and duty-free, its variety of fragrances largely untouched. A dining area, complete with tables and chairs, large black bin bags sloped around the tables like sleeping sentries.

Caz moved onwards, through security. She moved past the airport's old-style pub, past a newsagents and down a stalled escalator. Her steps against the ingrained metal echoed throughout the sparsely populated airport.

She reached the entrance. The sound was on top of her, all around her. It came from the door through which she and the others had earlier escaped.

It was a knocking sound, still coming in threes. In the pale light, Caz could make out red stains on the glass.

There was someone there.

A bloody palm beat suddenly against the glass, hammering out the steady rhythm, ONE, TWO THREE.

Caz narrowed her eyes, tracing the shape of the silhouette behind the glass. It wasn't one of the women. The profile looked male.

Her heart was beating so fast, Caz nearly swallowed it.

She moved closer to the glass, trying to make out more of the figure standing behind it. The head was bowed, and she still couldn't make out a face, but the frame was definitely male.

Tall and thin. A messy mop of hair.

Caz suddenly recognised him.

The face looked up at her, and she was sure.

It was Barry Rogan.

FOURTEEN

Reilly and Jeff stood looking at the man behind the glass.

Caz was crying, her face pressed against Red's chest. The doctor consoled her gently, stroking her hair.

The teenager's screams had woken up most of the survivors. A crowd now gathered around the glass doors, everyone staring at the trapped man.

"We have to help him!" Caz protested.

"Let me think, damn it," Reilly protested.

"Barry!" Caz screamed, not listening to the priest. "Barry, I'm sorry!"

Caz lunged for the glass, but Red held her back, his arms wrapping tightly around her small body. Reilly wished the doctor would give her some sort of sedative; she was making his job very bloody difficult.

Jeff shone his torch on the glass.

Barry Rogan looked out at them. His face was blank. His clothes were covered in blood, yet, save for his hands – bloodied and bruised from the insistent beating upon the glass – Reilly couldn't see any significant injuries.

The priest ran a hand through his hair.

He had to think this through. He didn't know what was going on here, where Barry had come from or what he wanted. Sure, the women were nowhere to be seen, now, but what if they were hiding out there in the darkness of Check In, using this Barry Rogan character as bait, waiting for the survivors to unseal the doors only to swoop in, fight their way through.

Jeff looked at Reilly, his torch beam still on Barry. "What do you think?"

Reilly shook his head. "So, he was on the bus with them."

Jeff shrugged. "That's what the girl says."

"He was! Tell them, Red!" Caz screamed.

The doctor seemed confused. "He was on the bus alright. But not like *that*. The guy I treated was real messed up. There's no way he could be walking. No way."

Caz struggled again. "Barry!"

Barry seemed to recognise her all of a sudden. He called to her, his words muffled through the glass.

"He looks human, sounds human…" Jeff offered, then shrugged again.

Reilly blew some air out. Nothing made sense in this godforsaken world. First those women and now some guy rising up from his deathbed, fresh as a daisy. He thought of Lazarus, of Jesus Christ himself – stories in the bible where people who'd been dead had risen up.

But that's all they are, right? Stories.

"You can't leave him there!" Caz petitioned. "Please! Help him!"

Reilly looked to Jeff. "She's right, we have to help him. Can you open that join up again?"

Jeff nodded his head. "It's only the riveted plate holding the doors together. I should be able to break the seal with a screwdriver, then prise it off." He tipped his head to the side, frowned. "If it was a TIG weld around the join instead of the plate across the front, it would be a different matter. You'd be looking a truck to pull the doors apart and – "

"Okay, you can do it," Reilly cut in. "Good. But I want Cole here, armed, in case something goes wrong."

"Okay, I'll see if I can find him," Jeff said.

Reilly watched the tradesman move back through to the airport mall.

He looked to Barry Rogan again, hoped to God he'd made the right decision.

FIFTEEN

Jock made his way to the airport kitchen area.

Sheepishly, he raided the cupboards. Threw a couple of bottles of water and some tinned foods into his knapsack. Added some cutlery and a can opener. Bottle of vodka as an afterthought.

He retreated back through the main sleeping area. There were few survivors there. Most of them had gone down to see whatever drama was happening at the entrance. Jock looked left and right before opening the maintenance door that led to the airport's holding rooms and the two women he'd picked up in Belfast's Botanic Gardens.

He entered their hideout, closing the door quickly behind him. Inside, he found Aida at the table. At the other side of the room stood Kirsty, wrapped in a blanket, the creature's head bowed, hair covering her eyes.

A sudden rattle of thunder. The rain continued to pound the roof of the airport.

Aida shivered, looked to Jock. "Did anyone see you?"

"No. There's something going on at the entrance." He handed one of the water bottles to her. "Everyone's down there."

"Did you get any food?"

Jock passed her a tin of soup. Followed through with the tin opener and a spoon.

Aida tore quickly through the tin, tipped it to her mouth. She drank its contents deeply. Wiped her face with the back of her hand.

Jock looked to Kirsty. "Does *she* need anything?" he asked.

Aida shrugged. "I don't know. I really don't."

"What's she doing?"

"Sleeping, I think. She's been like this ever since the rain started."

"She sleeps standing up?"

"Guess so."

Jock sighed. "Glad someone can. I don't think I've slept a wink since those bit– " he stopped, rephrased his words, "Since all of this started."

Aida's eyes fell upon Kirsty again. She smiled, like a mother looking upon her child. It unnerved Jock.

He began to wonder how the two had met. How deep their connection ran and which way Aida would swing if she had to choose a side. Of course, the enigma of it all made the young Egyptian woman all the more attractive to Jock, a man for whom the average woman was no longer appealing. He needed someone dangerous, unpredictable, and they didn't come more dangerous or unpredictable than this bird. He rolled his eyes. Bloody typical that he would find himself courting someone whose best friend was a fucking monster…

Which reminded him.

"I got us… this," he said, producing the bottle of vodka. "Figured we deserved it after all we've been through."

Aida smiled. "That's really thoughtful, but I don't drink," she said. "It's against my religion."

"Oh," Jock said. He placed the bottle on the table, as if embarrassed to even be holding it. "I didn't think of that, I'm sorry, I just – "

Aida reached for his hand, gripped it tight. "What I did," she said. "In the park. It was just panic. I-I…" A tear ran down her cheek, unchecked. The sudden emotion was welcome. Until now, the younger survivor had revealed nothing of herself to Jock, always guarded, always suspicious.

He fumbled in his pocket, finding an old hanky he'd changed the oil with a few days ago. Used it to dab at Aida's cheek. The tears were replaced with oil stains, but she didn't seem to notice or care. She just made more tears, and these too needed to be wiped away.

Something moved in the corner. Jock turned towards the creature. The blanket had fallen from her body, but she herself didn't move, still in whatever trance held her.

He looked back to Aida. "Look, everyone's done something they haven't been proud of. You ever wonder what I was doing out there when I ran into you?"

Aida shook her head.

"I was running." He pulled his cap off, ran a finger over its rugged leather. "When those creatures attacked the airport, and everyone was scrambling for their lives, I just scarpered. Never told anybody where I was going. Just ran." He looked Aida in the eye. "I panicked," he said, "Just like you did in the park."

She smiled gratefully, then buried her head into his shoulder. She cried softly for a while and Jock held her until the tears stopped coming and all he could hear was the steady rhythm of her breathing, ebbing and flowing like waves under the onslaught of rain.

SIXTEEN

Although it was approaching 2.00am, most of the survivors at the airport were wide awake. All eyes were on Barry Rogan, his lean frame bent over a table in the dining area, face arched over the plate of stew he'd been given.

Reilly sat opposite Barry. A mug of coffee rested in the priest's hands, but he hadn't as much as sipped it.

The priest cleared his throat, spoke: "I was led to believe that everyone on the bus had died," he said. "Yet here you are."

Barry dipped a piece of rusk into the stew then attacked it with his teeth. He looked up, smiled with his mouth still full, then returned to the food.

"I was also told," Reilly continued, "that you had been afflicted with… shall we say… *crippling* injuries?"

"Yet here I am," Barry said, glaring at the priest challengingly.

Reilly leaned back in his chair, folded his arms. Looked to the gathered group.

Caz stood up, walked to the table where the two men sat, signalling for Reilly to move. He did so, reluctantly – or so he wanted her to believe – but Caz could see the priest's very obvious discomfort with Barry Rogan.

She took a seat, leaned forwards and sighed. "I saw what those things did to you, Barry. I tried to stop the bleeding, bandaged your wounds as best I could." She paused, and in a softer voice added, "What happened? Tell me. You seem completely healed now, and that's – "

"Impossible," Red broke in. "From a medical viewpoint, that is."

Barry looked up from his food. Gravy stained his mouth, but he made no attempt to wipe it away. He looked to Caz and then to Red. His eyes lingered on Red for a moment, like he recognised him from somewhere but couldn't place it. "Well, what does your 'medical viewpoint' make of those fucking things out there?" he asked.

Red said nothing.

Barry laughed. It was an unpleasant laugh, echoing around the canteen like breaking plates.

He stopped, fixed his eyes on a blank spot on the wall in front of him, then sighed.

Looked to Caz, then said, "I know what you did for me, and I'm grateful. I really am. But right now, I don't need any questions. Not from him," Barry pointed his spoon at Reilly, "Or him," the spoon moved to Red. "I just need to eat." He looked towards Chef, gesturing to his empty glass. "You got any milk, mate? Or juice?"

Caz watched Chef's face turn pink. "Look, you little toe rag," the Australian man barked, "What do you think I am, eh? Some fucking Abo at your beck and call!?"

He stumped his cigar butt into Barry's unfinished dish.

Barry pulled away, outraged.

"Now," continued Chef, leaning his elbows on the table and staring Barry right in the eye, "you might want to answer some of that prick's questions," he pointed to Reilly, "or it'll be your skinny ass on the menu tomorrow. Got it?"

Chef pulled away, still glaring.

Reilly stepped forward, cleared his throat. He looked sternly at Chef, pulled a chair up, then sat down opposite Barry Rogan once more. "Okay," he said. "Now where were we?"

SEVENTEEN

Red rubbed his eyes, looked around.

The panoramic view in his surgery-stroke-bedroom had its advantages. But the dawn wake-up call was going to get tired real quick. Christ knew, with all that weirdness last night with Barry Rogan, he hadn't managed to get much sleep at all.

He could see the women. Gathered around the main airport building, even denser in number than the day before. Hungry looking, their weird-ass eyes sparkling through the glass of Gate 10.

"They're back," came a voice from somewhere behind.

Red turned to find Professor Herbert Matthews smiling at him.

"And so are you," the doctor replied, dryly.

"I should thank you for – "

"Don't bother. I didn't do much."

"All the same."

The old man heaved his body from the makeshift bed. His blankets fell to the floor.

"Here," Red said, recovering the blanket and throwing it back around him, "You should stay lying down for a while. Just until you get your strength back."

"Thank you."

"Don't mention it."

It was hard for Red to engage with Herbert Matthews without appearing angry. This was the man who had caused the bus to crash with his pathetic stand-off, a wanton display of selfishness that Red would expect from spoilt children, not grown men. In the doctor's eyes, Herb was responsible for the deaths of all those on the bus. People he'd grown to know, to care for and respect. Herbert Matthews had killed them. He'd killed all of them...

He killed Benny. Blew a chunk out of his head.

"You need to eat," Red snapped. "Keep your energy up."

"Whatever you say."

"I'll get us something right after my smoke. What would you like?"

"Whatever you can find me..."

Red nodded. Turned to go.

He fumbled in the pockets of his stained lab coat for cigarettes. Found the box of matches, given to him by Benny. Retrieving them, he smiled at Benny's writing scrawled across the box. *I am a dick,* it read. On the other side was a little stickman drawing that was clearly meant to be Red, with his thick curly mop of hair and lab coat.

"I want to say I'm sorry," came the old man's voice. "About your friend." His voice became louder. "Look, I made a mistake!"

But Red didn't reply.

He sparked up. Threw the used match at his feet and then just kept walking.

EIGHTEEN

Barry and Caz stood at one of the designer stores in the airport's Departures lounge.

The rails had been mostly pillaged; Caz had noticed quite a few of the survivors – young, old and everything in between – wandering around in Diesel jeans and Calvin Klein sweaters. Caz spent a little time sifting through the dregs, trying to find something suitable for both herself and Barry.

"What do you think of this?" she asked, holding a pretty little summer dress against her petite frame.

"Lovely," replied Barry, with little more than a glance.

He flicked through a rail of jeans, searching for his size. Caz looked at the jeans he was currently wearing, hanging out from under the shirt hanging out over his waist. The blood stains on the jeans were a reminder of the serious injuries Barry had suffered, now seemingly healed.

Caz paused, allowing the dress to slip back onto its rail. "Barry?" she said, drawing closer to him. "What *did* happen back on the bus? It's just that your injuries were so serious…"

Barry regarded her fondly. "I don't know," he said. "Please, stop asking me. What I told those fuckwits last night was the truth. I can remember nothing since the attack at Carlisle Circus, after – " His voice trailed off. "Sorry," he said. "Didn't mean to go there."

"Don't be sorry," Caz said. "You've nothing to be sorry about."

Painful memories once again invaded her mind. She'd been out in the car with Barry. They'd stopped for petrol, and Barry had left her in the car to go to the shop. It was then that Caz had been kidnapped, taken to that house and tied up. The violence she'd suffered, the humiliation... If it hadn't been for Barry pulling out all the stops to come and rescue her, she could have been killed.

But what those bitches had done to him on the return journey...

"Look, I trust you," she said, her heart doing the talking. "But *you* need to trust *me*, to open up and tell me what's going on. I care for you, Barry."

"Don't you *dare* care for me," he snapped, pointing his finger at her sternly. "Because if you do..." He turned away from her, still holding his new jeans on the hanger. His body started to shudder, and Caz realised he was crying.

"Barry?"

She moved to comfort him, but he pushed her aggressively. His eyes were red, bloodshot. "You don't know the kind of man I am," he seethed.

"M-maybe," Caz said, "But I know the kind of man you are *to me*."

He looked away again, face twisted as if ashamed. "The things I've done – "

"I'll never forget what you did *for me*," Caz cut in. "I would be dead if it wasn't for you, Barry. Why can't you see that?"

Barry looked to her, face still riddled with angst. He collapsed into her waiting embrace, still holding his new jeans against his lean frame. He balled uncontrollably, his body shaking profusely. "I'm sorry," he wailed. "I'm so, so sorry! Why won't they listen? Why won't they leave me alone?"

Caz held him as he wept, rubbing his back and whispering soothing words into his ear. She didn't know what his words meant, and she didn't care. He was talking, that was all that mattered to her right now. That was all that needed to make sense in this moment shared between them.

In the following days and weeks, they would work out the rest. Caz would grow to love Barry Rogan, just as she had grown to love Tim Adamson before him.

And true to form for the hapless teenager, something bad would happen.

NINETEEN

With the rising of the sun came a new day. White clouds sprayed along the deep blue like whipped cream. Last night's rain was quickly lapped up by the sun.

Cole stood alone on the roof of the airport's main building. He watched as more Dolls appeared, filling the airport car parks and runways.

There was a lot more of them today.

Using the scope of his rifle, Cole scanned their faces.

One of them turned, looked right at him.

Cole removed his eye from the scope, stepped back from the edge of the airport roof.

Showgirl was powdering her nose. She glanced down at the hordes of beauties filling the grounds. "It's a woman's world," she smirked, winking at Cole.

Cole didn't see the humour.

Rabbit was nowhere to be seen. Probably too scared to get out of his rabbit hole today. That suited Cole fine.

Cole removed the scope from his rifle and set the gun aside. It was embarrassing to even hold it, faced with such insurmountable odds, but the rifle comforted him in some small way. And a little comfort was all a man could expect in this Brave New World.

The sound of footsteps made him swing around.

It was Jeff.

Cole nodded as the other survivor approached.

Jeff returned the nod. "More of them today, I see."

"Yep. They left yesterday at sundown and returned at sunrise this morning." Cole looked the tradesman square in the eye. "I've been watching them carefully," he added.

Jeff sniffed, then rubbed his nose. Buried his hands deep into the pockets of his overalls, jingling keys and loose change. "It's kind of like a trade-off," he mused. "They get the daytime. And we get the night."

"They get the sun and we get the rain," surmised Cole. He thought about that for a while, then said, "What was it they used to call Jesus?"

Jeff's eyes narrowed. "Sorry?"

"One of the names they gave to Jesus," Cole repeated. "The Water of Life? That was it, wasn't it?"

Jeff laughed. "No idea. The wife would have known, but I was never that religious."

Cole shrugged. "Maybe it's holy rain we're getting. Blessed by God or something."

He retrieved the scope again, surveyed the airport's grounds in closer detail. There wasn't much movement from the creatures. Their eyes continued to flicker, switching colours like traffic lights. From his vantage point, Cole couldn't see the main entrance of the airport. He couldn't tell if the creatures were trying to breach the front of the building. But he could see some doors around the side of the building, a fire exit.

His eyes narrowed as three of the creatures from the crowd moved to the fire exit and started to beat their fists upon it. The doors were straining.

Cole lowered the scope.

"Jeff…" he said. "I think we might have a problem…"

TWENTY

The airport wasn't a place that was familiar to Herbert Matthews. Even though his 'condition' (*That's what the doctors called it, right?*) was diagnosed towards the latter part of his career working at the university, Herb never had much inclination to travel.

This had had been a bone of contention with his wife, Muriel. Unlike the good professor, Muriel liked nothing better than meeting new people, seeing new places and breathing new air. She never got to visit half the places she would have liked to before...

A terrible picture filled Herb's mind: his deceased wife rising up, a shadow of her former self, meeting the business end of his shotgun. Another picture bled through, featuring, yet again, Herb and his shotgun. This scene had been playing through his head all day, and he couldn't find resolution from it.

What exactly happened out there?

He recalled a stand-off on the bus. A sudden movement, jolting him in the wrong direction. The blast of his shotgun, the splash of red and crash of metal against glass, as the driver of the bus, a young, male nurse, was...

...murdered?

Herb winced as the scene played and replayed yet again.

Suddenly, Muriel was there too, her armchair exchanged for a hard back seat on the bus. In this new, revised version of events, Herb aimed then fired on the nurse with zeal. He then turned towards his wife, firing upon her too, his old shotgun suddenly developing the capacity to hold, lock and unload any number of shells into his dear wife.

But she wouldn't die.

In his mind, he could see her laughing at him, lips thick with lipstick. Beautiful eyes burning up, flames shooting from each pupil as if she was sucking in the buckshot like some kind of fire-eating, mythical beast.

And still Herb fired, shouting her name as if angry with Muriel – angry that she'd left him to this cruel and harsh world where he had to fend for himself, where he struggled without her there to do things for him, where he made the WRONG decisions…

He awoke with a gasp, finding himself in Gate 10's toilet. Someone had defecated in a bucket, and left it in one of the cubicles. The smell was putrid, scorching the back of his throat. Herb immediately threw up, partly from the smell and partly from the nervous energy surging through his body.

Crying, he fell back against the cubicle door.

He wished Muriel were here with him now. The *real* Muriel.

He didn't think he could go on without her.

TWENTY-ONE

Reilly was in the small office he used as his living quarters. He sat on the edge of his bed, staring at the wall. His priest's collar was loosened, his jacket slung over a nearby chair.

On the bed beside him lay a handgun.

It was loaded.

He could pick the gun up and put it into his mouth. Pull the trigger, and that would be that.

It was tempting. And Father Patrick Reilly was no stranger to temptation.

He looked at his hands. They still weren't clean. Pink speckles of blood persisted below the nails in those hard to reach areas. Reilly recalled the reasons why his hands were bloody. He had been thinking about little else since this time yesterday.

The awful decision he'd made.

He looked again at the gun.. It was still tempting him.

He lifted his eyes, as if to see heaven, finding only a dirty ceiling. Reilly felt trapped. He felt like he was going fucking nuts.

The door opened without a knock.

Jeff walked in, a perturbed look across his face, said, "We have a problem."

Great, thought Reilly. *Another fucking problem.*

"What is it?" he asked.

He noticed Jeff staring at the gun.

Maybe it was tempting him, too.

"Breaches."

"What do you mean, breaches?"

"Possible access points for those things outside," the tradesman explained. "The airport is mostly secured, or at least where we are is secure. We've sealed the interior doors by riveting metal sheets across the joins. But on the outside, we've mostly used TIG welding. It would normally take a lot to pull that join apart, as I was saying before, but those creatures are stronger than you'd think. There are a few points that look more vulnerable than I'd like them to look. It's unlikely that anything will happen immediately, but we need to act quickly in order to prevent any problems in the future."

More sealing, Reilly thought. *More drilling and hammering and fucking welding things to other things.* He envied Jeff for being able to wrap himself up in this kind of activity.

Reilly dropped his head into his hands.

"Are you okay?" Jeff asked.

"Gate 22," Reilly said, ignoring the question. "Is Gate 22 one of the problem areas?"

He looked up, watched Jeff's face grow red.

"Yes. It's one of them."

...

They called a meeting so that Jeff could explain to the group what was wrong and what they needed to do about it.

They had five problem areas in total.

The fire door that Cole had spotted was one. The glass doors leading to what remained of Check In was another. Three of the Departure gates leading out to the runway were also unstable – including Gate 22.

Jeff worked all this out from the map of the airport he'd taken from the control tower. He knew which doors had been sealed shut during their first few weeks at the airport and which exits had been blocked with the closing of Arrivals. Jeff knew all of this because he made it his job to know it. Planning and mending and securing kept him sane, focused. He did this work because he needed to do it.

The survivors divided themselves into five groups - one for each hot spot. Before separating, Jeff shared out the equipment they'd needed. He'd found a stack of 10mm-thick steel plates in the airport's maintenance bay and used them to create a simple doorstop for each of the problem doors. The horizontal plate could be anchored to the floor. The vertical plate could then be bolted and ratcheted to the alloy doors. Jeff reckoned this new approach would be as secure as they needed. And best of all, it wouldn't take much in the way of know-how to implement.

They were limited when it came to expertise: each team was allocated one member who had at least some DIY experience in the old world, and this person was to act as foreman.

Their arsenal was also limited.

Most of the weaponry had been brought by Cole. Some of the other survivors had arrived at the airport with personal firearms, only to have them confiscated by Reilly. With the exception of Cole, there was a zero tolerance to firearms within their community. It was meant as a precautionary measure, to keep the peace.

With his only patient, Herbert Matthews, up and about, Red decided to offer a hand. Seemed the right thing to do, he thought, after all the inconvenience their arrival had caused the airport survivors.

Reilly and Jeff opted to head for the furthest gate breached.

Red tagged along, even though they hadn't really invited him.

These two fascinated the doctor. They presented themselves as the airport's leaders, yet there couldn't be two people less suited to the role.

The priest was, maybe, at one time, an assertive type of fella. But right now he looked spent. A man on the edge. Folding beneath the ever-mounting pressure his position brought.

Jeff, on the other hand, was much quieter. Like an advert for that old saying, *Still waters run deep.* He would probably have made a better leader than the priest, were he to have wanted the job. Yet, the way Red saw it, the tradesman seemed keen to take a back seat. And not only that, he was clearly pushing the priest to the front seat, regardless of what the good Father wanted for himself.

The three men headed for Gate 22. It had been closed off from the survivors after the plane demolished nearby Arrivals. Some of the survivors had witnessed the scene unfold. They'd relayed the tale to Red the other night. Made for good conversation over a duty-free bottle of gin.

Jeff placed the doorstop, along with the 20KG masonry drill, the genny and other gear, onto a baggage trolley. He dragged the trolley, Red pushing from the rear. The priest took the lead, carrying a handgun.

They reached the entrance to Gate 22 in no time at all.

Red could recall heading for this very gate in a fit of panic not too long ago, just before the shit had hit the fan. It had taken him longer to get there that day, what with queues of people and overzealous security to negotiate. But today, there were neither crowds nor security. The airport was silent, only the faint noise of the creatures evident: their scraping, clawing, banging, flapping. These were the sounds of the new world.

They reached their destination. A half-arsed barricade blocked their way. It consisted of various strips of sheet metal stacked up against some overturned tables from the canteen. There was luggage, display stands from the mall, queue barrier posts, everything under the damn sun. It was a mess, crudely constructed, clearly not the work of a meticulous man such as Jeff.

A thick, acrid smell came from the corridor leading to Gate 22. The result, Red figured, of festering sewage from toilets that had been abandoned for weeks.

"So…What's the plan?" he asked, looking first to Reilly.

The priest didn't answer.

Red looked to Jeff.

The tradesman removed his cap, scratched his head. This was a man who took his time about things, looking at a problem from all angles. Red wasn't convinced the other groups would be so thorough, yet it would hardly matter: a man like Jeff would double-check everyone else's work, as well as his own.

"I guess we need to find a way through this," he said, gesturing to the messy blockade, "so as we can seal it closer to the exit."

"Maybe we could just secure this blockade," Red suggested. "It looks fine, just needs tightening up. We don't need to go right up to the runway exit to keep them out."

But Jeff wasn't convinced. "I just think we'd be best with two lines of defence, rather than one. If we could secure the runway exit with the doorstop," Jeff patted the contraption on the luggage trolley, "then we'd be in a much better position."

"Jeff, you know we shouldn't go in there," Reilly said.

"There's no other way," snapped the tradesman.

"Why. What's in there?" Red asked.

Reilly shot Jeff an acidic glance, and then looked to Red. "You don't want to know."

"Maybe he *does* want to know" Jeff countered. "He's a doctor, so maybe he *should* know. Maybe he'll understand."

"Guys, guys," Red laughed, raising his hands. "This is all very flattering, but there's no need to fight over me." The other two weren't amused. As Red watched on, becoming increasingly uncomfortable, they continued to stare each other down. The doctor could have cut the air between them with a plastic knife, never mind a bloody scalpel. "Look, whatever we're doing, we need to do it quick. Those exit doors aren't getting any stronger."

Jeff breathed out. Looked to Reilly.

"Okay, okay," the priest conceded. He pulled the slide on the handgun, chambering a round. "Let's get this over with."

TWENTY-TWO

Cole stood at the main entrance.

Beside him were the survivors from the bus: the young girl, Caz, and her mysterious friend, Barry Rogan.

All eyes were fixed on the glass doors dividing the survivors from the breached Check In lounge.

Although daylight now penetrated the main entrance, and the glass was clear enough to see through, the bus remained invisible. Instead, countless Dolls pushed against each other, fighting for the survivors' attention, their eyes constantly changing colour.

Barry stared intently at the Dolls. He seemed fascinated. Moved closer to them.

The young girl looked worried, stepping forward to grab him. "Barry," she began, in a half-whisper.

Cole stopped her, pulled her back.

Barry inched closer. Pressed his palm against the glass.

To Cole's horror, a hand reached out from the crowd on the other side, then pressed against the glass in imitation of Barry. It reminded Cole of the bathroom in Gate 10, the Dolls invading his mind, manipulating him, staring back at him from the other side of the mirror. But this Doll seemed different to the others. Softer. More human. She was beautiful. Tall and lithe, long red hair framing a narrow and well-proportioned face. Her t-shirt looked clean and white, as if she'd just put it on. It read 'FORGET ME NOT'.

Her eyes traced Barry, head turning to the side as she watched him. It was like he and the Doll were lovers, separated and pining for each other.

Caz stepped forward once again.

This time, Cole let her go.

She pulled Barry back, snapped, "What are you doing?"

Barry didn't answer.

The red-haired Doll slapped the other side of the glass, hissing furiously at the teenager, her humanity from before all but gone.

Caz turned back to Barry. "You're going to get us killed!"

Still, Barry said nothing.

The red-haired Doll attacked the glass again. Others joined her. Soon, there was a line of them along the sealed doors. Beating with their hands, eyes flashing, lips hissing.

One Doll rammed its head against the glass, leaving a bloody smear.

The three survivors backed away.

All eyes returned to the place where the doors had been resealed after Barry had been brought in. Jeff and the others had done a good job on it. The new metal sheet seemed to be holding, the double doors still pressed tightly together, despite the creatures' attack.

But for how long?

Cole looked down at the baggage trolley and sighed. He didn't know where to even start. Jeff had asked them to reinforce the seal using the doorstop; this was an external door now and needed to be stronger. Cole had done some building work in the past, before his time in the army, but he wasn't keen on hanging around here any longer to do this job.

He looked to Caz, reading similar thoughts from her face.

Barry's expression held a mixture of fear and intrigue.

"Come on," Cole muttered, glancing once more at the Dolls. He held a similar intrigue for them as Barry did, but after his experience on the bus and Gate 10's bathrooms, he'd also learned to fear them. In his mind, Cole could see Rabbit, both ears covering his eyes. "There's nothing we can do now. We'll need to come back when they're gone. We're only riling them by staying."

Rabbit was nodding furiously.

The survivors hurried away.

TWENTY-THREE

Rather than pick the barricade apart, Jeff reckoned they'd do best to enter Gate 22 through one of the toilets. He could clear a small space in the wall. It was pretty solid, so he'd require something strong to break through.

A sledgehammer would do the trick. Rather conveniently, he found one amongst the barricade outside the Gate, just another piece of shit thrown onto the pile. It was old, a little rusted, but strong.

Jeff took the lead, slamming the hammer repeatedly against the plaster. Each blow echoed throughout the bathroom like the bells of hell itself. With brute force, the tradesman finally blasted through the wall, creating a small hole – enough to peek through.

The corridor at the other side of the wall was quiet. It seemed relatively safe, for now, so Jeff attacked the wall again, making the hole big enough to get the doorstop and genny through.

It took a while to squeeze everyone and their equipment through, but it was manageable with the three of them working together: Reilly went first, Jeff and Red waiting at the other side. The three men then formed a line to pass along the doorstop and other gear they needed.

When they'd all climbed through the hole, Jeff offered Red the sledgehammer. Red took it without arguing. He didn't want any trouble – he was a lover, not a fighter, as the old saying went – but even a lover stood a fair chance in a fight with a sledge in his hands.

There was a familiar smell in the corridor. The smell of death. It was everywhere, of course, hanging in the air like some kind of bitter aftertaste to the world ending. But, here – in the approach to Gate 22 – it was particularly pungent.

"It is just me who smells that?" Red asked, in a hushed whisper.

There was no reply, but he noticed the two men exchange a knowing glance: they shared a secret that he was clearly being excluded from. It reminded Red of his time at school, trying to get in with the popular kids. They might have let him hang around, play footie once in a while, but there was always something he wasn't privy to, something that separated their sort from his sort.

Knowledge is power.

They passed along the corridor, slower with having to manually carry the gear. The smell became unbearable. Acrid. Stinging Red's throat. It was like those bitches had marked their territory down here, pissing in every corner.

"The main lounge is up ahead," Jeff said, looking vaguely to Red. "The runway door's just down the stairs."

"Roger that, boss."

Lounge usually meant bar, and bar meant drink. Red was feeling a little parched and fancied a drab of whiskey. Just enough to steady his golf swing, of course. He clasped the sledge a little tighter.

As they moved into the lounge, Red cast a glance at the large glass windows looking out. "Dear God", he breathed.

The view he saw now beat Gate 10, hands down. From Gate 22 you could look beyond the runways and car parks of the airport, out onto the roads and countryside. And all he could see was... *them*. Literally thousands, maybe tens of thousands of the creatures.

Red fell against the trolley, knocking something to the floor.

"Careful!" warned Jeff.

He felt suddenly dizzy. Red was scared of heights, and this was a similar feeling to that: fear and nausea combined, a head rush. He needed a cigarette *and* a drink. Badly.

Jeff quietly readied the genny, taking the breaker off, flicking both ignition and choke on. Before long, the damn thing chugged into life, its uncouth noise making the nervous doctor jump. Red watched as Jeff readied the extension lead, hooking up the drill.

"We'll need to get the doorstop down those steps to the runway exit," the tradesman said, pointing to the nearby stairwell.

It all seemed so simple to him. For Red, nothing they could do seemed enough to deal with the dense number of creatures outside. Glancing at them once more, Red could feel his heart not just sink, but pass into his bowels.

He dropped the sledgehammer. Dipped behind the nearby bar, quickly securing an unopened bottle of Jack Daniels. Red unscrewed the top and drank thirstily. Blew out some air before turning to face the others.

It was then that he noticed something else, something that hadn't struck him when he first entered the area. A large blanket stretched across the middle of the lounge waiting area. It was grey, almost blending into the pale tiled floor. Dry blood stains ran throughout its fabric.

There was something underneath the blanket, several *somethings*, in fact.

Red sat his bottle on the bar, edged closer to the floor. With one hand he lifted the nearest edge of the sheet and drew it back. "What the… fuck?!" he said, looking up to the other survivors.

Reilly stared back, handgun aimed at Red.

TWENTY-FOUR

"What the hell are you doing?" gasped Jeff. "Put the gun down, for Christ's sake."

But Reilly wasn't listening. He stepped forward, inching towards Red, his handgun aimed squarely at the doctor's head.

"What are you hiding, here?" asked Red. He slowly unrolled more of the blanket, still keeping his eyes on Reilly and the gun. Underneath he found a line of dead bodies, at least ten on first estimation.

But that wasn't the worst of it.

These weren't victims of those creatures outside. A bullet wound punctured each body. From the size of the hole, it looked to be the work of a handgun, no doubt the same handgun pointed at him now.

"These people weren't dead, were they?" Red said, accusingly.

"I'm fucking warning you," Reilly fumed.

"Not very nice language for a man of the cloth, is it?" mocked Red. "But, let's face it, even the dirtiest tongue fades into insignificance when compared to this."

Jeff raised his hands, stepped forward. "Patrick, you need to – "

"You think I give a shit about *language*?! You've no idea what it was like on that first day they attacked, what we had to do to keep ourselves safe!"

"I *do* know!" Red protested. "This madness touched us all, every last fucking human being that was left behind!" He was enraged, now, furious with the priest. *How dare this asshole think he has a monopoly on grief!* "My little girl is out there, somewhere, and it fucking kills me every second to think of that – *every fucking second*! But we have to keep going. We owe it to ourselves." Red pointed to the bodies on the floor, "And we owe it to each other."

A sudden noise startled all three men. It came from under the blanket. Red gingerly reached for a corner and folded the cover back. On the floor, shaking and shivering in her own bodily waste, was an old woman. She was alive.

"Oh dear God," Reilly gasped. "Dear God, what have I done?!" He stumbled back, almost as if the old woman might lash out and attack him.

"You fucker," Red said, his voice shaking with rage. "How could you do that to an old woman!"

"No, it wasn't like that," Jeff started.

He was interrupted when Reilly raised the handgun and inserted into his mouth, sucking on the business end like a baby's dummy. He glared tensely at the other two men. His breathing was strained, coughs spewing into chokes as he fought to keep the gun in his mouth.

"Patrick, please…" mouthed Jeff.

A sudden noise from downstairs.

All three men stood motionless.

The sound came again. Something breaking. A door pushing open, as if forced through by a crowd.

Another sound, this one closer.

The survivors turned in time to watch three figures rise up from under the blanket. They looked like young women, but their eyes told a different tale, flipping back and forth between various colours as they surveyed the three men in the room.

"Oh shit," was all Red could think to mutter.

His arms found the old woman, scooping her up like a broken doll. She weighed nothing.

The priest's gun hand exited from his mouth to point in the direction of the three creatures. "Run," he said to Red.

Red sprinted as fast as his accelerated heartbeat would allow. He could hear Jeff's voice behind him, the tradesman still trying to reason with Reilly. But Red kept running.

He made it to the toilet wall, allowing himself a cautious glance in the direction from which he came. He could see more of the creatures, crowding into the lounge area. He couldn't see anything or anyone else.

Carefully, Red fed the small frame of the old woman through the gap in the toilet wall.

He clambered through himself.

Turned to look once more through the gap.

A hand grabbed his arm, and Red immediately slammed it with his fist.

"Ahh!" came a scream.

Red pulled away from the wall. Watched as Jeff appeared.

"Fuck me," he breathed as the other man climbed through the gap. "You scared the hell out of me!"

Jeff was sweating, out of breath. He paused to wipe his forehead.

"Where's Reilly?" Red asked.

Jeff shook his head, still recovering.

But then he looked at the gap in the wall, and his face fell. "The genny and drill," he lamented. "I grabbed the trolley, but forgot the genny and drill!" He turned to Red. "We won't be able to reseal the wall. Those creatures will get through!"

Father Patrick Reilly could hear his own heart beating, the sound seeming to echo throughout Gate 22's waiting area.

He swung the handgun between the three bitches – now closing in on him like hungry wolves.

He heard another sound, this one a crash. The exit at Gate 22 continued to take abuse. Its doors led to the runway. If those bitches broke through, they'd be in the airport's main building in no time.

Reilly needed to do something.

He looked at each of the creatures, stared them down before making a sudden and unpredictable dash for the stairs leading to the runway exit. One of the creatures made a clumsy lunge, but Reilly managed to dodge it, sending the bitch sprawling across the lounge floor in the process.

He made it to the stairs, scrambled down to the lower level. The huge glass windows looked out onto the startling sight of thousands of creatures, fighting against each other and the reinforced glass in an attempt to breach the airport.

Reilly found the exit.

The doors' barrier lock strained against the pressure, threatening to buckle at any second.

He looked quickly for something to push against the doors, noticing a large drinks vending machine right by the exit.

A sudden shriek from behind caused Reilly to turn.

One of the creatures from upstairs was on him.

He raised the handgun, emptying two rounds in succession. The first went wide, burying into the wall. The second struck gold, piercing the creature's face, sending chipped bone into the air, and knocking her to the ground.

She writhed angrily on the floor.

Reilly emptied a further two rounds into her head at close range, finishing her.

His heart was still racing.

"Fuck," he whispered to himself.

He noticed the other two creatures, descending from the upstairs lounge area. Reilly kicked some chairs against the stairwell, hoping to stall their approach.

Next, he fought against the bulky vending machine, trying to slide it across the floor. The thing was heavy, most of its weight in the base, but Reilly somehow managed to slide it across the smooth floors, successfully closing off the strained runway doors. He could hear the efforts of the creatures on the outside to fight against the jam, but it would all be in vain.

Satisfied, Reilly turned, again, to the stairwell – just in time to catch one of remaining creatures lunge at him.

She caught his arm, sinking her teeth through his skin and shaking the flesh like a dog with a rubber toy.

Reilly screamed, immediately pushing the barrel of his handgun against the bitch's head and firing several rounds. The first couple met their target, spraying blood and brain against the nearby pristine white wall. The third round tore through Reilly's own arm, the pain and shock causing him to drop the handgun like a hot spud.

He fell to the ground, nursing his wounds. Blubbered without restraint.

Another shriek to his left.

Several hundred shrieks from outside.

Reilly swallowed hard. Felt along the ground for the gun. Retrieved it, firing wildly at the remaining creature scrambling down the stairwell.

The shots went wide.

Reilly took to his feet, making a pained and strained dash for the stairwell, pushing past the creature. He scrambled back up the stairs, pausing only to kick one of the chairs against his pursuer, tripping the bitch more out of luck than skill.

His heart was banging in his chest now. He could taste blood in his mouth, and his head was starting to spin.

He noticed the genny on the floor, the drill beside it. Using his good arm, Reilly lifted the attached drill, dropping it on top of the genny. He dragged the whole shebang across the floor. Struggled towards the toilet wall, nervousness and desperation helping him focus, as well as keeping the pain at bay. The shrieks of the felled creature were vivid, and he fought to quicken his dwindling pace.

He reached the toilet wall, looked in finding Red and Jeff, the tradesman's hand outstretched to help him through.

"No, take the gear," Reilly said.

Jeff didn't argue, all three men working to pass the contents of the trolley, along with the genny and drill, through to the other side.

There was a screech from Gate 22's corridor, and Reilly turned to look towards the lounge. Two more creatures rose up from the blanket. The bitch from downstairs joined them, all three closing in on him.

Reilly checked his gun, then looked through the hole in the wall. "You have to seal me in," he said.

"No, you can – " Jeff began.

But Reilly cut him off. "You have to. There's three of them here. I can hold them off while you do the work."

"Jesus Christ!" Jeff protested.

But Red grabbed the tradesman, shook him. "Come on, man. Reilly's right. We have to seal this place."

Swearing once again, Jeff turned to the equipment on the floor.

Back in the corridor, the first creature edged its way towards Reilly, the other two hanging back. He raised the handgun, fired once, twice, the second shot clipping her on the shoulder, spinning her around and knocking her to the floor.

Reilly moved forward, stepping over the creature as she struggled to get up and pumped a further two rounds into the head, stilling her.

Back in the toilet, Jeff's drill fired up.

Reilly startled at the sound, and the second creature was on him like a rash. She stretched her fingers out, raking her nails across the priest's face.

Reilly screamed, dropping the gun and raising both hands to protect himself.

The creature kept raking, tearing through the skin of Reilly's hands, forcing him to the ground, and then lighting upon him. But Reilly brought his legs forward, then kicked out, knocking the creature off her feet.

Jeff's drill continued to whine as the priest fumbled along the floor for the gun. Blood flowed down his face, getting into his eyes.

He found the gun, drawing it up in time to pump several rounds into the creature as it attacked once more, dropping it to the floor. He aimed again, firing another round into its head.

He turned the gun on the final creature and fired, but all he got was a click.

The damn thing jumped on him, jaws snapping as she bit into Reilly's neck.

The priest screamed out, beating her head with the gun as he crashed to the floor.

She tried to pull away from Reilly, suddenly intrigued by the noise ahead, but Reilly grabbed her foot, dragged it back.

She lit upon him again, angrily lashing out. Her nails tore into his stomach, digging up his guts and shoving them into her mouth, biting down on the tough flesh.

Reilly felt himself gag, the puke clogging his airways, pain and lack of air stealing him from consciousness.

The final whirls of the drill were the last thing he heard.

TWENTY-FIVE

The rain beat sternly upon the runways and car parks of the airport, washing all trace of the creatures away and affording humanity another breather.

Despite the loss of their would-be leader, the mission of the survivors to secure the various weak spots within their solace had been successful. Under the safe embrace of night, further work could be done from the outside. Jeff was confident that they could do enough to 'satisfactorily' secure the building. It was such a Jeff word to use.

No one really spoke of Father Patrick Reilly. It was like his memory too had been washed away by the rain. Only Jimmy the Saint showed visible grief. He sat alone at his table, meal untouched in front of him. His face was red and puffed up, tears spilling down his cheeks, glistening in the poor light. A few people went to comfort the lad. Most of the group just ignored him, quietly eating their own food and then leaving.

Caz and Barry sat at their own table.

They watched as the airport community continued to line up for their food.

The canteen had the feel of a soup kitchen. Gruel and wit were dealt out in equal measure by Chef. His sidekick, Archie, stood next to him, playing no other role than that of laughing at everything the loud-mouthed Australian said. It made quite the double-act, and Barry found himself smiling at their routine.

"That guy's a dickhead," Caz said, furiously.

"Yeah, but he's funny," replied Barry.

"You weren't thinking that last night," Caz said, referring to the interrogation of Barry by the airport survivors.

"Well, you know that they say: 'keep your friends close, and the bloke who cooks the nosh closer,'" Barry replied, still smiling.

He was in much better spirits.

Maybe it was his deepening affection for Caz. Or the fact that they could all relax a little, now that the airport was secure. Or maybe Barry had decided not to question things in a world with no answers, the 'whys' and 'wherefores' of how he came to be healed from would-be fatal wounds somewhat irrelevant when just about nothing else made any sense.

Whatever the reason, Caz was glad.

"Can't believe Star and Sean are gone," he said.

Caz shrugged.

"I really liked Sean. And Star was alright too. For a dyke."

"Barry!" Caz protested. He couldn't talk like that. Not in public.

"What? She *was* a dyke. Fucking looked like one, too."

"You're awful," Caz giggled.

She picked at her food. Listened to the steady tattoo tapping the window. "This rain thing," she said, head tilted to one side, "It might just be nature's way of sorting things out for us."

"What do you mean?"

"Well, those creatures: Professor Matthews said they're alive. Just like us, only they've evolved to be stronger and," she searched for the right word, "weirder, I guess." She sat her fork down, thinking some more. "Maybe that's why they come out during the day. Maybe they need the sun even more than we do – to energise them, feed them, or something."

"Evolved? Did he really say that?"

"Yeah. He said that humanity had been switched off, upgraded somehow, then turned back on again. Those things are like the next step of evolution or something."

"That's utter bullshit," Barry stated bluntly.

"How do you know?"

"Because I studied evolution. Got my A-Level Biology, so I did. And that's just not how it works. Evolution doesn't just happen overnight. It takes millions of years. And it's a lot more complicated than turning a switch off and on, again. What kind of professor is he, anyway?"

"Some kind of engineer, I think."

Barry laughed. "Well, he knows fuck all about biology, that's for sure."

Caz looked perturbed. "He's been in touch with some people from England," she insisted. "A team of scientists who've been studying this all."

"What are you talking about, team of scientists?" snapped Barry. He shovelled some food into his mouth, pointed his fork at Caz. "You ask me, that old man's been feeding you and everyone else around here a load of bullshit."

...

They didn't take umbrellas. They didn't even wear macs. It wasn't an intentional thing, but some subconscious part of Jeff Craig and Professor Herbert Matthews perhaps felt more comfortable feeling the rain's cool sharp slap upon their heads.

They'd left the main building through one of the more easily secured doors and were now heading across the runway towards the control tower.

"So, have you visited the tower yourself, er…"

"Jeff. My name's Jeff. And yes to your question. We cleared the control tower of bodies when we first arrived."

"I'm sorry," said Herb. "I'm very bad with names. Seems odd after a lifetime of teaching, but there you have it."

"It's okay." Jeff looked to the control tower as they made their approach. "So, tell me what you're planning to do, here, Professor."

"Make contact with a colleague in Manchester," Herb beamed. "You see, Terry – his name is Terry – has set up some kind of collective, much like you have achieved here, er… "

"Jeff."

"Jeff. Sorry, I knew that. Just takes longer these days, what with the old mind not being what it used to be." He cleared his throat, continued. "Soon as I make contact with Terry, we can start to make more plans – set up better connections, better communications. He's based at an air strip as well, you see."

"Shouldn't be a problem. We already had a couple of ham radios rigged up to an aerial."

Herb stopped, turning to look Jeff in the eye. "Have you talked to Terry? Or found others?"

"No, nothing like that," Jeff sighed, rubbing his head as he thought back to the first days after they'd arrived at the airport. Everything was chaotic back then. Even worse than now. Were he to guess the reason for setting up the radios, it would probably have been Reilly's idea. A way to communicate with other locals, tell them there was a place that was safe and secure. Reilly had been that kind of bloke, once upon a time. Before this world had twisted him.

The two men reached the control tower, Jeff fumbling in his pockets for his bunch of keys.

"Haven't been here in a while," he said.

He found the right key, opened the door.

Both men stepped in.

They climbed the dusty staircase to the main control room.

Inside, they found cluttered work stations and a messy ensemble of wires. The wires led from a couple of car batteries towards some radios. Jeff watched the old man run his hands over everything, like a doting grandfather. "This is just… perfect!" he said, eyes lit up like Christmas.

Jeff smiled back. The professor seemed harmless enough, despite the stories doing the rounds back at the airport. He dropped his bags, smiled approvingly, like Jeff were some landlord showing him around.

"Here's the key," the tradesman said, tossing the master over to Herb. "Keep in touch with the rest of us, hear?"

But Herb Matthews was gone. Lost already to a world of electrics and cables and machines that may or may not work.

Jeff quietly left the room. Descended the stairs and exited the tower.

He walked across the tarmac, back to the main airport building. Glanced once more up to the control tower where he could just make out the profile of Herb Matthews, standing by one of the windows.

TWENTY-SIX

Red looked out across the large window onto the runway from his makeshift ward at Gate 10. It seemed so empty without the sight of thousands of women.

He fumbled in his pocket for the mobile phone. Flicking its cover, he ventured another few seconds of precious power. The message came up, as usual:

NO SIGNAL.

He flicked through the address book, stopping at the only entry he cared about: DADDY'S LITTLE GIRL.

Red pressed the button, watching as the little green phone symbol teased him the way it always did.

And then that message, again:

NO SIGNAL.

No life. No little girl.

"Where are you, Julie?" he said.

The sound of footsteps from behind grabbed his attention. He turned to find Cole strolling in.

The Derry man's face was made-up to the nines. A little messy, as if applied in a hurry. Red hadn't had many dealings with the man since their rescue from the bus. He realised he hadn't even thanked him.

"I see they've gone, again," Red said.

"Yep," replied Cole. He seemed distant. His eyes had an alert quality about them, as if he were running from something, or someone, but couldn't quite get away.

"You know my daughter could be out there," Red said, smiling weakly. "That's what I always think when I look out the window. Julie's her name. She would have been twenty-one today. I never forget her birthday, even though her mother and I – "

"Heard you had some bother," interrupted Cole.

Red was taken back. For a moment, he just looked at the other survivor. Then he spoke: "We lost the priest. Found this old girl in the process, though." He pointed to his one remaining in-patient laid across a line of seats in the waiting area.

Cole drew beside her. Smiled affectionately. "I know this woman," he said, running his hand across her cheek. "Her name's Peggy." He looked to Red. "She seems frail. Does she have much chance of pulling through?"

Red shrugged. "She's lost a lot of blood. I need to get some fluids back into her. Saline, O NEG blood. Painkillers, antibiotics, something like co-amoxiclav, maybe some penicillin, flucloxacillin…" He shook his head, suddenly aware he was rambling. "It doesn't matter. I don't have any of the equipment I need, never mind the blood or medicine."

Cole looked away, suddenly distracted. It was like he'd just received a phone call from an invisible phone. He snapped out of his trance, looked to Red, then asked, "Where would you get that?"

"Get what?"

"The stuff you need: blood, equipment, whatever."

"You'd need a hospital," Red said. "Haematology lab or theatre fridges. There's other stuff I'd need too, for example, a – "

"I can get it," Cole interrupted. "Just jot down a description of everything you need and where I might find it, and I'll get it for you."

Red looked to him. "I don't know, man…"

"Look, I can do it. Trust me. I *want* to do it." He wandered over to the glass, looked out onto the rain soaked runways. "Peggy was the first person I met when I arrived here," he said. "She met me at the door, smiling, holding a cup of tea in her hands. She looked at me and said, 'That's a lovely dress you're wearing, young man.'" His eyes found Red. "It was a nice thing for her to say. I'll do everything I can for her."

TWENTY-SEVEN

Jock made his way down the disused corridor leading to one of the airport's storage areas. He looked to his left and right before opening the storeroom's tinny door and slipping in quickly, closing the door behind him as quietly as possible.

The hungry glare of Aida Hussein met him, her deep brown eyes falling upon the small knapsack around his shoulder.

Jock fumbled in the bag, found a packet of biscuits which he then passed across.

Aida snapped the biscuits from him, retreating into the furthest corner. Ripped the packet open, crumbs falling to the floor, before ravenously devouring the first couple of biscuits in one bite.

"What kept you?" she mumbled between bites, sweet meal spraying from her mouth. "We've been starving down here."

She referred to 'we', but Jock knew the other occupant in the room wouldn't want any biscuits.

"Any change?" he said, gesturing to the blankets in the corner.

"What do you think?"

Jock sighed. Kirsty Marshall didn't look well. Slumped like a dog, she hadn't stirred in hours. It was like she'd given up on life. Or afterlife, or whatever…

Jock sat on the edge of the bed, reached for the bottle on the table. He poured himself a healthy drab of vodka.

"Priest's dead," he said, simply. "Not sure how, but it seems – " and here Jock whispered, as if he were talking about a child, "That *one of them* might have got him."

Aida didn't reply, still eating.

"Did you hear me?"

"Yes I heard you," she snapped back, eyes suddenly alert again. She shoved another biscuit into her mouth, chewed quickly. "I just can't seem to care about someone I haven't met." She was right, of course. Jock realised that while he had been wandering freely throughout the airport, Aida had been cooped up in this godforsaken room like some kind of prisoner.

"He wasn't a bad sort," Jock said. "A bit prissy, but alright at the end of the day."

He sank the remains of his glass, looked to Aida. She'd finished eating, and now just stared into space.

"I'm can't stay here for much longer," she told him. "I'm crawling the walls."

"Well, what's the alternative?"

Aida sat the packet of biscuits down, then moved across the room. Sat herself on the bed beside Jock.

"We could leave," she said. "Just the three of us."

Her face drew closer. Jock could nearly taste the sweetness of her biscuits. Sweat hummed around her body like thick mist, but it wasn't unpleasant. Nothing about this woman was unpleasant to him.

"There's nowhere to go," Jock said. "You said it yourself. Nowhere's safe out there. Not like here."

Aida turned away, dejected. Stared blankly at a bulletin board on the nearest wall. A newspaper cutting from 1993 looked back at her.

A sudden noise caused both survivors to look to the corner. Kirsty had rolled over, a whining sound escaping her mouth. Her head appeared from under the blankets, hair dishevelled and matted. Fresh tears ran down her cheeks as she looked over to the survivors, her eyes glittering like she was possessed.

"What's wrong with her?" Jock said.

Aida didn't answer him, instead moving quickly to Kirsty's side. "It's okay," she said soothingly. "I'm here. It's okay."

"Why's she crying like that?"

"I don't know."

She pulled the blankets back to take a closer look.

Kirsty shuffled away from her reach. Settled in a far corner, still whimpering, fixing both survivors a look that suggested she would attack if they approached.

Jock watched the creature squirm in the corner, his eyes widening as he realised exactly what the problem was: Kirsty's belly was swollen, hands curled protectively around the mound.

"Oh my fucking God," he gasped.

TWENTY-EIGHT

The rain was constant, hammering the windows near the bed.

The girl's long, sleek hair shone in the paleness of the moonlight.

Barry felt his hands on her breasts. They were firm and vibrant.

Her hands travelled south, sliding under the waist of his shorts.

He closed his eyes. His head fell back as he drank in her gentle caress, his heartbeat quickening as he became more and more aroused, the girl working the shaft of his cock.

"Caz," he whispered, allowing his eyes to open.

But it wasn't Caz who was touching him.

The teenager lay beside him with a knife through her neck. The book she'd picked up earlier in the mall lay dead on her lap, its pages soaked in fresh blood. Her new specs were smashed across her face. Splinters of glass peppered her brow.

Barry looked up, found FORGET ME NOT mounting him.

She was laughing, her eyes dancing between a myriad of colours. Her laughter seemed to speed up, as if on fast-forward. Her eyes kept time, the sound of wet, slippery skin slapping against his ears, louder and louder.

Barry pushed her away. "What did you do?"

She paused, looking him deep in the eyes. "It's not what I did. It's what you did."

Barry turned to look at the corpse beside him. "No way."

"Yes way," the creature said. "But that's not all..."

She held up the hand she had been using to caress him. Her palm was bloodied.

Barry ran his own hand under the shorts, finding his crotch area to be damp and frayed. Torn, just like it was before he'd been healed.

"No, this can't be happening," he cried.

There was a sudden bang. Like a drum roll. Again it came, muted and heavy like his heartbeat. FORGET ME NOT was saying something. That word again, the one she'd been singing to him on the bus. The three syllables bounced to the beat of the drum. Still barely audible. Still lost to him.

But this time Barry didn't care what she was saying.

He pulled himself up from the bed, moved to Caz's body. Tears began to roll down his cheek, thick and coppery like blood. He realised he couldn't see anymore, feeling for his eyes, finding mangled sockets.

His mouth went to scream.

He woke up.

Caz was lying peacefully beside him. Her glasses sat on a nearby coffee table, intact.

Barry felt his eyes, then his crotch. An erection was throbbing for attention.

There was a thud. It must have been the drumming sound in his dream.

He looked to the large window, peering out onto the runway. Another thud – and this time he could see it was the result of a large brick or stone hitting.

Barry got up, pulled on his jeans.

He walked over to the glass. Leaned in closer, trying to get an idea of where the stones were coming from. Another one struck the window at eye level, causing him to jump back.

"Jesus," he whispered.

Barry looked to the bed, but Caz was still fast asleep.

He pulled on his shirt, slipped into his trainers.

Moved back through the main airport, along the tiled floor of the Departure gates towards the security door on the lowest level.

He found the side door, the only door not welded shut, their new route in and out of the airport. Carefully, Barry rolled back the barricade, unlatched the security catch. He pulled the door open, looked out onto the darkness of the runway.

A solitary figure stood in the rain, soaked to the skin.

"Barry…?" she said, clearly shocked to see him.

It was Star.

PART THREE
THE MALL

ONE

Over the weeks, normality slowly ebbed its way back into the lives of the airport survivors. Before long, they wanted something different. Survival, alone, was no longer deemed a privilege. The survivors began to hanker for the things they used to have, the things which had given them enjoyment in life before The Great Whatever.

They wanted better food.

They wanted tobacco, alcohol and narcotics.

They wanted entertainment, something to pass the time, to make them forget what had happened to them.

They wanted purpose.

An entrepreneur arose from their ranks in the unlikely shape of Cole. Here was a man who had never given up on the finer things in life, whether it were Gucci shoes or Calvin Klein lingerie. And now, the burly man with the full face of Chanel saw a market for other people's desires. And he responded to that with zeal.

With Cole's nightly trips out of the airport, the survivors were able to stock up on all kinds of things. Bartering became common, those courageous enough to join Cole on his pillaging escapades trading with the main players in the airport for other goods and services.

Everyone was forced to play some kind of role, gaining employment either in the kitchen, with Chef, or any of the other businesses springing up from within the airport's mall area. Over time, people began setting up all kinds of shops and services: clothing outlets, electrical shops (anything that was battery powered became a commodity), food outlets – providing international cuisine that Chef either couldn't prepare, or couldn't be arsed to prepare – and a newsagent. Even a newspaper became available, printed by several survivors using a laptop and printer combo.

Competition forced the airport to evolve into a dynamic and exciting market place.

And so a new natural order evolved. By night, under shelter of the rain, the survivors conducted life. By day, they hid, most sleeping through the stifling silence and ever-present, picturesque views of the bitch-infested runways.

...

Jimmy the Saint worked at the bedside of the airport's oldest resident, Peggy. He emptied her catheter bag before helping her to freshen up. Peggy seemed to be getting stronger and more able every day. Although she still couldn't walk, she was able to wash herself in the basin of water Jimmy held for her.

She could also feed herself.

Jimmy took the small plate of unfinished food the table beside her bed, grinning at the old woman as he shoved the bit of sausage she'd left into his own gob.

Peggy smiled back.

From the sidelines, Red looked on proudly. In his freshly laundered scrubs, Jimmy was looking like a proper nurse these days, and the gate didn't look a million miles away from a proper hospital ward. They had drip stands, catheter stands. A portable suction machine. An arrest trolley with everything ready to go: cannulae, needles, blood pressure cuff, Volplex and giving sets, oxygen. With a change of lab coat for each day and a bright shiny stethoscope around his neck, Red felt like a proper doctor again.

Beside him stood his unlikely supplier; a burly Derry man with perfectly manicured nails. "Does she need anything else?" he asked.

"Not a thing, mate," Red said. "She's doing great with young Jimmy here on the case."

Jimmy smiled as he approached the other two survivors. "I'm back here at two o'clock, yeah?"

"Three, Jimmy. You're back at three," Red corrected. "Show me your watch, lad."

Jimmy enthusiastically rolled his sleeve up, proudly showing off the new watch he'd bought with last week's wages. Red pointed to the number three, tapping it with his finger: "When the small hand gets *there*, I want to see you *here*."

"Okay", replied Jimmy.

He hurried off, no doubt to carry out his other errands for the day.

"He's doing okay, then?" asked Cole.

"I told you, he's doing great. Apparently, he used to look after his grandma before this all happened. There was very little I had to teach him."

Cole nodded. "That's good." His eyes found Peggy. The old woman smiled at him, but he looked away.

"Why don't you go over to her?" Red said. "She'd like the company."

Cole's face reddened. He shook his head. "Not today."

"Go on. Seriously, she won't bite."

Cole smiled. "No, not today," he said again. He looked nervous, like he wanted to go over but was scared. His fists began clenching and unclenching by his side.

"Another time, eh?" Red said, ushering him away. "It's good of you to check in on her. She thinks the world of you and Jimmy, you know."

"Sure," Cole said. "It's just that…" He allowed the sentence to die. "I don't know," he added.

"What?" Red encouraged. "Go on, mate. You can tell me."

But Cole raised his hand. "Never mind," he said.

Red let it go, not wanting to pressure the man. Cole was a strange fish, he knew that much. It wasn't the clothes and make-up – hell, none of that mattered in the new world – there was just something about the man that bothered Red – and just about everyone else at the airport. There were the mood swings, for starters; the talking to himself; the twitching; the random shouts from the bathroom; the cuts just under his skirt, which Red suspected were self-inflicted…

His unhealthy fascination with those things outside.

Cole watched them arrive every morning, as the rain receded into the final shadows of pre-dawn. Perched on the main building's rooftop, sometimes firing upon them, picking them off one-by-one, the POC-POC-POC of his rifle ringing out through the airport like fireworks. And then, when the rain came back for its nightly vigil, Cole would see the creatures off before deciding whether to sit alone with his rifle in the dark or head out on one of his scavenging missions.

Red wasn't a psychologist, but he'd covered a little mental health while studying medicine. Were he pushed for a diagnosis, he might have put Cole down as schizophrenic, with a little personality disorder to boot. The polite way to describe him would be 'eccentric'. Whatever spin he put on it, Cole wasn't a people person. In fact, Red wondered if the new world they found themselves in suited the big man better than the old world.

As Cole went to leave, Red stopped him, placed a hand on his shoulder. "You know, she wouldn't have made it were it not for you, big lad," he said. "Getting that stuff from the hospital really helped me keep her afloat."

"Sure," Cole replied. "I know that."

"Just checking," Red said, releasing his hand.

He looked over to Peggy and frowned, wondering if the old woman's remarkable recovery was *really* due to his medical prowess and all the new gear. Or if something else was at play, something that Cole could somehow sense but wasn't keen on talking about.

TWO

"You're late," said Star, without an ounce of irony in her voice.

She stood at what used to be a souvenir shop, sweeping the remnants of a broken mug into a dustpan. The shop sat opposite the canteen, in the main part of the airport mall.

"I had to change Peggy's – " Jimmy the Saint attempted.

"Floor needs mopped," Star cut in. "I've brushed it, so you just need to mop. Mix a little disinfectant in the bucket first. You know how to do that?"

Jimmy nodded.

"Good. Then get to it."

Jimmy sighed. "Then can I get a tattoo?"

"Then," Star said, "I want you to spray this shit," she handed Jimmy a plastic spray bottle containing Isopropyl alcohol, "all over the work surfaces. Clear?"

"Clear," Jimmy said. "And then can I get a tattoo?"

Star breathed a heavy sigh, and said: "What did I tell you before, Jim Bob? You have to think hard about what you're putting on your hide."

"I still got my picture," he said, patting the pocket of his ruffled shirt with pride.

"Well, keep it by your bed, like I told you. And if you get bored waking up to it, then you don't need it as a tattoo."

"But if I still like it next week?"

"We'll see after four weeks."

"AW!" protested Jimmy.

"That's my final offer, Jim Bob. I can mop my own floors if you don't like it…"

Jimmy snapped up the mop bucket, filled it with bottled water, and then added some disinfectant. He stabbed the mixture with his mop, slopped it on the floor.

Star cuffed his head playfully, left him to it.

She finished sweeping around the front.

The place was perfect for a tattoo shop, with its non-porous lino flooring and wipe-clean surfaces. It had a little sink room in the back for cleaning and sterilising her tubes, another job she might get Jimmy to do for her, or some apprentice wannabe, if such a freak existed amongst the airport survivors.

She spotted Cole strolling by and walked out to meet him. "Hey there."

"Hey," answered the Derry man, typically monosyllabic.

"You going out tonight?"

"I go out most nights," he replied. "Why? Want something?"

"Yep, sure do. You going into Belfast?"

"Think so."

"Well, I'm going with you, then."

Cole's eyes narrowed. "I can get whatever you need. You don't have to come."

"Tattoo gear," she replied, shortly. "I'm opening a new shop here in the mall. Need to move all my gear from the old shop." *If it hasn't been pillaged*, she thought to herself.

"It'll take a lot of room in the van," Cole said frowning.

"I'll get another van," Star persisted. She wasn't going to let this one drop.

"So, you want a lift into town, then? That's what you're asking for, isn't it?"

"Pretty much. And a hand lifting the gear."

"It'll cost you."

"Yeah. I'm thinking a classy pin-up girl would suit that arm of yours nicely."

Cole's eyes brightened. He rolled up his sleeve, studied his arm intensely, no doubt imagining the tattoo. He licked his lips. Looked back at Star, a faint smile spreading across his face.

"Deal. We leave at sundown, when the rain starts."

"Cool," Star said.

Been a while since she'd done a pin-up. She'd enjoy it, maybe base it on an old Bettie Page photo. That would suit the big guy down to the ground.

Star watched him walk away, still checking his arm.

"Hey, stranger," someone called.

Star looked, finding Barry Rogan coming towards her.

"What's up?" she said.

Barry shrugged. "Not much. You setting up a new shop or something?"

"Yeah. Just need to get my gear and all, but that's the plan."

"Good for you," he said.

But he didn't look so thrilled. He looked good – *too* good when you thought about it – but far from happy. Of course, Barry Rogan's miraculous recovery didn't interest Star the way it interested the other survivors at the airport. She didn't care, to be frank. Didn't want to think about or dwell on it in any way. Because to do so would get her thinking about *her own* miraculous recovery.

"Look," he said, "We need to talk."

"We are talking, Barry."

"I mean *really* talk."

"God, here we go…" Star looked away, her eyes finding Chef. The Australian was lecturing Archie about something. The smaller man was just nodding, accepting everything Chef told him, a glazed look across his face.

"I'm serious," Barry said, grabbing Star by the shoulders.

"Fuck off," she said, pulling away.

Barry was persistent. "Look, if what I've heard is true, then you're in the same boat I'm in. One minute you're on the ground, with a pack of those whores chewing your bits, and the next minute you're up and walking again." He looked to Jimmy, still mopping the floor. "Setting up a fucking tattoo shop."

"Your point being what?"

Barry leaned in closer, his voice little more than a whisper. "Jesus, girl, they tore my fucking dick off, poked my eyes out. And now look at me! Standing right in front of you, not a scratch on me."

"What do you want me to say, Barry? I know it's fucked up, but what isn't? Nothing makes sense anymore. So, sue me, but I've decided not to fucking dwell on it. To just get on with life. What's so wrong with that?"

A deep sigh crossed Barry's lips. He balled his hands into fists. Looked furious, so furious that he might strike out.

The tattooist stepped back from him, prepared for the worst. But his face softened, tears watering the corners of his eyes. "Fuck, Barry," Star said. "Don't pull this weepy shit on me, I don't need it."

"Wait," he said, but she was already walking away. "Please," he cried, but a raised hand called time on their conversation. "I'm scared, damn it! Scared of what they've done to me!"

Chef and Archie looked up, both men staring across the mall at Barry Rogan.

"What are you looking at?" he seethed, dabbing the corners of his eyes with his sleeve.

The two men looked away.

Barry took a moment to compose himself, then turned and headed back towards the Departure gates.

THREE

Kirsty Marshall was pregnant.

Her belly was bloated, skin stretched over the mound. To Aida's untrained eye, she looked a few months gone, but how could she tell what that meant, how could anyone tell what it meant? There was simply no way of knowing how or if this would play out like a regular pregnancy.

The creature seemed to be in pain. Her back was pressed against the wall, eyes flapping slowly, building momentum.

Aida kneeled by her side, careful not to get too close.

Jock reached for his revolver, and with shaking hands, began to load it.

Aida glared at him. "What do you think you're doing?"

"This is fucked up," he said. "If she's pregnant, if that's what's really happening here, God knows what's going to pop out of her."

"A child, Jock! That's what normally *pops out* of women."

"*Normally*?" Jock laughed. "There's nothing *normal* about this, and that's no fucking woman." He wiped some sweat from his brow, continued loading the gun. "I should never have brought that thing here. I'm going to put an end to this right now."

Aida raised her hand at Jock. "I'm warning you, put the gun away."

"Or what? What are you going to do about it?"

"Look, you're going to rile her," Aida said in a quiet voice. "Is that what you want?"

Jock was reminded of what Kirsty had done to those people at the park when she'd last been riled. He looked at his revolver, wondering how many shells it would take to put her down, wondering how good his aim would be and how far it would take her to travel from one end of the small storeroom to the other, if threatened. Even when in pain. "There's something wrong with her," he said, lowering the gun. "Complications of some sort, anyone can see that."

"So you were just going to shoot her? Put her down like an old dog?" Aida shook her head. "You're scared, Jock. Admit it. This has nothing to do with Kirsty, it's about you. The man who runs, who lashes out whenever he's scared."

A shrill wail escaped the creature's mouth.

Jock leapt in shock. "Jesus Christ, can you stop her doing that?"

"Admit it! That's what this is about! She scares you, doesn't she?"

Jock slammed his fist on table. "Of course she bloody scares me!"

He turned away, walked to the other side of the room. Took a deep breath, then said, "Let's think about this rationally. Maybe she needs a doctor. That's what you'd do if this was a *normal situation*, if she were a *normal woman*."

"Are you insane?"

"I must be fucking insane to have ever brought that *thing here,*" he spat.

Aida glared at him once again. "She's a pregnant woman, for God's sake. Show some respect."

"*Show some respect?* Respect for what?"

"The miracle of new life, Jock."

"*New life*?"Jock laughed bitterly. "You don't know *what* that is growing inside her, whether it's alive or dead, human or inhuman! How could you?"

Aida didn't answer.

"Tell me," Jock persisted. "Tell me how you know what's growing inside her. Because, God knows, I need convincing."

"I can feel it," Aida cried. She tapped the side of her head, "Right in there, I can feel everything she feels." Her voice came louder than expected. "You have to trust me," she added in a quieter voice.

Jock shook his head. "All I've done is trust you."

"I know that," Aida conceded. She moved closer to him. Touched his cheek with her hand. "And I'm really grateful for that. We're *both* really grateful."

Jock looked to Kirsty, a heavy sigh moving through his lips. He was tired. Tired of worrying, of hiding. He felt very close to giving up, to blowing the lid on the whole damn thing, or taking that chopper on the roof and running again.

"Jock," Aida said, pulling his face back to hers. "There's a *real* baby in there, I can feel it like it were inside my *own* body."

Jock held her gaze.

Was it normal for women to sense these things? Was there something ritualistic, something spiritual about the birthing process that only women could relate to, that a Philistine like him would never be able to understand? Jock had bedded more women than he cared to count over his forty odd years as a heterosexual male, flying that damn bird of his across the seven seas, an international man of fucking mystery. But standing here right now, it was plain the Scotsman knew damn all about the female species.

He couldn't take any more, went to leave the room.

"Where are you going?"

"I just need to get out."

"Jock, please…"

"Don't worry, I won't say a word out there." He paused by the door, sighed again. "Maybe she needs some food," he reasoned. "Maybe that's what's wrong with her." He thought on that for a while, then added, "I'll go to the canteen, grab some canned meat or something."

He looked to Aida, reading fear in her eyes, concern. "Have you got that other gun handy?" he asked. "The one I picked up yesterday in the mall?"

Aida nodded.

"Well, keep it close. It's filling up out there. More shops than ever. They'll need more space, more places to stock goods. I don't know how much longer we can remain here undetected."

He reached for the door handle.

"Jock," Aida said. "I need you. I can't do this on my own."

The pilot looked at her, then at Kirsty Marshall. The liquid sound of her flapping eyes filled the room now, faster, her eyes darker. Her face still creased in a painful grimace.

"God knows, I'm *trying* to help you," Jock said.

Then left.

FOUR

Jeff cleared his throat as he walked into the lounge where Red had set up his surgery, outpatients clinic, Emergency Room and just about anything else medical that the survivors needed. He looked over to the only occupied bed on the makeshift ward – Peggy's. She was sleeping soundly, something she seemed to be doing every time the tradesman made an appearance. He was beginning to feel paranoid, suspecting that the old bint was trying to avoid him.

Red sat in one of the chairs by the corner, working on a crossword. He looked up at Jeff, nodded.

Jeff nodded back. Cleared his throat, gestured to Peggy. "She's doing well, then?"

"Same as the last time you visited"

Jeff smiled. "That's good."

Red returned the smile. Went back to his crossword.

"Look, I was wondering if you could maybe take a look at the professor some time today," Jeff said.

"Why, what's wrong with him?"

"Nothing. It's just that he hasn't left the control tower."

"Hardly an illness. Isn't he working on some kind of project, or something?"

"That's the thing. I don't know. He won't let me in. Jimmy drops him over some food, leaves it by the door. But the old man won't as much as answer the door when I call. I'm kinda worried about him…"

Red looked Jeff in the eye. "That's big of you."

Jeff was silent for a moment. He looked out across the runway. The sight of thousands of women was hardly surprising anymore, but it never failed to unnerve him. Were any of the exit points to fail, those bitches would be inside within seconds.

He looked to Red. "You know, Father Patrick Reilly wasn't as much of a monster as you think," he said.

"I wonder if Peggy would agree with that," Red snapped. "Did you know I found a bullet hole in her dress? I wonder how that got there…"

"I knew him before all of this," Jeff continued. "He was my wife's priest. She was Catholic," he added, as if it mattered anymore what religion a person followed. "Eventually, she talked me into going down to mass with her, and that's when I met Patrick."

Red sighed, looked at his watch. "Will this take long?"

Jeff smiled. "Unlike you, Red, Patrick wasn't a particularly charismatic man. In fact, it was very obvious that he was going through the motions: sit down, stand up, bless this, hail that. You know how Catholics get on…"

"Not really. I'm atheist. So were my folks."

"Well, they do things rather theatrically, shall we say. And Patrick was hardly a theatrical man."

Jeff was quiet for a moment, as if thinking. Then he said, "About two months prior to the whole world-ending thing, I was involved in a car accident. Reckless driving, they said. Mangled a wee lad of six years old."

Red looked up, set his crossword on the table.

195

"Felt terrible about it, as you can imagine. The wife convinced me to go and see Father Reilly, try and get some kind of peace. Well, like you, Red, I'm no god botherer. Quite the opposite, in fact. But I was willing to try anything – and, to be honest, it didn't take long to realise that Patrick's own faith was less than steadfast, shall we say."

Jeff breathed a heavy sigh, looked to the floor.

"So I met Reilly, and he poured me a drink. Twelve-year-old single malt," he remembered with a smile. "I talked, and he listened, and at the end of it all, he didn't really offer very much at all. I waited, but all he said was I could come back and see him any time I wanted.

"Well, I visited him every day after that. We worked our way through one bottle and then another. And here's the thing, Red: Reilly never as much as breathed a prayer or sang a Hail Mary in all the time I spent with him. None of that stuff. He just listened. And poured."

Jeff removed his peak cap, holding it in front of him like a penitent child. His overalls were filthy, even more stained than usual. The med school psychologist in Red might say the tradesman was working even harder, avoiding any free time where his mind could wander and allow dark stabs of guilt to creep through.

"You know," Red said, standing up and fumbling in his pockets for a cigarette, "you didn't take that kid's life, Jeff. Not really." He paused to light up. "You took a couple of months from him, at worst. Hardly that bad in the scheme of things."

Jeff thought about that, weighed it up. It wasn't a perspective he'd considered before now. "You're probably right," he shrugged. Cleared his throat, suddenly embarrassed. "I'm sorry, I know you're busy. I'll let you get back to – "

"I think my daughter's out there," Red said. He pointed to the runway. "With that lot, I mean."

The tradesman looked to Red, and then to the runway. Hell of a thing for a man to think his daughter had become one of those creatures. "Chances of seeing anyone you know are slim," he offered. "It's a big crowd."

"Let's hope," Red said.

He looked to Jeff, warming to the man. Asked, "Why did Reilly put all those people under that blanket?"

Jeff thought for a minute, like he'd rehearsed what to say and wanted to get it right. "It was my idea, not Reilly's. After the first attack, most of the survivors retreated into the mall. They were scared, and I mean *really* scared. Things were tense, and we knew it wouldn't take much to tip some folks over the edge. People like Chef. People who could be a danger to themselves or the others…

"So, when we managed to secure the place, we decided to hide what we could from the survivors who'd retreated. Reilly got rid of the bodies. Jimmy helped him. They brought the wounded to Gate 22." Jeff pursed his lips, glanced at Red. "They were hurt real bad, you know. Some beyond recognition. They wouldn't have made it through the night… he did what had to be done."

Red looked over to Peggy, raised his eyebrows. "What *had* to be done? You sure about that?"

Jeff frowned. "Look, didn't you say that young lad, Barry, was in a bad way when you first met him?"

"Yeah, but – "

"Well, Peggy was the same." He moved a little closer to Red. "You see that's the thing," he said. "She didn't look like she does now. She was all torn up, pretty much dead."

FIVE

Herbert Matthews sat alone in the control tower just across the way from the main airport. Plates with half-eaten food surrounded him. A window was open, allowing a few speckles of rain to drift in – Herb's last remaining link to the outside world.

He stared at the radio on his desk, twisting the dial.

Scratched at his beard, shooing away yet another fly. Pulled his dressing gown close, feeling the nip of cool air coming through the window.

Herb continued to work the dial. Several wires ran from the radio, linked to the car battery under his desk. A single reading offered the professor an idea as to how much power was coming through.

He pressed the button on his mic, and spoke: "Professor Herbert Matthews from Belfast International Airport, calling for any receivers…"

The distinct fuzz of dead air came back at him.

He tried again: "Hallo. Can anyone hear me?"

Still nothing. Just white noise. "Where are you, Terry?" he muttered to himself.

He heard a knock, coming from the entrance to the tower, at the bottom of the stairs. Looked at his watch, but it wasn't suppertime.

The knock came again. Slower than that of Jimmy the Saint, who normally delivered his food.

Herb decided to ignore it. Was just about to return to his work when he heard a voice calling.

It was the doctor.

Herb felt a sudden pang of guilt. He was reminded once more of the doctor's friend, Benny, and how his recklessness had led to the man's death.

And then Muriel, Herb remembering that Sunday when he woke up to find her dead on the sofa of their Ballyclare home. Watching over time as she changed, looking more and more like the young girl he'd courted all those years ago. Herb could see her in his mind as she came for him, eyes spinning, like a woman possessed, his damn shotgun firing like it had on the bus, the splash of blood and brain across the wall.

He buried his head under his old gown, shamefully. Squeezed his eyes shut and sobbed.

But Muriel's face remained in his mind.

Another knock.

Then a voice from the radio.

Herb's eyes snapped open. He twisted the dial, listened again.

"Muriel?"

He'd heard her voice before. As he'd made his way to Belfast, the rain beating upon the windscreen of his van, Muriel had been there in the seat beside him. Her gentle encouragement had kept him strong, propping him up as he addressed the survivors, telling them about his plans, about the group in Manchester.

He strained his ears to listen to the static from the radio. He'd definitely heard something, and it had definitely sounded like Muriel.

Another knock. Herb swore, covered his ears. "Go away!" he cried.

He cranked up the radio's volume.

"This is Professor Herbert Matthews from Belfast International Airport," he repeated, "calling for any receivers…"

The knocking persisted, seeming to swell around him, filling the room as if amplified. Hammering in his head like some huge bloody drum. And then it was gone, the static on the radio the only sound remaining once more.

Herb looked to the mic. Was just about to press it once more when he heard a voice cutting through the static.

It wasn't Muriel.

It was Terry.

SIX

The rain beat upon the red-headed doctor as he walked briskly from the control tower. The old coot wasn't answering. He didn't care what Jeff thought; he didn't have time to stand there all night, hammering on that door like an idiot.

He had work to do.

He noticed Cole and ran to catch up with him.

The big man was just about to close the driver's door to the lorry he'd been packing, all set for another night's pillage through Belfast city. "Wait up, mate." Red panted, doubling over on himself. "Last minute order."

Cole looked a sight to behold, the rim of his trucker's cap hanging over his powdered face. The young tattooed woman sat in the cabin with him. A couple of others were in the back, no doubt the hired help for the evening. "We're pretty much booked up", he shouted over the rain and lorry's revving.

"This one's important", Red shouted back, still breathless. He patted the piece of paper in his hand. "Medical stuff again. I've drawn a map for you, as usual."

Cole frowned, taking the paper off Red, looking at the directions. "What is it, anyway?"

"Microscope, slides, other bits and pieces."

Cole pursed his lips, flipped the paper over, reading the list of items, no doubt considering how much room it would all need.

The tattooed woman spoke: "I'll take it in my van, if it doesn't fit in here."

Cole looked quizzically at her. "You don't even *have* a van."

"Yeah, but I'm getting one, aren't I?"

"I'll leave it with you, then," Red laughed, banging the door closed for them. They were still bickering as he left.

On his way back through the airport's main mall area, Red noticed the hustle and bustle of business starting up for another night. More survivors had arrived, some travelling back with Cole after one of his runs, others perhaps attracted by the activity and bright lights of the booming airport mall.

Eating habits had adapted around the new natural order, meaning dinner was often served around 4.00am. Of course, some people still preferred to stick to their old routine. Retailers, therefore, were forced to employ staff around the clock to capture as much business as possible.

Red smiled to himself, noting how even under these bizarre conditions, the airport was starting to feel and look almost normal. It was a reminder of the 24/7 culture of before. Humanity was crawling back onto its feet, and, just for a moment, the doctor felt proud to be part of that.

He noticed a number of survivors sitting by the airport pub, drinking. Alcohol had been a welcome addition to the survivors' lives. They'd tried religion with Father Reilly and found it wanting. Booze was much better.

Amongst the crowd, Red noticed Caz and Barry, laughing and holding hands in one of the stalls of the pub.

His smile faded a little.

He recalled his chat with Jeff about Barry Rogan's miraculous recovery. Red hadn't imagined those injuries he'd seen back on the bus: something had happened to Barry, and whatever it was hadn't been natural.

He watched the young survivor head off to the bar, no doubt to grab some more drinks for the pair.

Approached Caz, smiling. "Hey, aren't you underage?"

Caz laughed. "Who cares?"

She looked pretty relaxed. It was the first time that Red had seen her kick back and enjoy herself. In fact, it was the first time Red had seen *anyone* enjoy themselves in what seemed like a very long time.

"That boy of yours treating you okay?" Red pried.

"Oh, Barry's a sweetheart. Did I ever tell you about the time he saved me?"

"Once or twice," laughed Red. It was more like double figures.

"Well, he's... one of the good boys."

"I'm sure he is." Red clicked his fingers, as if casually remembering something. "Say... would you tell Barry to call by the surgery tomorrow, some time?"

"Why? Is something wrong?"

"No, don't worry. Nothing like that. Just a routine test I wanted to carry out. Just to make sure – "

"I can't believe this", Caz cut in, suddenly irate and a hell of a lot more articulate. "First the priest, now you. Why can't you people LEAVE HIM ALONE?"

The pub silenced, the other drinkers turning towards them.

Red smiled, waved his hand at the other drinkers, then leaned in to Caz. "Who's 'you people'?! Come on, it's me here, girl. Red, your friendly neighbourhood doc. I just want to – "

"Run some tests. Poke and prod at him, like he's some kind of FUCKING LAB RAT! Don't you think he's been through enough?" Her face was bright purple. She was practically spitting at him.

"Wait, that's not fair, Caz."

"What you're doing isn't exactly *fair*, is it? If he needs your… doctoring… he'll ask you. That's how things are working now, right? No pressure. No obligation."

"I guess so…"

"Good. I think we're done here, then." Caz lifted her drink, took a long swig, then slammed it to the table.

"I guess we are," Red said before moving away.

From across the bar, he could see Barry Rogan eyeballing him.

SEVEN

Humanity was no longer the dominant beast in Belfast.

Every building throughout the city stood quiet and solemn.

The rain provided the city's solitary soundtrack, dutifully falling from the sky as if directed by God Himself, humanity's only solace in an otherwise brutal landscape. Bodies littered the streets, a plague of flies feasting on their flesh. Swirling tumbleweeds of rubbish danced lazily in the breeze. A hurried scrawl of spray paint, simply reading KILL BITCHES, stained the front doors of a church.

Star shuddered as she stared out the van's window.

Cole continued through town, then up the Dublin Road.

"Not stopping in the city?" asked Star. "There's a Tesco's in the centre."

"We've cleaned it out already," Cole said. "There's another Tesco's up the Lisburn road. It's much better. Good storeroom."

Star shrugged.

Found herself looking at Cole with appraising eyes.

"What?" he said, checking his face in the mirror.

"Nothing," she said. "Just wondering what your story is."

"My story?"

"Yeah, why you're all dolled up like that. Ain't normal, is it?"

Cole laughed. "Are you calling me a freak? Because if you are, glass houses and stones come to mind…"

Star smiled. "Nah, not calling you anything. Just saying it like I see it. You're a bit of a square peg in a round hole, that's all." She sniffed, rubbed her nose. "And yeah, maybe I know something about that feeling too."

Cole looked at her, sizing her up. "Ex Army. Spent some time in Iraq, Afghanistan. Saw what people see out there, but if you're looking to lay it all there, then think again." He looked back to the road. "I was the model fucking soldier. Clean shaven, buzz-cut hair, the works."

"So what happened?"

"I woke up on my twenty-fifth birthday, heard a Voice in my head that I didn't recognise. By the end of the week, there were two Voices in my head. I tried to ignore them, but it was pretty impossible – like ignoring someone who's standing right in front of you."

"What did they say to you?"

Cole shrugged. "Just stuff. Banal things, interesting things, whatever came to their mind, I guess. It's a bit like having a commentary running all the time."

"Are they talking now?"

Cole's eyes moved as he listened for something. "Yeah," he said. "Showgirl likes you. Says you remind her of…" He bent his head to one side, "Lori Petty? Is that right?"

Star laughed. "That's fucked up, man."

"Yeah, well there you have it."

Cole was quiet for a moment, negotiating his way around a broken down blockade across the road. Star could spot the charred remains of bodies amongst the wreckage: something bad had gone down here.

"Doesn't explain the drag."

Cole laughed. "You want to know about the drag?"

"Sure I do," Star said.

"It's a disguise," he said. "I tried to hide from them at first. The Voices, I mean. Locked myself in cupboards, switched all the lights off in the house. None of it worked for very long, though: they'd always find me. So I started wearing disguises. And that worked really well. I'd wear funny hats, false beards, that sort of thing."

"Oh, come on, man," Star laughed. "You're not serious."

"Deadly serious. And here's the clincher: drag worked best. I could fool them for hours at a time wearing women's clothes. Longer if I used wigs and make-up." He laughed. "But then I kinda got into it, and it became less of a disguise, felt more... well, more like me."

"Are they always there? The Voices?"

Cole smiled. "Most of the time," he said. "I can scare them away sometimes. If I get angry or smash things up or hurt myself." His face reddened. "But most of the time, I kinda like them there. The doctors and psychiatrists, they always wanted to make them go, gave me tablets and little tricks I could use to get rid of them, but I guess deep down I always wanted them to stay."

He looked sheepishly at Star. "Sometimes," he said, "I can hear the Voices in other people's heads too. Like tuning into my own helps me tune into others..."

He looked back to the road, sighed. "Look, I'm sorry. You probably didn't want to hear all that. It's kinda weird. People get freaked by it…"

"Tesco's," Star said.

"Sorry?"

"Tesco's," she said again. "I noticed the sign in the headlights. You've gone past it."

"Fuck," Cole said.

He glanced in his mirror, sank his foot on the brake, the van skidding a little. He did a little three-point turn, then headed back down the road towards the supermarket.

"But you haven't freaked me," Star said. "It takes a lot to freak my ass. Your bullshit don't come close."

She met his gaze for a second, before smiling. There was warmth in the smile.

"Come on, let's go shopping," she said, then climbed out of the van.

EIGHT

The place was in darkness. Streetlamps drooped above them, like giant fingers, poised but useless.

Cole snapped his torch on.

He pulled the back shutter up, allowing the other two men to dismount the van. Empty rucksacks hung from their shoulders, torches in their hands. Everyone seemed ready for business; this was a well-oiled machine in operation.

"Okay, let's see what's on the agenda for tonight," an older man called Noel said, flicking through some pages. "There's the usual stuff for Chef, plus additional cigars and alcohol." He looked up from his clipboard, laughed: "Like he's got a hope!"

"What about the *unusual* stuff?" asked Cole.

Noel raised an eyebrow, flicked through the pages again. "Sushi rice…That's got to be a first. Oh, and we've got all that stuff for the doc that you mentioned to me, earlier. There's a load of electrical stuff on here as well."

"Busy night, then." Cole said. "Let's get to it."

"What about my gear?" Star said.

"We can stop on the way back," he said. "If you give us a hand with this lot, we'll help with your stuff. Noel can go with you while me and Bert hit the hospital."

The younger man, Bert, nodded.

"Okay by me," Star replied.

All three men pulled surgical masks and goggles over their faces.

Noel handed the same to Star and she donned them. They were probably for the smell; the survivors' tolerance to the acrid stench of decay had somewhat waned while living in the airport.

Cole handed Star a torch and a handgun, checking she knew how to use it.

She tucked the gun into her belt, snapped the torch on, ran her beam along the front of the building, but she could see nothing through the dark glass. The store's branding remained fixed above the doorway.

The men padded towards the building. Star felt glass crunching under her Doc Martens as she followed.

They entered.

A dull hum filled the air, as if there were a freezer still working somewhere.

Star moved the beam of light along the floor, noting a smear of blood.

"Watch your step," Cole warned her. In his free hand, he carried a handgun. He flicked the safety off, eyes darting around the shadow-infested store.

As they moved deeper, Star realised that the noise she could hear wasn't a freezer running. It was the sound of flies. They haunted the place like tiny demons, swarming against the survivors' faces. The goggles and mask took the worst of it.

Noel handed out lists to each of the men.

The survivors spread out, seeking their bounty. Star followed Cole, not wanting to admit that she would have felt somewhat unnerved on her own.

The flies continually assaulted her goggles. She slapped at them uselessly.

The beam of her torch found several mutilated bodies. "Some of these are fresh", Cole said, shaking his head. "Don't people know, by now, to stay away during the day?"

"Darkness maybe scares them more than the bitches," Star muttered.

Cole grinned. "I'd have put you down as the vampire type."

Star rolled her eyes.

They found what they needed, Cole filling his own rucksack, then made their way into the storeroom at the rear of the building. The other men were there already, the younger of the two, Bert, busily stacking a pallet full of goods, while Noel poked his head into a nearby office.

Star noticed Noel suddenly drop his torch, and pull away. "What's wrong?" she said, moving to where he stood, shining her torch into the office.

"Over there!" he pointed, still breathless. "Shine your torch over there."

Star did as she was told, cautiously moving the light over to an area close to the desk. She noticed another streak of blood, this one beside a few spent shells and blackened walls.

"Further right" Noel guided her.

And then she found it.

At first, she thought it was another body. On closer inspection, Star realised that this wasn't just another hapless survivor. It was *one of them*; she was sure of it.

Its eyes were caught mid-twist, from one colour to another, stalled like a broken slot machine. A bullet hole, neat and clean, pierced its forehead.

"Jesus," Star breathed. "Some bastard got lucky."

Cole sidled up beside the two survivors, peered into the office. "I don't get it," he said. "I shoot those things all the time. Aim for the head, watch them fall into the midst of the others. But they're always gone by nightfall. The others take the bodies with them."

"Well, maybe this one got lost," Star said.

Cole didn't answer.

Removing his jacket, he gently laid it flat across the creature's face.

The other two men eyed him suspiciously.

NINE

Caz zipped her raincoat up tight.

She had purchased it at one of the shops in the airport mall. People were selling all sorts of things there, and, with the little bit of work she did for Red, as well as occasionally helping out at the newsagent, Caz found herself on something of a comfortable income.

Enough to get drunk on.

She made her way across the tarmac, towards the control tower. It was an errand that Red had wanted her to run – a penance sort of thing. To be honest, she'd have probably refused to do it, Herbert Matthews not being anyone's favourite person after the whole bus thing, but, what with shouting at Red earlier, she was feeling a little indebted to the doctor. Barry had gone to bed. Caz had stopped by Gate 10 simply to apologise, and here she was now.

Damn you, Red.

She still felt a little tipsy, the wind nearly blowing her over. The rain hammered down, Mother Nature perhaps as tetchy as Caz felt around this time of month. Caz was worried it might be some kind of omen, that things were not going to stay as good for the survivors. There was too much that remained unanswered: the origin of those creatures; their thirst for violence; why the rain scared them away.

And then there was Barry. Red was right – there were unanswered questions about Barry Rogan, and even Caz was getting a little curious, despite what she'd told him. He'd been mortally wounded by the creatures, eyes torn out, his private parts mutilated. Caz had watched it happen with her own two eyes. Yet, now he looked healthier than ever. *And everything is working fine down below*, she mused, smiling to herself.

Caz arrived at the control tower door, knocked.

There was a man inside who once claimed to have the answers to some of the questions she asked herself. But these days, the professor seemed incapable even of answering his own door.

Caz knocked again, this time calling out: "Professor Matthews? Are you in there?"

She knew he was. He hadn't been anywhere else in weeks.

"Professor!" she persisted, hammering on the door furiously. "Come on! Open up, it's cold out here! I really need to talk to you! It's Caz! There's something I need to ask you!"

Nothing.

She was just about to leave when she heard movement from inside. Shuffling on the stairs. The rattle of keys at the lock.

Caz stepped back.

The door unlocked. Slowly opened.

"Are you on your own?"

"Totally."

The door opened all the way, and Herb stepped out briefly and checked the runway.

Caz nearly gagged at the shape of him: under the harsh light of the moon, Herb looked barely human. His hair was bedraggled, his skin flaky, looking raw and sore. The dressing gown and pyjamas, which had clothed him since they'd met, were literally sticking to him, no longer seeming to have any colour about them. And then there was the smell. Wafting into the cold, damp air like a poisonous fume.

Caz swallowed a little sick from the back of her throat, tasting the booze from earlier.

He stood aside, held the door for her. "Would you like to come in?"

She wouldn't, but Caz forced herself through that door, cursing Red under her breath as she went.

Herb directed her up the stairs and then towards the main part of the control tower.

The room was foul.

A single desk lamp offered light. Empty cartons of half-eaten food were scattered along the floor and desks. Clear plastic bottles filed along the windowsill, containing what looked to be the man's piss. Assorted wires and tech ran along every wall.

"It's a little messy," the old man said, apologetically. "Muriel would have a fit, if she saw the state of…" His voice trailed off, a faraway stare drawing across his bedraggled face.

Caz stood awkwardly, looking at the old man, trying desperately to think of something to say.

With the feigned normality of the airport, she hadn't been prepared for this. Herb's dishevelled chic served as a bitter reminder of the outside world, the world the rest of the airport survivors tried very hard to hide from.

"You said you had something to tell me," he said.

"Yeah", Caz remembered. "People want to know if you've made contact with anyone on the radio."

A huge fly landed on her face, and she swatted it away. Caz reached for a window, but Herb cautioned her manically: "No! Keep it closed!" He pushed past her, locking the window tight and closing the curtains over it. A bottle of piss toppled over, spilling across the desk.

"Sorry," Caz said, stepping back.

Herb waved his hand dismissively. "It's okay, it's okay." He wiped the piss with the sleeve of his dressing gown, then replaced the bottle. "Now," he said, "You wanted a progress report. Well, the answer is yes, I have made contact with the Manchester team."

Caz swallowed hard. "When? And what did they say?"

Herb laughed, the laugh becoming a cough. His face grew red as he steadied himself on the corner of a table. "I've only just reached them," he said once recovered. "It's very early days. There's so much to consider. We're still in the early stages of discussion." He paused, plucked his glasses from his eyes and cleaned them before adding, "I'll be in touch once I have something concrete to offer."

Caz nodded. Smiled weakly, before turning to walk back down the stairs.

"You don't believe me, do you?" she heard him mutter.

Caz paused, looked back at him. "Sorry?" she said.

In the poor light, she couldn't see his blotchy skin or the grime on his clothes. He looked like the Herb she'd first met, the mad professor from one of those old Sunday matinees.

"I said you don't believe me. No one does," he said.

Caz was reminded of her conversation with Barry, of how he'd questioned the science the old man was proffering. Looking at Herb now, there was no reason to believe anything that came out of his mouth.

"It's okay," he said, smiling. "I sometimes doubt myself, you know."

A fly lit upon the side of his face, and he swatted it dead, without even as much as blinking. He studied his hand, staring at its tiny corpse. "What if I'm wrong?" he mused. "What if those creatures aren't some kind of next step in the evolution of life?" He looked up, his face very solemn. "What if it's *death* that has evolved?"

TEN

Star stood at the reception area of her shop.

Noel stood beside her, hands in pockets, whistling as he looked around. He didn't seem impressed. He didn't seem unimpressed, either, just out of place. Her shop wasn't the kind of place people like Noel would ever have set foot in. Not in the old world.

Star glanced around, eyes surveying all the things that were once so familiar to her: her workstation in the centre of the shop, the shelf still loaded with books and CDs, the flash art tacked to every wall, a few paintings she'd just finished leaning against the counter waiting to be hanged.

The place hadn't changed a bit.

Star didn't know why, but a part of her had feared the worst: maybe the gaff would've been trashed, her gear stolen since the last time she'd stopped by.

Instead, it felt like she was in for another day's work.

She walked to the counter, flicked through her appointments book. All those names in there. Booked right up to August and beyond. Some of them were regulars, people who'd been coming to her for years. Others unknown to her. Maybe in for their first tattoo, never to happen.

She pulled her old stool up by the workstation, sat on it and rubbed her hands together, thinking.

"Maybe I should, er, leave you for a bit," Noel said.

Star nodded.

Noel smiled sheepishly, took one last look around. "You kept it well," he said.

Star glared at him. *What the fuck was that supposed to mean, "kept it well"?*

Catching the look on her face, Noel excused himself, whistling as he went.

Prick, mused Star.

But he wasn't a prick. He was just someone who felt uncomfortable in a tattoo shop. She'd met a lot of people like that over the years – most of her customers to some degree, even some of the regulars. Some people would overcompensate, try to act big. Others would camp the nerves up way more than they actually felt, making a big drama when there was no drama to be had.

Star didn't like drama.

She didn't like people too much either.

Star liked art and needles and skin.

She recalled her last tattoo here, the black and grey pentagram on that young student girl. She'd finished the piece on the girl's body, right there on the floor where she'd fallen, yet now the girl was nowhere to be seen. Risen with the others, Star reckoned. Pretty fucked up, were she to think too much about it.

Slowly, Star rose up herself and started to pack her stuff together. She'd made a quick call before, packing the basics for inking on the go. But with their bus having crashed into the airport, all of that stuff had been lost. Star needed to get the whole shebang tonight, to clean this joint out, load up the van Noel had found for her.

She started at her workstation, packing three machines, one for lining, another for shading, a third for packing colour in. Next she grabbed her needles, her tips 'n' grips, the full range of inks, throwing it all into the same box she'd packed the machines in. She unplugged her lamp, added it with the powerpack, footswitch and clipcord.

Star kicked that box away, pulled up another. In this one, she threw her spray bottle, alan keys and leatherman. She found a few packets of latex gloves, the nice black ones she liked, and threw them in. Some plastic clipcord covers went in next, followed by a few tubs of Vaseline and some clingfilm

She called Noel in to lend her a hand with the heavier gear. Together they packed her autoclave, ultrasonic and the hot seat itself: her dentist's chair.

Finally, she grabbed her old wooden stool and tucked it under her arm. Took one last glance around the joint. Lifted her appointments book, as an afterthought, tucking it under her other arm, and then left.

ELEVEN

It was dangerously close to first light by the time Cole had parked by City Hospital at the lower end of Belfast's Lisburn Road. He unrolled the piece of paper that Red had given to him. He'd need to find the Haematology lab for the stuff the doctor had requested. Thankfully, it wasn't Cole's first time at the hospital, and Red's map was as good this time as all the others he'd drawn for Cole over the last number of weeks. He should be able to wrap this errand up fairly quickly.

Grabbing his handgun and shoulder bag, Cole pulled the keys from the ignition, then opened the van door.

"Bit late for another stop," came Bert's voice from the seat beside him.

Cole sighed. "I've been here before, know where I'm going. It'll only take ten minutes."

"Alright, but leave the keys, would you? Don't fancy being stuck here on my own."

Cole rolled his eyes, dropped the keys on the driver's seat. Continued climbing out.

He moved across the car park towards the entrance to the hospital. The building had been around since the early part of the 19th Century, in one form or other, beginning life as a workhouse for the poor. It still looked formidable today, with its distinctive yellow tower block pointing into the sky, housing nine hundred beds within its numerous wards. In the old world, a lot of sick people populated those beds, some perched up on white pillows, others doped up on pain meds or kept alive by some machine. Cole dreaded to think how many of those bodies had risen up from their beds in the new world, haunting the hospital corridors before spilling out into the streets.

He pushed through the revolving doors of the entrance, tasting the stench in his throat. The usual disinfectant odour had been replaced by the same smell of death Cole had experienced at Tesco's. A swarm of flies met him as he entered, and he pulled the mask and goggles across his face like before.

Cole clicked his torch on.

He made his way through reception, his beam scarring the walls. He passed a notice board covered in posters, mostly health service campaigns warning of the dangers of smoking, obesity, alcohol, things that really didn't seem to matter much since the world went tits up, and getting your arse bitten off became a genuine cause for concern. He passed a small shop on his right hand side, with its rotten fruit and dead flowers, and headed on down the main corridor on the ground floor.

He spotted a lift, its double doors half ajar, several mangled bodies lying in its gloomy corners. A slathering of blood coated the metal of the doors, black like oil until Cole's torch fell upon it, and the deep red came out in the light.

Cole found a sign on the wall. Traced the list of wards with his finger to find the Haematology lab. He checked the directions against the map Red had drawn, making sure that he knew where he was going.

He pushed through a nearby stairwell, his footfall heavy on the stairs. Even though it was summer, Cole felt a biting chill. Bodies lay strewn across the banisters and stairs. Cole hadn't noticed so many before, and he wondered if there'd been a fresh attack on the hospital since the last time he'd visited, if some hapless group of survivors had tried to make this place their base.

He pushed through to the second floor, lighting up the pale, bare walls to find the ward markings. Satisfied once again that he was where he needed to be, Cole continued down the corridor.

Within minutes, he'd found the Haematology lab. The door was locked, and he tried to force it through with his shoulder. It was too strong. In the end, he had to blow the lock with a couple of blasts from his handgun. The loud crack echoed around the nearby wards.

Cole entered the lab.

He rummaged through the place until his torch found a microscope. Cole fed it into his shoulder bag. Added the slides and other materials Red had asked for, then quickly left.

As he retraced his steps, he noticed the purple hue of pre-dawn assault the window. Cole glanced at his watch and swore. The sun would be up soon.

Something moved in the shadows, and Cole swung his torch to find the shape of a woman at the stairwell door. He raised his handgun, but she put her hands up, said, "It's me. Put the gun down."

Star.

Cole blew some air out, lowered the weapon. "What are you doing here?"

"Noel thought you could do with the extra van space. We packed a load into your van at Tesco's, after all."

Cole gestured to the shoulder bag, said, "I'm fine. It's only a microscope."

Star raised her hands. "Okay, just trying to help – no need to bite my fucking head off."

"I almost killed you."

"Forget it. Look, it's getting light soon; we have to move."

"You think I don't kn– "

A sudden noise interrupted them.

Cole's torch beam flew out across the corridor, searching for the source of the noise. Fresh pockmarks on the walls confirmed his suspicions that there'd been some sort of conflict here recently.

He strolled down the corridor, gun at the ready. There was a fork at the end, leading towards Ward 7. Cole hung a right and followed the new corridor around, Star behind him.

"Where are you going?" she complained, but he shushed her, still listening, still tuning into the sound he heard.

They passed a nurse's station. Spent shells littered its floor. A fresh corpse lay sprawled across a desk. A man with half of his face missing, the other half gnawed to the bone, staring up at the ceiling. Cole wondered just how many places like this existed: last chance saloons, where desperate men and women had fought bitterly for the right to live.

And lost.

"What are we looking for?" Star asked.

"Don't you hear that?"

"Hear what?"

"A sound… like bird wings."

Star's head leaned to the side, left ear tuning in to find the noise.

"It's coming from the next ward over," Cole whispered.

He moved past the body, through to the main ward, Star following.

He killed his torch. There was a little light coming through the window now, and he knew they should be out of there, but curiosity was getting the better of him.

They passed a row of beds, and Cole noticed one with its curtain half pulled, blood soaking the fabric. The body of an old man was stretched across the sheets, still hooked to various tubes and machines. Flies swarmed furiously around his mutilated torso. Those whores had feasted on him where he lay.

"The flies, that's what you hear," Star said, swatting one.

"No, it's something else…"

He spotted the day room, just down the corridor. Moved towards it.

Its door was closed over, but the sound he heard seemed to be coming from inside.

Cole rubbed his hand across the dusty glass fronted door, looked through. Inside he found a line of creatures, maybe ten or twelve. Some of them wore nursing uniforms; others dressed in hospital night gowns and pyjamas. Their eyes were flapping backwards and forwards between various colours, but the noise they made was more gentle than he was used to.

Like birds' wings.

"Jesus Christ," Star said, as she peeked over his shoulder. "We need to get out of here."

But the Derry man ignored her, drawing closer to the door, pressing both palms against the glass.

Still the creatures didn't move, remaining perfectly still within their regimented lines. Their eyes were focused dead in front, flickering. The sound of skin flapping against skin filled the ward.

"What are they doing?" Star whispered.

"Sleeping?" suggested Cole.

Star looked down the corridor, a new shiver of pre-dawn light piercing the nearby window and catching her eye. "Fuck, we need to move," she said. "Come on!"

But Cole remained firmly rooted to the floor.

"What's wrong with you? Come on!" she said, this time tugging his arm.

He went with her.

...

As they reached the ground floor, dawn broke through the windows, spilling its yellow glow through the windows of reception.

"Hurry!" Star called, her pace quickening.

A screeching noise rang out from behind them, followed by footfall on the stairwell. Cole could hear his van skidding off from the car park, Bert apparently deciding not to hang around any longer.

Noel was at the front door calling to them, the other van's keys in his hand.

Cole threw his shoulder bag to Star. "Go! Get the engine started and wait for me. I'll hold them off."

He killed the safety on his handgun, chambered a round, and waited for the double doors of the stairwell to open. He was surprised when a nearby storeroom burst open instead, a dark haired Doll crashing out onto the corridor. She wore a white uniform, the badge reading 'Staff Nurse Adamson'. The uniform was torn and bloody, hat still pinned to her messy hair. In life, the woman's eyes had been a deep oceanic blue, but now they burned red.

She hissed, lunged for Cole's throat.

Cole stepped aside, tripping her, sending the hapless Doll sprawling across the smooth floor. He raised the handgun, but the Doll was quick, scuttling behind the desk at reception.

The stairwell doors burst open, the entire contents of Ward 7 spilling out into reception. Cole swung his arm, firing into their mass, the rounds punching through the crowd, pushing them back.

Nurse Adamson came for him again, but Star got there first, bursting through the doors again, her handgun pumping several rounds into the Doll's pale, heart shaped face. The nurse shrieked, struggled briefly on the floor, and then was still.

"Hurry!" Star called to Cole.

Together the two survivors exited the hospital, racing across the car park, towards the waiting van. Its engine hummed against the still, post-rain air and coarse shrieks of the Dolls giving chase.

Noel was hanging from the driver's window, his gun in hand.

The two survivors climbed aboard, hardly having time to close up the van's back doors before the wheels were spinning, the van skidding away from the hospital.

TWELVE

The roads were filled with Dolls.

Cole could feel the engine rev as Noel pressed his foot down harder on the van's accelerator.

Star grabbed hold of the wire cage as the van picked up the pace.

Gear from Star's shop was stacked high around them. Cole's rucksack, containing Red's microscope, rested on the floor.

"We're too late," she said.

"What do you mean, too late?"

"Those whores will be all over the airport car park; there's no way we'll get back in."

"Shit," Cole fumed, clearly annoyed with himself. He leaned on his hands, thought for a moment.

Rabbit poked up from his hole, then glanced around. He looked worried. He always looked fucking worried. Cole focused on his burrow for a moment until something clicked. "That's it," he said.

"What's it?" Star asked.

Cole ignored her, leaning to the driver's cage, shouting in to Noel, "Take a left here. I know somewhere close we can bed down for the day."

"Where?" Noel asked.

"My house," Cole said.

...

They rolled into a housing estate just off the Doagh Road in Newtownabbey. High rise flats pierced the sky. There were Dolls everywhere, but Cole reckoned they could avoid them.

"Pull up right beside there," he instructed Noel, pointing towards the tall brown fencing around the backyard of an end terrace. It was where he had called home for the last two years.

"Wait, those things are out there," Star warned.

"Best be quick, then," Cole said.

He fumbled in his pocket, pulled out his bunch of keys. Ran his fingers over them, picking one out. Exited the van through the back doors, ran for the back gate to his house and opened it.

"Hurry," he called to the others.

Noel and Star followed, sliding through the gate just in time. Cole slammed the gate on the face of a shorthaired Doll with bright red lips, then latched it tight. They'd probably get over it eventually, but not before the survivors were in the house.

Cole found another key, used it to open the back door. "Go on in," he told the others, stepping aside politely.

...

It was an average Housing Executive terrace. Downstairs had a kitchen and dining area and a small front room that looked out onto another high fence. The windows were double glazed, adorned with thick black curtains. There wasn't much light getting in.

"You liked your privacy," Star remarked.

Cole smiled.

"Go on, make us a cuppa," Noel said, setting himself down on the sofa.

"Would beer do?" Cole offered.

"Job's a good 'n'," Noel smiled.

"Make that two," Star said.

Cole went into the kitchen, opened the long-defrosted fridge and pulled two lukewarm beers out. He plucked a bottle opener magnet from the fridge door, used it to pull the bottle tops off. Returned to the living room with the beers.

"What's that meant to be?" Noel said as Cole entered the room. He was staring at a painting on the wall.

"Art," Cole said, handing him the beer.

"One of yours?" Star asked.

"Sure is."

"Didn't know you painted."

"I don't. It was part of some therapy session. Get your inner demon out and all that." He laughed.

"I like it," Star said.

"I don't like it," Noel said, turning his nose up. "I like a painting to be something you can recognise. Like a house or beach or some bitch's face, that kind of – "

"Some bitch's face?" Star laughed. "Charming."

"Just saying what I like," Noel protested. "No need to go all women's lib on me, okay?"

"Bet you made someone a great husband," Star said.

Noel looked hurt all of a sudden. He lifted his beer, took a sip.

"So what is it?" Star asked Cole.

"What's what?"

"The painting. What's it meant to be?"

"Some bitch's face," Cole said.

Noel laughed, spitting some beer out in the process.

"Seriously," Star said.

"Seriously?" Cole sighed, studying the canvas. He could see the various shapes running along the top like jagged teeth, oils thick and raised, giving way to what appeared to be two bodies in the middle drawn close together, dancing, maybe. "They asked me to paint what I could see inside my head," he said.

"What's it like being a loon?" Noel asked.

Cole smiled. "I've good days and bad days. Just like everyone else." He looked again at the painting, frowned. "That was a bad day."

"You've got something, big guy," Star said. "The way those colours blend with each other, I like it." She thought for a moment, then said, "You know that tattoo you're looking for, the one on your arm? I'd like to work with you on the design, see if we could get a little of what's going on here," she pointed to the painting, "in there. What do you think?"

Cole looked at the painting, then to Star. "I'd like that," he said.

There was an awkward silence. Outside, the Dolls worked at Cole's fence, their nails scratching on the wood, but nobody inside seemed to give a shit. They were used to being surrounded, living in the airport.

Noel yawned, said, "Well don't know about you two, but I'm knackered."

"There's a couple of beds upstairs," Cole said. "Pillows, duvets, the works."

Noel's eyes widened. "You serious?"

"Yeah, go grab one. Be nice to sleep in a real bed for once."

"Bloody right it would," Noel said, leaving his beer and making for the stairs.

Cole waited until he was upstairs before looking to Star and saying, "And then there were two."

He lifted a cushion from the sofa, beat his hand against it. "I can sleep here," he said. "You take the other bedroom."

But the tattooist stood up from her chair, took a step towards him. "We could always share it," she said, reaching her hand to touch his face.

Cole didn't flinch or back away from her. Instead he looked into her eyes and again said, "I'd like that."

They drew closer to each other, arms wrapping, hands searching, lips pressed against lips.

Outside, the Dolls continued to work the fence.

The sun climbed the sky, oblivious.

PART FOUR

THE RAIN

ONE

Every night.

Barry had the same dream every night.

The redheaded bitch crawling over him, her hands sliding over his skin, caressing, teasing.

Tonight she was on fire. Heaving, sucking in air. Her nails digging into his back. Teeth sinking into his neck. Mounting then riding him like a dog in heat.

Barry tried to fight her off, yet failed. He was too weak. His eyes clouded, starting to wane. Blood ran down his face. Pooled out across his groin.

FORGET ME NOT was laughing. Pointing to the body of Caroline Donaldson in bed beside him, singing to him in her nonsensical language, the same song as before with the three-syllable word he couldn't make out.

BLAH-BLAAH-BLAH.

BLAH-FUCKING-BLAAH-BLAH.

He woke as he always did, sweat slick on his skin, heartbeat racing. He looked beside him, finding Caz fast asleep, unharmed, the gentle noise of her breathing a relief to him.

He searched beneath the sheets, once again finding the stiffness of an erection.

Standing up, he wiped the sleep from his eyes, went to the window and looked out. It was raining outside, the car parks and runways bathed in moonlight.

Barry watched as a van pulled up to the side entrance of the airport.

"What is it?" asked Caz, stirring.

"Cole and the others," Barry replied. "Looks like they're back."

...

"So there you have it," Cole said, finishing his tale.

He was tired. The last thing he needed was an interrogation. But it seemed the other survivors had been worried about them, fearing the worst. Bert hadn't made it back at all. A whole night's takings lost. Made Cole mad.

Showgirl was mock-yawning, making fun of his low, dulcet tones.

Cole made a face at her.

"What?" Chef asked, thinking the face was for him.

"Nothing," Cole replied. "Just knackered, like."

Chef shrugged. "Fair enough."

Cole looked around the table. The main players were all present and accounted for. Jeff held his cap in one hand, scratching a sizeable welt on his head with the other. The doctor stared into space, looking as tired as Cole felt. Jock hovered in the shadows. Near him, Chef and a few others from the kitchen. Even Barry Rogan was there, sat at the back of the group, drumming on the table as if bored.

Chef mumbled something to Archie beside him, the smaller man laughing.

It was Showgirl who was the first to speak out. "Here's the plan, Stan," she said, her voice more affected than ever. "Go back to the city tonight, when the rain starts. Find those sleeping beauties. Shower them in gasoline. Toss a match. Boom."

To be fair, it was a fairly solid plan; Cole wished, for once, that the others could have heard it. If the Dolls had stayed in the hospital one night, there was a good chance they might be doing the same the next. Even if they moved around, there was still a good chance the survivors would find them. Starting out at dusk, when the rain started, would give them a good eight hours. Hell, they could maybe find a few nests in the one night.

Chef seemed to agree. "Well, that's it settled, then," he said, looking around the table.

He was met by blank faces.

"Jesus, it's obvious! We get some people together; we search for them, nest by nest; then we torch the bitches."

Still the blank faces.

"Oh, come on!" Chef protested. "We could actually win this fucking war…"

Archie threw a fist into the air, muttered something inaudible.

"But is it a war?" asked Jeff.

"Of course it's a war!" Chef protested. "They attacked us, don't you remember?"

"Remember? I was right in the middle of it," Jeff snapped. "Doing my bit, while most of you were hiding." He ran a hand through his hair, scratched again. "But that was a long time ago. Since the rain came, things have been different."

Chef grumbled under his breath.

"Look, I'm just wondering if we already have the best deal we can expect," Jeff continued. "We've survived this far, and things are actually starting to look kind of normal around here. So why upset the balance? Why anger them?"

"Because of what they've done and what they're capable of!" Chef fumed, slapping the table with his hand. "Have you all forgotten that?"

"No, we haven't forgotten," Jeff argued. "In fact, it's exactly why I'm urging caution."

Chef threw his hands in the air. "For the love of God," he lamented. "Look, the only reason those bitches don't attack is because they *can't*. We have to remember that, instead of playing happy fucking families. Come on, we're fucking prisoners in here; let's not fool ourselves! I say we show them how vulnerable they are, and maybe they'll think twice about messing with us in the future."

There was a lull in the debate, both Jeff and Chef looking around the table for support.

Red decided to throw his oar in. "Thing is... you're both right. In a way."

Everyone looked at the doctor, waited for more.

"We either make peace with the way things are and leave it as it is," he continued, "or we fight back. Now, I reckon most of the fighting spirit's been kicked out of yours truly, but if somebody wants to rally the troops and go burn themselves some witches, who am I to stop them? Bloody hell, those things don't seem bothered either way. I mean, if they aren't riled by Flossy over there," and here the doctor pointed at Cole, "taking pot-shots every day from the roof, what's a few burning beds going to do?"

There was another silence.

Rabbit looked up briefly, then tucked his head back down the hole.

Showgirl rolled her eyes, tutted. "Y'all are waaay too rabbit-like," she said in a deep-south drawl. "Need to grow a set, take a stand." She looked to Chef, turned her nose up at his soup-stained apron.

"Fatboy over there's the only one with any testicles around here."

Cole sighed. Rubbed his mouth. The lipstick was hard and dry, and it crumbled against his hand "I'll take the van out as usual tomorrow night," he stated, looking around the table, "Any of you want to join me, cool. We'll take out one nest – just to test the water – then come right back." He looked to Jock, thought for a moment. "Unless you want to fly some of us in, Jock?"

Jock raised his hand. "No way, man! I'm not getting involved in this shit."

"Why not?" asked Chef. "Planning another recon, are you?"

"Just you watch your mouth…"

"Or what?" Chef's eyes narrowed. "You're not as indispensible as you think, Flyboy."

"Is that so?"

"Fuckin' right."

"Woo-hoo!" danced Showgirl, waving pom-poms, spelling out 'Go Chef'.

Cole shushed her, feeling his face blush. "We're good with the van," he said quickly. "With Bert AWOL we lost a lot of supplies last night, so we'll need to do more shopping anyway."

Jock pulled his chair back, stood abruptly. "Fucking maniacs," he said under his breath, before storming off.

"What's got into him?" Chef protested, holding both hands up in defence.

"Just leave it," the doctor warned. "He's not worth it."

Showgirl leaned forward, whispered in Cole's ear. "Watch him," she said. "The Scottish guy. He's up to something."

TWO

Jock slammed the door angrily.

The noise echoed out into the empty corridor, but his anger wasn't spent. He kicked a chair, watching it crash into the back wall, near where Kirsty sat, nose buried in some tinned meat.

The creature didn't react, but Aida recoiled. Back in the old world, her husband was fond of that same routine after a bad day at work. The slam of a door was an all-too-familiar harbinger of woe; Aida could usually expect a beating to follow. It was one of the many things about the old world she didn't miss.

"What happened?" she asked.

"We're leaving," Jock snapped, fumbling some things into a sports bag as he talked. "This place is fucked." He pulled his revolver out of his belt, checked it. "Those silly bastards are planning to go out and hunt those things. It's only a matter of time before someone comes sniffing around here. Especially if they get a taste for blood."

Tears welled up in Aida's eyes. She looked to the pregnant creature sitting on the blankets in the corner. "We can't leave."

"We're fucking leaving!" Jock yelled, snapping the revolver closed.

"And going where? Come on, we've been over this! You've said it, I've said it: Where is any better than here?"

"Any-fucking-where!" The pilot's face was red and puffy, freckles bursting from his cheeks like sunspots.

Tears clouded Aida's eyes.

Jock looked at her guiltily. Softened. "I'm sorry," he said.

He ran his hand over her face, collecting the salty moisture on his fingers, then looking at it like it was something rare or precious.

Aida pulled away, wiped her face. She composed herself, forced a smile. "It's okay."

Jock rested on the edge of the camp bed, near Kirsty. He reached for his bottle of vodka, tried to pour himself a glass, but his hand was still shaking. "I can't keep doing this," he said.

Aida went to him, taking the bottle. She found another glass, lined them both up on the small table, before pouring a healthy shot in each. She handed him one, then downed the other in a short, sharp movement.

Jock regarded her curiously. "Thought you didn't drink."

She smiled. "I do now."

Jock smiled too. He hated getting angry. Needed to keep a cool head for everyone's sake.

He looked over at Kirsty. The creature looked a lot healthier since eating, the painful spasms from before having calmed. In fact her belly seemed even larger now, and Jock found himself wondering, once again, just what was growing in there, what exactly he was so anxious to protect. But then he looked to Aida. He knew damn well his actions had nothing to do with the creature; it was blind love, a teenage crush on Aida that kept Jock loyal. Nothing else.

Aida drew close to him, pulled his cap off and ran her fingers through his hair.

He closed his eyes as her lips met his.

And in the warmth of their embrace, Jock found himself wondering just how far he'd go to protect her.

THREE

The Rain hit harder the next night. It came down in sheets, bouncing across the runway.

Cole pulled the hood up on his parka as he refuelled the van.

Jeff stood at the side, waiting.

"Hey," a voice called.

Jeff swung around, finding the doctor under an umbrella. In his hand was a little bottle. He handed the bottle to Jeff.

"It's for your head," he said. "That gash you've been working at. Could get infected if you don't look after it."

Jeff looked at the bottle, held it up to the moonlight. He unscrewed the bottle, dipped his finger inside. Sniffed the ointment, recoiled a little.

"Yeah, minging, isn't it?"

Jeff nodded. "Wee bit." He looked to Red, smiled, then said, "Thanks."

"It's nothing, mate. Just doing my job."

"No, for the other day too. That chat we had. It really helped put things into perspective with, you know…" He pulled his hat off, studied it, was about to scratch his head when he checked himself.

"Glad to hear it," Red said, then added: "You were getting a little worked up in there, during the meeting. You sure everything's alright?"

Jeff looked to the airport, eyes surveying its various windows and doors. "You know, I've spent a lot of time behind those walls, doing my damnedest to keep those things out. Building barricades, welding and riveting one thing to another. Blending in like some kind of chameleon." He looked to the sky, smiled. "Since we had that chat, I feel like a new man." He patted his belly, the keys in his front pouch jingling. "Got some fire back in there. Don't mind speaking up for myself. Want to get out, again. To be free. Does that make sense?"

"Sure it does."

Jeff nodded, went to leave.

"Be careful out there," Red called. "And grab us a nice bottle of whisky, would you? I'm thinking you and me could have a drink together. Talk some more. What do you think?

"Sounds like a plan," Jeff said.

FOUR

The team was in the van and ready to go. Chef had notably shied away, despite his earlier zeal, Archie and his other yes-men disappearing with him. In fact, most of those gathered were the quieter members of the group; Noel was there, as was Jeff. A solemn-looking middle-aged man named Thomas and a younger, equally forlorn-looking lad called Binks joined them. Several others made up a team of about twelve.

The group had armed themselves to the teeth, both with weapons and the homemade explosives that Cole had conjured up. This was a job that needed to be done as quickly, safely and violently as possible.

Some of the men, Cole worried, would be emotionally invested in their mission, having lost friends from the earlier attacks of the creatures. Now that there was a weakness to exploit, an Achilles Heel, they might be looking payback.

For Cole, this was nothing to do with revenge, and little to do with survival. He'd studied the creatures every day for weeks now, watched how they moved, the noises they made, those eyes… That nest in the hospital intrigued him. He wanted to look at them up close, watch their reactions as the survivors unleashed their attack.

The journey to the nest was tense. There was little chatter save for Cole, quietly reciting over and over again how the mission was to proceed. Even Showgirl remained respectfully mute, dressed down in denim shorts and a t-shirt that simply said 'That's my boy.' She smiled when Cole caught her glance, blew him a kiss.

Rabbit, on the other hand was muttering and shaking in the corner. Smoke poured from his rabbit hole, as if someone had thrown a stick of dynamite down there. His eyes were red and sore looking, his tall ears crooked and frayed. Cole looked accusingly at Showgirl and frowned, but she remained the picture of innocence.

Jeff interrupted: "Are you okay?"

Cole looked around, focusing on the real world. Everyone in the van was looking at him. He realised he must have been talking to the Voices out loud. "Yeah, nothing to worry about," he said, then wiped his brow.

He looked out the back window of the van. The rain hammered hard, building like a thick mist on the road behind them. Cole watched as something formed within its mass, playing like some movie on a screen. He rubbed his eyes, but the film kept rolling, reaching out from the gray mass of rain to fill his mind.

He pictured Red, wandering through the airport's mall. Chef and the others working away in the kitchen. He even saw the old man, Herbert Matthews, working on the dial of an old ham radio at the control tower.

He saw Barry Rogan.

Cole sensed something brewing, something about to change. His mind swirled, the thoughts and feelings of the doctor suddenly filling his head. Cole could read the man's mind. This was new. Sure, he'd had feelings before; tuning into his own Voices made him sensitive to what was going on inside the heads of others – their emotions, their thoughts – but he'd never experienced anything as intense as this.

This was fucking terrifying.

Cole shut his eyes, tried to blot everything out, but he couldn't.

He wasn't able to control himself. The images and sounds from each film accelerated in his mind, making him want to scream. The picture sharpened and Cole was drawn further into the doctor's head…

…

Red had left Jimmy the Saint to attend to Peggy, taken himself off to do some shopping. As he moved around the stalls, he thought of what Jeff had told him, about how messed up Peggy had been when they'd buried her under that blanket at Gate 22. The microscope Cole had brought would allow the doctor to look more closely at the old woman's blood, but Red was stalling. Perhaps he was in denial. Perhaps a part of him wanted to wait until there was a reason to be worried.

Either way, the old lady wasn't his real concern.

Barry Rogan worried him more.

The young man who'd crawled from bitch-infested wreckage, only to worm his way into the affections of Caroline Donaldson, a girl Red had quickly grown attached to. Caz reminded him more and more of his own daughter, right down to the cherry tints in her hair.

He thought of the phone in his pocket. The number saved under DADDY'S LITTLE GIRL. He had spent many sleepless nights reciting those digits, wondering where she might be.

"She's a real beauty, isn't she?"

"Sorry?" Red said.

He'd been staring at a guitar. The trader, a small and well-turned out man, was smiling at him, hungry for a sale.

"The guitar. It's a Fender, twelve strings. She's in good condition, not a scratch on her." He ran his hand across the fret board. "Have you ever played a twelve string?" he asked. "Such a smooth sound – it's like playing two guitars at once."

Red picked it up, looked the guitar up and down. Its smoothly polished belly was impressive. Most of what they recovered from the Great Outdoors looked weathered and chipped, but the trader was right: this old girl was perfect.

"Is she tuned?" Red asked.

"Give her a strum. See for yourself."

Red weighed the instrument in his hands, amazed by how light it was. He hadn't touched a guitar in years, not since his student days, when he'd been known to drag one out for parties, entertaining everyone with a bit of Dylan. He sat the guitar on his knee, one foot placed up on the market trader's low table. Shaped his fingers into a simple G-chord and strummed.

The sound of the guitar radiated through the nearby restaurant. A few people looked up from their supper. Red suddenly realised that since everything had gone to hell, he hadn't really heard much in the way of music – especially not live music. And it seemed, by the way the gathered diners were looking at him, most people were in a similar boat

He strummed again...

...

Cole was pulled momentarily back to his own body.

He checked himself up and down, finding his hands shaped around his rifle as though it were a guitar.

He searched the faces of the men in the back of the van, as if suspecting one of them to be playing a trick on him.

His vision blurred again, his mind superimposing onto another canvas, this time the mind of Professor Herbert Matthews…

…

Herb was in the control tower. The window was open, allowing the wind and rain passage through the room.

Yet the old man could still hear Terry. Even though he had switched off his radio, unplugging it from one wall to slam it against another, the dulcet tones of Terry's distinctive Mancunian accent persisted.

All of the plans, the hope, that Herb had poisoned the other survivors with was most definitely lost. Terry had been merely a figment of his imagination. A symptom of his ever-decreasing handle on reality and the grief for his dear wife, Muriel.

In a vain last attempt at silencing the voice, Herb lifted the radio and threw it out of the window.

There was momentary silence, before – from another radio which had never worked until now – Herb heard the voice of Terry once again

The old man buried his head in his hands and cried.

FIVE

Cole flipped back, his mouth open as if he were crying.

Everyone was looking at him now, their faces bemused.

His view shifted yet again, this time to the sleep-stained mind of Barry Rogan...

...

He woke, drenched in sweat.

On the end of the bed sat the creature he knew as FORGET ME NOT.

Her red locks glimmered in the moonlight. She was staring at the sleeping Caz in an almost maternal way.

"You stay away from her," Barry warned.

The creature shushed him. "You need to listen to me," she said. "Things are going to change, and you're going to have to decide just who is important to you in the new world, Barry Rogan."

"No, I can't hear you, can't see – "

"I can help you, Barry," she persisted. "I can help you find peace within yourself, solace from the demons."

Barry shook his head, closed his eyes tight and prayed to God that the creature would be taken away from him, that she would leave him alone for good.

He woke again, this time for real.

The creature was no longer at the end of his bed.

Caz was still sleeping peacefully.

He rubbed his eyes, the first pang of guilt ebbing into his mind. He was reminded, once again, why he was being haunted, playing back in his head what he'd done to those three girls.

The pills.

Their doped-out eyes looking up at him from the bed.

His hands reaching for the belt on his jeans…

…

Cole switched back to the van, the scenes playing in Barry's mind leaving a bad taste in his mouth.

He hawked, spat on the floor.

The others in the van continued to stare at him. "What are you all looking at?" he snapped.

They looked away.

Cole waited to be flipped again, to be inserted into someone else's head, but the picture in his own mind held. He searched desperately for the Voices. He needed some comfort, some answers to what was happening, but couldn't find them. He called for Showgirl. God knew, even Rabbit's sorry ass would be welcome right now; that damn hole he lived in would make a very good hiding place – and fuck, did Cole feel like hiding right now.

Something touched his hand, and he jumped.

He swung his head around to find Showgirl right beside him, breathed a sigh of relief. She was dressed as a nurse. Inserted a thermometer in his mouth, wiped his brow. "This is fucked up," he said to her. "What's happening to me?"

"Dunno, kid, but I'm working on it." She pulled the thermometer from his mouth, took a long hard look at it. Glanced up, eyes full of concern.

SIX

The van pulled up by City Hospital. The engine stilled. Noel opened the back doors, stepped back expectantly, but none of the survivors moved.

"Come on, move! We need to do this quickly," Cole ordered, ushering the others out. He felt like he was going mad. Waiting to be torn from his own mind again, inserted into that of another survivor. "What are you waiting for?"

They ran across the car park, gathered under the canopy of the hospital's front entrance, rain crashing down around them. Cole moved through their number, trying to divide them into groups to search the building. They seemed terrified. He needed to get them in there and out again quickly, before someone lost it...

...or before I lose it.

Noel shifted amongst the men, doling out the gear they'd need. It was proving hard to organise everyone, and Cole wondered, briefly, if it had been a mistake to take so many survivors with him. It had seemed like a good idea at the time – safety in numbers and all that, but...

Oh Christ, no.

He switched again, this time entering Red's mind.

...

The doctor sat on a stool in the restaurant area of the airport. He was laughing, applause ringing throughout the seated crowd. He took a little bow from his makeshift stage, thanked everyone. He cleared his throat, feeling the strain on his voice. He hadn't played for years, and his fingers were feeling the nip of the strings.

Red had never witnessed such craic in the airport. Perhaps it was the faint hope offered earlier, the fact they had found a weakness in the creatures, or maybe people were simply enjoying the kind of relief that an acoustic guitar and several old sing-a-long classics could bring. Either way, people were enjoying themselves. They were all having fun.

"Hey!" Red looked down from his perch finding the market trader. Dude seemed irate. "You haven't paid me yet!" he protested, a look of 'hard-done-by' etched across his face.

"Oh come now, sir," Red quipped, half to the man and half to his adoring fans. "What has a poor NHS doctor such as I to offer you?"

A round of laughter rang out at the trader's expense.

"You have to give me something," the man replied, looking at the crowd and then back to Red. "You can't just take it without paying."

The crowd was quiet, waiting.

Red turned to the man, mock-whispering to keep the crowd in on his joke, "What about a private health plan?"

More laughter.

The trader seemed interested. Ignoring the laughter, he asked "What would that give me?"

Red looked again at his audience, before proclaiming: "Drugs! Lots of them!"

More vicarious laughter.

The laughter faded, and Cole again switched from the mind of Red to that of Herbert Matthews, finding himself in the control tower…

The wind blew harder, and the rain fell more furiously, as if building to an almighty momentum. If Herb had been a betting man, he'd have put money on a spat of thunder. But his betting days were long gone. Everything was long gone.

He sat on the control tower's generous windowsill, looking out onto the wild, stormy night.

He buttoned up his pyjamas, tied his dressing gown.

Herb had been brought up to look his best when meeting someone special, and Muriel was without a doubt the most special person he had ever met. She would hate to see him so scruffy looking. But then again, knowing Muriel, she would probably have his Sunday best awaiting for him on the end of the bed or on the chair, just like she always had.

From behind, Herb could still hear the radio, Terry blethering on in his Manc accent. Making plans, talking of things that no longer made sense.

Herb could bear it no more.

He checked his rope, making sure it was tight. Slipped into the noose and awaited his moment. Herb was enjoying the feel of the cool rain upon his face, so he waited a while longer.

The time had to be right…

…

Cole noticed his hands curled around his throat when he flipped back. He stood in the car park. The cool rain upon his face shocked him back into his own reality.

He saw Noel in the van, waiting at the wheel, ready for a quick getaway once they had done what they needed to do.

Cole swallowed hard. He needed to do this as quickly as possible. There were too many unknown quantities working against them, not least this new weirdness with mind-switching.

He turned back to the survivors. They stood by the hospital entrance, readying their weapons. They were still scared. Even Jeff looked spooked, the normally calm tradesman breathing heavily as he waited. For a man who would usually enter the room without anyone knowing, this was a big deal.

"Come on! Let's go!" Cole barked, moving to the entrance and then opening the door.

SEVEN

Thomas held the rear as the survivors inched through the doors of the City Hospital, entering the reception.

They made their way up the pale corridor, past the lift with its bloodstained doors. Found the stairwell, ascended, broke into groups to search each of the hospital's floors.

Cole moved towards Ward 7, Binks and Jeff behind him. He could hear the same fluttering bird noise he'd heard the other night.

They passed the nurse's station, the same shells from before scattered on the floor, pockmarks on the walls. They moved through the ward, past the curtained bed with the mauled body.

Found the day room.

Gingerly, Cole looked through the glass. The Dolls were there like before. Standing in line, perfectly still. Oblivious to their presence.

Cole entered the room, the other two men following.

The Dolls didn't flinch. Only their eyes moved, flickering slowly. The wing-like sound was almost pleasant.

Cole motioned to Jeff to set the explosives. Reluctantly, he obeyed, carefully laying the necessary charges in each corner of the room, not daring to move anywhere he didn't have to.

Cole primed his detonator, ready to blow seven shades of shit out of the sleeping beauties. He motioned to the others to exit the building.

Yet Binks stayed put. For some reason unknown to Cole, the lad held a knife in his hand. Tears filled his face, the young survivor staring into the eyes of one of the Dolls, a brunette with bleach-white skin.

"Fucking bitch," he said, then drew the knife across the creature's throat.

Cole froze, a dry rasp leaving his mouth, but the Doll didn't react – it merely jolted, slightly before falling back into line with the others. The blood continued to flow down her neck, covering her breasts, soaking the waistband of her skirt, then dripping to the floor, where it gathered in a pool by her naked feet.

Yet Binks wasn't done. Still weeping, the troubled survivor dropped the knife, fumbled about in his coat pocket, then produced a firearm.

Cole was on him like a rash, disarming the younger survivor, then dragging him out of the day room like a petulant child. Binks went quietly, didn't fight back.

They moved along the corridors and down the stairs.

Reached the van. Most of the others were clambering in the back. Cole shoved Binks, the younger survivor taking the hint and climbing in with the other survivors.

"Did you find anything?" he asked the others. "Any more nests?"

"No," someone said.

Cole frowned, looked back to the hospital, his eyes finding its tall yellow peak. A streak of lightning ran across it, a rattle of thunder following.

Cole watched the sky for a moment longer, then looked at the small box in his hand. Satisfied they were a safe distance from the building and under cover, Cole went to press the detonator switch.

He was interrupted by Jeff.

"Listen," the tradesman said.

"What is it?" Cole snapped, frustrated at the interruption.

"The rain...I think it's s-stopped."

"What?"

Cole raised his hand to the sky, checking for rain.

And then he switched.

EIGHT

He found himself in Red again.

Pissed as a newt, the doctor swigged his bottle of Jack Daniels. A young woman lit his cigarette for him, and Red winked at her in thanks. She seemed cute – he'd have to remember her.

"So, ye bastids," he slurred, "What do you want next?"

"Whisky in the Jar!" someone shouted from the back.

"What? Again?"

"You haven't played it yet!" someone else shouted out.

They were still laughing.

The rain had stopped, but everyone was laughing…

…

… And then Cole was back in his own body.

Everyone was screaming. Some of the men climbed out of the van, ran across the car park towards the hospital. Cole shouted after them, but panic had set in, and no one was listening to a damn thing he said.

Noel was in the van, revving the engine, ready to shoot through. Several Dolls worked at the doors, long arms swiping at the survivors inside.

Another creature was on Jeff. The tradesman screamed for help. There were more screams from the hospital, survivors running everywhere, covered in blood. The Dolls followed. Cole didn't know what to do or where to go first.

He swore loudly.

There was nothing for it. He had to act now.

He found the detonator in his hand, snapped its the switch. The explosion tore through the night, the hospital building shaking. Several bodies were flung from the entrance.

More men screaming, more people bloodied, more limbs dropping to the rain-drenched ground.

Cole stumbled away, suddenly feeling queasy.

He found Jeff on a nearby patch of tarmac. The tradesman was staring right back at him, shaking like a wounded animal, face grimacing and eyes pleading. Two Dolls were working on his gut.

Cole dropped his detonator, slinging his rifle from his shoulder. He fired in Jeff's direction.

The tradesman's body jerked and then was still.

The Dolls continued to feast on his corpse.

Firing small bursts, Cole moved towards the van.

Its wheels were spinning as it shifted backwards and forwards to shake the Dolls hanging onto the sides. One of the doors was flapping against the wind like paper. Cole grabbed it, used it to gain purchase up into the back of the van. Fired against the face of a Doll that was trying to climb in, kicked another back.

He noticed several other survivors hiding in the back of the van.

Pulled the doors closed. "GO!" he yelled at Noel, who wasted no time in putting foot to metal.

Then he was back in the mind of Herbert Matthews…

The old man stood at the window of the control tower, looking down. The creatures gathered below, as if in anticipation of some new and exciting magic trick.

But Herb had no tricks left.

He knew it was the right time to bow to the crowd and exit stage left.

Gently, he pushed himself from the edge of the windowsill, feeling the wind on his face as he fell towards the runway, before the sharp jolt of the rope. His vision blurred, tired old body continuing to swing like a pendulum, hanging over the crowd of creatures, before darkness filled his head.

Cole switched quickly to the head of one of the Dolls.

She watched with the others for a few moments longer, the to-and-fro of the rope hypnotic. There was the sense of enjoyment, of curiosity, but these were nothing compared to the hunger burning within her. The taste of Herb's raw emotion flowed through her veins. She wanted to devour the old man's flesh, to drink his blood, to taste more.

Like all the others, this Doll functioned only to feed. And function was the only word to describe what she did, because she sure as hell wasn't alive. Cole was quite sure that what the old man had suspected, what had been going through his head as he dangled on the rope, was true: these creatures were death personified. They were the very evolution of death.

Growing bored, the Doll turned towards the main airport building. There were a lot of tastes in there,

all kinds of emotions to feast upon. As she looked
towards the nearest door, her hunger intensified.

...

Cole switched again, finding himself in the back of the van.

Noel was shouting, swearing to himself as he drove. The van was belting up the M2.

Cole pursed his lips, breathed out some air. His heart was beating so fast that it felt like it might explode in his chest. He'd never died before in someone else's body. It hadn't been pleasant.

Showgirl looked at him, a single black tear painted on her china-white cheek. She was dressed in a black satin suit and netted hat, as if attending a funeral. "Damn shame," she said, dabbing the corners of her eyes with a handkerchief.

The van moved off the motorway, cutting through Templepatrick, towards the airport. Cole noticed more Dolls crawling out of the woodwork. But Noel wasn't hanging around. His foot was so close to the van's floor that Cole could almost feel the revs in his throat.

Beside him, the others lay in various states of health. Binks glared back, crying again, angry, and Cole wondered what it was the younger man saw in that Doll's face back there.

The Derry man moved to another survivor, whose blood pooled out along the floor of the van where he lay. He tried to administer first aid. Everything and everyone was a mess. Cole couldn't imagine things having turned out any worse.

"What the fuck happened back there?" Noel said to him.

"It's the rain," Cole spat, fingers pressed on a wound that wouldn't stop bleeding. "The fucking rain stopped."

"How the hell are we going to get back into the airport? Those fuckers are going to be everywhere!" yelled Noel, eyes flaring in the rear view.

Cole shook his head.

He caught a glimpse of himself in the window. Looked like one of those fucking Dolls, all panda-eyed and smudged lipstick.

Showgirl was beside him again, dressed now in a 50s-style green khaki shirt. A military hat rested on her head. She held a clipboard, removing a pen from her mouth to scribble something down. "Listen, tiger," she said, "You have to get this sorry crew in order. They'll all die, and you with 'em, if you don't kick 'em into line!" She tipped her glasses with one painted nail, peered over the frames. "So look lively, laddie!"

Cole swallowed hard, turned to the other survivors. "Listen to me!" he screeched, his voice croaking with the strain. "Everyone needs to fight their way inside when we get to the airport."

There were immediate protests.

"If you don't fight, you won't live," Cole insisted.

He looked through the cage to Noel. The older man's hands clung to the steering wheel like his life depended upon it. The roads were becoming progressively more difficult to negotiate, such were the building numbers of Dolls.

This was bad.

NINE

Chef slapped his hand on the bench. He hadn't laughed as hard in God knew how long. He bent over as the stitch in his side grew sharper, his shapeless belly shaking with each wheezing guffaw.

Onstage, Red was the most pissed Chef had ever seen a man. In the doctor's mind, he was no doubt rocking out like Keith Richards, yet to the audience, he sounded more like Keith and bloody Orville.

Chef heard the two-way radio splutter into action. He'd almost forgotten about the bloody mission, what with all the fun.

Slowly, he picked up the receiver, still smiling. "You guys better get back soon or – "

Noel's voice: "Chef! Open the fucking doors!"

Chef placed a finger in one ear, blotting out the noise from the canteen. "Noel? That you? What's wrong, mate?"

"Everything! Get the side door open, and be ready for all hell to break loose. The rain's stopped, Chef. They're here. The bitches are here!"

Shit.

Chef cast a glance to the nearby window. He could see the beads of rain dotted over the glass. But there was no patter, no movement.

He hurried over to the stage, snatched the mic away from the drunken doctor. "Listen up," he said. "Noel and the others are on their way back. I need volunteers to arm up and get down to the side door."

The laughter cleared. Nobody spoke. A pin could have dropped, and no one would have missed it.

Chef rubbed his mouth, cast a glance around the canteen. "Listen, you dimwits, the mission's fucked! We need to get down to the side door, let them back in. Now!"

Still no one moved.

Chef swore, then dropped the mic.

He grabbed Red by his lapels, pulled him close. "You better sober the hell up," he warned. "Cos they're gonna fucking need you down there." He let the doctor go, then moved through the canteen, rallying the crowd. "Come on, people, this is serious. Let's go!"

TEN

The van burst through the gates of the airport, skidded towards the side entrance.

A crowd of Dolls moved in from the car park.

Cole looked to Noel, fear and desperation etched across his face. "Did you get through?" he asked.

"Y-yeah," Noel managed. "Chef answered. Told him to meet us here."

Cole looked out. They were right beside the side door, only metres away. But the Dolls were closing in thick. They needed to move, now, or it would be too late. "Ok, let's go," he said to everyone.

"You must be joking," quizzed Noel. "That door isn't open yet!"

"If we wait any longer you'll not get these fucking doors open!" He kicked his way through, stepped onto the tarmac with baited breath. Raised his rifle, ready for action.

Noel jumped out the driver's door, joined Cole.

The two men stood at either end of the vehicle, Noel armed with a Heckler and Koch USP handgun, Cole with the HK33. They wasted no time in firing at the incoming creatures, Cole's automatic firing in wide arcs to repel the incoming herd.

The other survivors struggled out the back of the van, protected by the covering fire, some helping their comrades. Binks ran ahead on his own. Made it to the side door, started banging furiously and swearing.

The door opened.

A scramble ensued to get indoors.

Some in the airport moved quickly to help Cole's team. Others backed away, shocked by how the bloodied men looked.

One of the Dolls managed to squeeze through the door, but a blast from Chef's shotgun sent her back outside. Another was feasting on Thomas, one of Cole's crew, the poor bastard screaming as she tore into him . Chef's second barrel made the sure he didn't suffer any more. "Get that fucking door closed!" he cried, as he waved the last of the men inside.

Several survivors pressed against the door, while others hacked away at the reaching hands of the Dolls. Several men were pushing a huge metal bin from the kitchen towards the door, hoping to create a temporary blockade. They managed to get it closed, the bin jammed against the join to prevent any further breach.

Chef looked to the wounded men who'd just come through the door, some of them collapsed on the floor, others wandering around in shock. "Help them, for God's sake!" he cried to the doctor.

"I'm trying, damn it!" Red protested. But he was hardly fit to tend to the men. Jimmy the Saint worked to make up for the doctor, and Caz and Barry were ready with blankets and water, approaching the wounded men as they stumbled towards the canteen.

"Jesus," Noel said to Chef, looking around at the carnage. "They've got us now. We're done for."

PART FIVE
THE END

ONE

Weeks passed, and tensions were rising in the airport.

Supplies of just about everything were running low.

The airport looked and felt smaller. A heavy, dull heat gathered throughout the less-ventilated parts of the complex. Condensation broke upon the panoramic windows, rolling down the glass like sweat, a bitter reminder of the rain that used to protect them.

Thousands of creatures waited outside, pining for the survivors within.

But that wasn't all there was to fear.

Chef stood armed and waiting for scavengers at his kitchen. Most of the other food retailers had been ransacked. Men and women were fighting over tins of dried peas and out-of-date Pot Noodles. Water was all but drying up, crude devices placed around the windows to gather the misty sweat from the glass.

Not very many of the survivors had anything to trade.

Star had.

She was busy inking, trading tattoos for cigarettes and alcohol. Her clients were often high or drunk, hoping to distract themselves from the grim reality of their situation. One man quipped how he wanted to be like Jimmy Dean, leave behind a good looking corpse, another survivor asking for script across her neck that read 'Bite Me'. But Star never judged. She just kept inking.

Today she was tattooing Dave Philips. Dressed in pure white linen and wire-rimmed glasses, Dave wasn't the most likely of clients. But he seemed comfortable in the chair, not taut and poised for the bite of the needle like most of her clients. Dave accepted the pain. Acknowledged it as an essential part of the tattooing process.

Red stood by the shop, smoking. He watched Star as she worked. It seemed to relax him.

From the surgery came a different vibe. Cries of pain filled the stagnant air of the complex. The buzz of Star's needle provided momentary relief from the sounds. But they were still putting her off her game.

Star cast an acidic glance at Red. "Can't you shut them up?"

The doctor shook his head, eyes still fixed on Dave's arm. Ink and blood mingled in thick pink streams, inching towards the man's elbow. "I've run out of pain meds. Another one died last night, and there are three others at death's door as we speak."

Red shrugged, continued to watch Star as she worked. It was making the tattooist uncomfortable.

"And what do you want me to do?" Star said, still working the needle. "Perk you up? Tell you it'll be okay?" At that, she stopped tattooing. "Because it won't be okay," she said. "We're all going to die. Simple as."

Red took another drag. "Who pissed in your pants?"

Star smirked, somewhat surprised at the resilience of Red's humour.

She noticed Dave smiling, too. He looked to Red, said, "Death's a part of life. They blend, much like the blood and the ink." He looked down at his arm, watched as Star worked. "It's kind of all I think about, now. It's what this tattoo means for me."

Star pulled back on her chair, looked at what she'd done with the tattoo so far. The pink of the lotus flower was radiant against Dave's pale skin and the deep, dark ebony of the chair's leather. It looked good.

"Go to the top drawer," she said to Red.

She began to work again, continuing to add colour.

Red did as she said, rooting through her top drawer. "What am I looking for?"

"Small envelope at the back."

Red retrieved it and went to give it to her.

"Nah, it's not for me. You take it."

"What is it?" asked the doctor.

"Dope," Star replied, simply. "Cole scored it for me."

Red smiled.

"So, roll yourself a fat one," she continued. "And while you're at it, roll a few for some of those screamers up there." She looked to Dave, winking, before adding, "See if you can help them find their inner peace."

"You big softie," Red said.

"Fuck off," came the reply.

The sound of Chef's voice bellowed from across the way. As Red turned, he noticed the Australian front up against a burly man waving a credit slip at him. "I don't care what that would have bought you before, it'll buy you fuck all now, mate. No more credit. Go and try the sushi parlour or the fucking Chinese around the corner. We're closing up sh– "

Red recoiled as Chef took a punch to the head. Another two men appeared, trying to bulldoze their way through the barriers that the mouthy Australian and his team had erected.

One of the attackers was rugby-tackled out of the way by young Binks.

The other met the business end of Noel's shotgun. "Don't be a bloody fool," he warned.

The man scrambled to his feet, hunger visible across his face. "For fuck's sake", he cried, "I haven't eaten since last week!"

"Not my problem" Noel said. "It's every man for himself now. Go find something of real value to trade, not those fucking credit slips."

The poor bastard looked beat, but there was still venom in his eyes. Red hoped to God it wouldn't get any nastier and was just on his way over to defuse the situation when something else happened.

What looked to be a young woman, her face covered by a hood, ran for the kitchen while the others were distracted. Without warning, Chef turned his gun on the woman, blowing a large chunk of her skull away.

A strike of scarlet spread across the nearby wall like thrown paint.

Red jumped, as if he, himself, had been shot. "Fuck," he swore.

Even Noel looked shocked.

Chef climbed onto the counter of his eatery. Brandished the shotgun like some kind of revolutionary. "L-let that be a warning," he announced. "None of you fuckers try anything, or there'll be more blood spilt. If you've got what we want, we'll trade for food. If not, fuck off somewhere else. I'm fucking serious."

Red moved to the felled woman, his hands in the air to show Chef he meant no harm.

Chef allowed him to come closer.

Red checked the body, finding the young woman still alive, somehow, fighting for breath. She reached for his hand, grabbed it. Her grip was strong, her nails digging into Red's skin.

"Shhh," he said. "It's okay."

But there was nothing okay about this situation. The young woman had lost a large part of her brain. Blood and gore pooled around her body. Her lips were moving. She started to cough, managed to clear her throat, and then took one final breath before her body fell still.

Red felt her grip weaken. He lowered her hand onto her chest.

Stood up, regarded Chef sternly. "Why?" he said.

Chef didn't answer, hands still wrapped around the shotgun, as it worried Red might come and have a go now.

Everyone was watching.

"Somebody help me," Red said.

Nobody moved.

Finally, Jimmy the Saint appeared. In his arms, he carried a blanket. Together Red and Jimmy wrapped the woman's body, then lifted her and took her to Red's surgery.

The other survivors simply stood and watched them leave.

TWO

Where was he?

Caz was worried about Barry Rogan. He'd been missing for a couple of hours. Upped and gone before she woke. Left his few possessions just lying on the floor. His clothes, his shoes. All just sitting where he'd laid them before getting into bed the previous night.

None of the other survivors had seen him.

Caz was beginning to fear the worst.

There had been an increasing number of suicides over the last few weeks, since the rain had stopped. Mostly hangings. Some wrist slicing. A few people had even thrown themselves from the airport roof, into the clutches of the Dolls.

She heard gunfire, reckoned it was another suicide, or maybe Cole on the roof shooting down at the creatures.

None of that concerned her. Barry was the only person she cared about. He had become increasingly withdrawn. Looked awful, his skin pale, sweating a lot. What little sleep he took seemed plagued by nightmares.

Caz needed to find him.

She decided to check back at their bed space again. Maybe he'd simply gone for a walk and was there now, waiting for her.

As she headed back towards the Departure gates, she heard a sound from a nearby set of bathrooms. She stopped, looked towards the sound. Moved closer. Eased the door open and peered in.

The smell nearly caused her to gag. Most of the bathrooms were no-go areas now. Nobody was cleaning them or replacing the chemical toilets that used to be in there. Most people used slop buckets.

Caz covered her nose with the cuff of her sweatshirt, took a few steps through the door. She found the urinals, the white of their ceramic now jaundiced. Next to the urinals ran a line of sinks, a mirror above them. Caz could see the reflection of the cubicles in the mirror. Most of the doors hung open.

One was closed.

The sound of heavy breathing filled the room. It was coming from the closed cubicle.

"Barry?" Caz said.

She padded across the floor, careful to avoid an overturned chemical toilet. Powdered excrement spilled from its mouth. Caz gagged again, fighting to stop herself from throwing up.

She reached the locked cubicle. "Barry?" she said again. "Is that you in there?"

The breathing stopped.

Caz gently knocked the door. "Barry?"

No answer.

She pressed against it, but it was locked. "Barry, it's me. Caz. Come on, I'm worried about you."

Still nothing.

Caz entered the next cubicle across. Flipped the lid of the toilet, climbed on top.

She peered over the side to the locked cubicle, found Barry. He sat on top of the toilet. Head between his legs, a bloody splash of puke on the ground before him. "Jesus, Barry, are you okay?"

She was just about to climb her way over to him when he looked up.

His eyes were spinning.

"Barry?" Caz said.

He stood up, reached for her.

THREE

Barry awoke on the floor of the bathrooms, a pool of blood surrounding him.

He felt pain. It ran through his body in waves, intense around his eyes, his groin – the places where those things had done the most damage to him.

He was cold, shivering.

Yet neither pain nor cold seemed to bother him anymore. He almost enjoyed these feelings, the sting of pain rich and warm, the icy chill of the bathroom floors like some fucking chaser.

What the fuck is happening to me?

Barry pulled himself up, looked around. His eyes were blurred, and he blinked, adjusting to the light pouring in through the windows. He went to the mirror. It was covered with something, and he instinctively wiped it clean with his sleeve, peered in at his reflection.

He looked as he'd always looked. Paler, maybe. Thinner. As his eyes adjusted, he realised that what he'd wiped away from the mirror had been blood.

What the…?

Barry snapped around, eyes searching the length and breadth of the bathrooms. There was blood everywhere, covering the walls and floor like a bad paint job. There were handprints, writing, symbols and pictures, all in blood.

At first, the writing made no sense to him, as if written in a language he couldn't read. But then it clicked with him: the writing was in reverse.

Barry snapped around, stared at the mirrors. This time instead of seeing his own reflection, he saw that of FORGET ME NOT.

She was talking to him, reciting a single word. Barry recognised it as the chorus line from that song she'd been singing to him while he dreamed. The three syllables, recited over and over again:

BLAH-BLAAH-BLAH.

But he could hear it clearly this time.

RE-DEMP-TION, she sang.

The same word was written on the walls of the bathroom, one after the other in long lines.

"No," Barry said to the reflection. "No, leave me alone."

But still she sang, over and over again.

As Barry searched around the bathrooms, he could see the word written in more places. Across the urinals. On the floor, the corners of the mirror.

He checked his own hands, found them covered in blood.

Have I done this?

His eyes found the cubicles. He noticed one was closed.

Barry inched towards it, pressed the door.

Locked.

He stood back, kicked the door once, twice.

The lock broke, the door swinging open.

On the floor by the toilet lay the body of Caroline Donaldson. Her clothes were ripped open. Blood pooled on the floor between her legs. In her hands, she gripped the little crucifix she liked to carry around with her.

Barry went to her, pulled her close, sobbing heavily.

He turned to look at the mirror.

FORGET ME NOT was still there, still singing that word over and over again:

REDEMPTIONREDEMPTIONREDEMPTION.

"It was you," Barry cried. "I'll fucking kill you for this!"

But FORGET ME NOT shook her head, pointed her finger at him.

Barry pulled away from Caz's body, staring again at his hands. "No," he said. "I didn't do this. I couldn't do this!"

He stared back in the mirror, finding the reflection of FORGET ME NOT. Her eyes were no longer Doll-like. They looked through Barry instead of at him. Like she was doped. Barry noticed he was holding something. A brown medicine bottle with pills inside. He knew what these pills were: Rohypnol. He'd used them on FORGET ME NOT and those other girls.

FORGET ME NOT's lips moved. "Redemption," she said, once more.

Barry fell back from the mirror. "No," he said again.

He watched as FORGET ME NOT's eyes changed, starting to flap between various colours. He reached for his own eyes, noticed that they too were flapping in time with hers. He squeezed his eyes shut, held them tight. The sound of flapping seemed to echo around the bathroom. Filling the room.

"No," Barry cried, "No, no, no!"

His eyes snapped open. Looked in the mirror.

FORGET ME NOT was gone, his own reflection where hers was.

He looked back to the cubicle, hoping it was all some dream.

But Caz was still there.

And her body remained still.

Like the rape of those three girls, this had actually happened.

FOUR

Red shook the little box in his hand, finding a single match left. He pulled it out and struck it against the side of the box, lit the joint between his lips. He took a long deep drag, held it for a few moments, before blowing the smoke out again.

He looked at the few remaining patients littering Gate 10's surgery.

The poor fuckers hadn't been fit enough even to take a smoke, so he'd had to feed the dope to them by mouth, using a little whisky to wash it down. It took a little longer to take effect, but they were mostly quiet now. With the screamers doped up, Red felt a little better: watching a man die was bad enough, but the sound effects made it a hell of a lot worse.

But death still thrived in the airport.

Another patient, one of the men who'd been out with Cole, had died that morning. He'd passed while Red was at Star's studio, around about the time of the showdown with Chef.

That made two more bodies in his surgery now.

Jock stood by one of them, the young woman from the canteen. His face was white as a sheet as he looked down upon the young woman's face. She was barely recognisable.

Cole was due any minute. With Jimmy's help, he'd drag the two new bodies up onto the roof, and then throw them over the side. They used to burn them first. Now, even matches were in short supply.

"Real waste," Red said, glancing down at the young woman's body before taking another drag.

Jock looked at the doctor blankly. He was crying.

"Hey, you okay?" Red said, placing a hand on the taller man's shoulder.

Jock wiped the tears away with his sleeve. "What happened?" he asked in a low voice.

"Hell of a thing. She tried to take some food from the canteen. Chef shot her."

Jock looked up, eyes wide with disbelief. "He *shot* her? In cold blood?"

Red shook his head. "Pretty much."

"Did you see it?"

"Yeah, I was there."

"And you did nothing to stop it?"

"It all happened so quickly," Red protested.

Jock was trembling all over. His eyes looked down at the young woman again. "I told her to wait for me," he said, "That I'd get her what she needed, bring it to her. Why didn't she wait?"

"Hey, don't look at her," Red said, leading Jock away. He found a blanket, covered the young woman's face.

Cole and Jimmy showed up, the Derry man nodding to Red as he entered. The doctor pointed to the two bodies and together the two survivors moved to the young woman's body.

Jock watched as they carried her away.

"So you knew her," Red said to him.

"Yeah, I knew her," the pilot replied.

"Had she a name?"

"Aida. Her name was Aida."

"Pretty name," Red said. He patted Jock on the back.

The pilot left the surgery, still in shock. Had Red any more of Star's gear, he would have offered him some. Poor bastard was taking the girl's death pretty bad.

Jesus, she was so young.

He thought again of his own daughter. The phone in his pocket that would never work again with a number that meant nothing, connected to nowhere. Red felt empty inside. Even his own little girl seemed lost to him. He tried to imagine her face but only got the messed-up face of the young woman Cole and Jimmy had taken away.

He turned his attention to Peggy.

Peggy was something of a medical miracle: while the rest of his ward withered and died, the old woman was thriving. She looked about ten years younger. Red wondered why she stayed in the ward at all. He seriously doubted that she was as weak as she made out.

With all that had happened, Peggy had been forgotten. Red had planned to examine her further. A complete blood count was out of the question. It was a long process in the old world, requiring the use of specialised equipment such as a haematology analyser to get the full picture. But Red could improvise manually with the microscope, slides and counting chamber Cole had picked up for him. It would allow him to examine the blood's physical activity more closely, check the blood's basic chemistry.

He remembered back at Whiteabbey Hospital, when Benny had been bitten by those things. The poor bastard's wound had looked peculiar, the blood in particular reacting very abnormally. He remembered it looking darker than it should. Red knew then that there was something wrong with Benny, and he suspected that the same might be wrong with Peggy and Barry, and just about anyone else those things had left their mark on. He'd mulled it over in his head, considering how the human body acted like an alkaline battery. Thus, when its blood pH level became too acidic, it wouldn't function properly. As a result, energy would decrease, cells wouldn't communicate properly, and the body's natural defence would deteriorate. Red could examine the blood cells, look out for increased activity within the white blood cells, see if there were something new in the system trying to manipulate or destroy the body.

Carefully, Red took a fresh needle and pricked the skin of the old woman's thumb. It took a while, the blood seeming reluctant to come at all. Red squeezed until enough dripped onto the slide, near the edge, then pressed some cotton wool over the laceration, pausing to secure it with a sticky plaster.

Red then took the slide over to his desk. He picked a second slide, holding it at a forty-degree angle and dropped it onto first slide, sandwiching the blood. He then placed the sample onto the tray of the microscope, above the light source, and leaned in closer to look at it through the eye piece. Red adjusted the magnification to around 500/1.

What he saw was quite spectacular.

He rubbed his eyes, looked again, lest he was getting the colours wrong. But it looked the same. There was a new blood cell attacking the others. At first, Red had thought it might be a dark red, but it was deeper than that: this new blood cell was black. And it was killing all the other blood cells, then adopting their functions.

He retrieved the scope, looked at the blood with his naked eye. Even then he could see a difference: the blood seemed to be behaving like that of Benny's: pulsating, congealing when it should still be fluid.

Red leaned back in his chair, thinking for a while. *What the hell can this all mean?*

Behind him, Peggy's eyes suddenly opened. Red pupils stared at the back of the doctor's head. Her skinny little arm reached forward, pulling herself up. She rose from the bed, clambered to her feet. Reached for the doctor, just as he turned, curled her veiny hands around his neck.

Red recoiled from her attack, but he was unable to shake her off completely. Her grip was tight. Red's eyes welled up as he slapped uselessly at her face. No air was getting in. He couldn't even scream.

Then it was over, as fast as it began: Red felt a splash against his face – a sickly, mucus-like substance clouding his eyes. The hands on his neck loosened. Peggy's body fell dead, crashing to the floor by the feet of Barry Rogan.

The young survivor stood wielding a large kitchen knife in his hand.

"What have those bitches done to me?" he said.

FIVE

Cole watched the corpse of Herbert Matthews swinging in the wind from the rope that hung down from the control tower's window.

In his hands, Cole held his HK33 rifle. It was loaded with a fresh clip. A scope was fitted to the top, and he looked through it, finding the old man's face. Flies circled around the decaying flesh, the old man's eyes wide open, looking dry and sun scorched, like the eyes of dead fish.

Cole moved the crosshairs of the scope, finding the thin fibres of the rope. He aligned the crosshairs with the rope, waiting until his hand steadied before he fired.

The first burst was off.

Cole readjusted his aim before firing again.

The second burst connected, dropping the body like a bag of coal into the waiting crowd of Dolls below.

Cole looked up from the scope, studied the scene.

The Dolls moved in like a pack of hungry dogs, dipping towards Herb's fallen body. An almighty din filled the airport complex as they became excited, their eyes changing.

Cole looked again through the scope, finding one Doll in particular. She was blonde. He liked blondes, liked how this one's hair glistened in the sun. He watched as her eyes switched between colours. Her body, lithe and fresh, swayed with the rhythm, as if every limb was connected to the same fucked-up socket as her peepers. A raw, primal energy raged through her like a wild dog – feral, hungry and frothing at the mouth.

She was dead – they all were dead – but death seemed to have changed in Belfast. That was pretty much the conclusion Cole had come to.

He knew this because, ever since the night when the rain had stopped, Cole had been spending a lot of time in the minds of others. Survivors, Dolls, it didn't matter. With the survivors, all he felt was hopelessness. The dull, heavy beat of their hearts. Heavy breathing. The knotted feeling in their guts and dry throats. These were people who feared death, who expected it every second, yet still feared it.

But inside the Dolls felt different. There was no fear. No sense of mortality. These were creatures who had already tasted death, who had gone beyond death, to a realm of existence that made no sense to Cole.

Herbert Matthews had known that. Cole had seen it in his mind as he sat on the control tower's window ledge, staring down at the Dolls. And now that Cole knew it, it changed everything for him.

A banshee-like shriek rang from the blonde's lips. A shrill, glass-splintering anger that was like a riot in his brain. It was annoying his *other* Voices. The ones that had been in Cole's head since fuck-knew-when – the ones that were articulate, that helped him make sense of the world. These Voices didn't like her Voice. It seemed uncouth. Showgirl was using her bra-cups to cover her ears. Rabbit was trying to ram his imaginary head up his imaginary arse and, what with being an imaginary Voice with an imaginary, self-deprecating personality, seemed to be succeeding. That made Cole smile. Sometimes he hated that fucking bunny.

Cole set the rifle down. Rubbed one hand across his shorn head, hoping to ease his clanger of a headache. This was all he needed. Something had to be done.

He lifted the rifle again. Loaded one bullet – only one. He aimed squarely at Blondie. Waited until his hands had steadied. Breathed in and then fired. The blast of the rifle cracked against his face like an electric shock. He watched Blondie's head snap back like an elastic band, a thin spray of scarlet dampening all around her. She fell into the throng. None of the others seemed bothered.

Cole looked up from the scope. He sat the rifle down carefully. Breathed in and then out again.

He waited once again for the Voices inside his head. Showgirl lifted one of her bra cups from her ears, listening as if for a change. Rabbit had managed to shove the entire girth of his head well and truly up his arse – ironically, Cole thought, he probably couldn't hear shit.

"Did you get her?" asked Showgirl, her pouting lips poised.

"Yep."

"Good boy!" She blew him a kiss.

"Just don't tell Rabbit…" he whispered, smirking.

They both laughed.

Nearby, ninety-nine pairs of eyes stared back from ninety-nine expressionless faces. One of their number began to shake, as if dancing. Her eyes were glittering.

Death was on the move, again.

SIX

Jock was going to kill Chef.

He couldn't do it now. He was too fucked up; he'd get himself killed. No, he had to wait, gather his senses.

Think things through.

Pick his moment.

He made his way back to the storage rooms. He'd gather his stuff, get himself ready for a quick getaway after he'd taken care of business. The chopper was still on the roof. He would make straight for it after he'd –

Jock stopped in his tracks. Narrowed his eyes.

In the gloom of the corridor, he could make out a figure. Someone at the door to the storeroom they'd been staying in.

Fuck.

"Hey," Jock called.

The figure stopped, looked around. "Jock?"

Fucking Binks. Jock knew that high-pitched little whine of his anywhere. "Yeah, it's me. What are you doing out here?"

Binks sniffed. Turned to face Jock. "Chef sent me. We're looking somewhere to store some stuff. Keep it safe. Didn't know anyone came up here. Guess we'll have to look elsewhere, eh?"

"Nah," Jock said. "This isn't a bad spot. And I can keep a secret, just as long as you cut me in on the deal."

Binks looked uncomfortable. "Maybe," he said. "I'll run it past Chef, see what he thinks…"

"Why don't you take a look inside?" Jock said. "Get a feel for the place. Size, storage space, that kind of thing."

"I don't know…"

"Sure you do," Jock said.

He grabbed Binks by the hair and slapped his head against the door. Pulled him back then slapped again. The attack left a smear of blood across the dirty wall. Binks cried out, but Jock pulled him close. "Want you to meet a friend," he said.

He opened the door, shoved Binks into the storage room, watching as the younger survivor tumbled to the floor. It was dark, the power in this side of the complex cut off to conserve what little juice the generator had left. Kirsty was in the corner waiting, hissing. The sound of skin hitting skin filled the room.

"Aida's dead," Jock cried, tears breaking from his face. "They killed her. This little cunt was one of them." His voice grew louder. "Do you understand me?" He yelled to the creature. "Do you understand a single fucking word I've just said?"

Kirsty emerged from the shadows, her eyes the deepest shade of red that Jock had ever seen. She lit upon Binks like a starving wolf, tore into him with abandonment. Peeled his skin away, gutted him. Sliced his throat, drank his blood greedily.

"Yeah," Jock mused. "You understand alright…"

…

When she was done, Kirsty returned to the shadows.

Jock leaned against the wall, tears streaming down his face in thick salty trails. He wiped them with his sleeve, but more came. His belly felt hollow, like Binks wasn't the only one who'd been gutted. His mouth was dry, coarse. Still the tears came.

In his hands, he fumbled with the revolver. It was loaded, was always fucking loaded; all he ever seemed to do was load and unload that damn thing.

He looked at the bloodied body of Binks.

Cunt had had it coming.

God, what Jock would give for Chef to come up here on his own. He'd been the one who had pulled the trigger, after all. Kirsty had the taste for it now; Jock could feed them all to her. Throw Noel and that dimwit Archie in to boot.

But that wasn't what he wanted. He needed to take care of business on his own. He'd slice their fucking nuts off, then finish the job with the gun. Three bullets would do it if he got right up close, one for each of the cunts. Hit them between the eyes. Straight through the fucking brain.

That left three more bullets.

He thought of Red. The doctor hadn't given a fuck about Aida. Left her all messed up, lying like a slab of meat. No respect for the dead. He'd get it too.

Two bullets left.

The final shot was for himself. God knew, he didn't want to live any more. What the hell was there to live for? Once the creatures got in, it was game over. They wouldn't go easy on any of them.

And the other bullet?

He looked towards the corner of the room.

Kirsty.

He should have killed her a long time ago, he knew that now. But Aida wouldn't have liked that.

Well, Aida was dead now.

Kirsty was hiding. It was like she knew what was happening, what Jock was thinking. As she saw the gun, she twisted against the wall, covered her belly protectively with her arms.

The gun shook in Jock's hands. "Fuck," he swore. "Do it, for Christ's sake!"

But he couldn't. Something stopped him.

He remembered that Asian girl he was banging, back when he was running dope in Tibet. She was only a child. Barely sixteen. Christ, he wasn't that old himself at the time, but sixteen was still a bit of a stoop even then. He remembered her old man coming for him one night. The stupid bitch had gone and got herself pregnant and hadn't told him till it was too late to do anything about it. Jock had tried to run. Her daddy caught him in one of the local watering holes, beat seven shades of shit out of him while his little girl stood and watched.

Yeah, I'm a real boy scout.

Christ knew, he was far from it. Jock had treated women horribly through his life, didn't give a damn, and now one had gone and got herself killed, and broke his fucking heart.

He lowered his revolver.

Sat down on the bed, put his head into his hands.

He felt something touch him, looked up to find Kirsty. She reached for his hand, unclenched his fist. Dropped something into his palm.

Jock raised his hand, straining his eyes to see what she'd given him. It looked to be a string of grass, only thicker. It was dry, decaying. He could make out a bud, some petals. Looked like the stem of a small flower.

A daisy, maybe.

Jock closed his fingers over it.

The creature turned away, shook her head angrily. The eyes started flapping again, and Jock looked up to see what had disturbed her.

He found someone else in the room...

SEVEN

Red primed his needle for taking another blood sample. His hand was still shaking from the attack, the corpse of his attacker still on the floor, amongst the beds of his makeshift ward.

Barry Rogan waited on the nearby seat. He looked terrible.

"Look, are you sure about this?" Red asked him.

"Yes," he said. "Do it."

Red inserted the needle, struggling to puncture the tough skin. He strained, pressing the needle with greater force.

Barry grimaced.

Red finished up quickly, pressed some cotton wool against Barry's skin.

He held the slide up with his other hand, looked at the contents, then carried it to the microscope. Recoiled with shock as the slide exploded in his hand, glass and red-hot blood showering his white lab coat and tearing a hole right through it.

"Sweet Christ!" Red pulled the coat off, threw it to the ground. The blood continued to burn through, working its way through the floor as it disintegrated the coat.

He turned to Barry, only then noticing how the younger man's eyes had changed colour, flashing a deep shade of purple.

Red backed away.

Barry stood up, closing his eyes and then shaking his head as if possessed, fighting to retain control.

"B-Barry?" Red probed.

The younger survivor cried out, his deep voice finally giving way to a vile shrill. Before his eyes, Red watched as Barry swung around to glare at each bed beside him, then descend upon the wounded, dipping his mouth into their heavily-doped bodies like a dog into meat. He ripped chunks out of their still-breathing torsos, shoving the flesh into his mouth, guzzling at the fountains of blood that squirted with each tear.

"F-fuck me," mouthed the doctor.

Barry stopped, looked up at him.

Red ran.

EIGHT

"It's one of them," said Cole, eyes fixed on the heavily-pregnant Kirsty Marshall. "You brought one of them here?"

"It's not that simple," Jock tried to explain. "She's different…"

"How?" Cole asked. He wasn't angry. He seemed more confused than anything. But his rifle remained fixed on both Jock and the pregnant creature. The Scotsman knew he needed to make his case clearly and quickly; both patience and humanity were wearing thin at the airport.

"She's pregnant."

"She's what?"

"Pregnant. Up the fucking spout."

"Fuck." Cole gingerly lowered his rifle.

As Jock watched on, the Derry man stepped towards the bed, reached his hand out, ran it across Kirsty's belly.

The Doll allowed him, staring up at his eyes, as if reading something there.

"Christ," Cole said, pulling his hand away again and stepping back. He looked to Jock again. "When is it due?"

"What?"

"The baby. When is it due?"

"How the fuck do I know?" Jock protested. "I'm not even convinced it is a baby in there."

"Well, how long has it been?"

"How long has what been?"

"Since she got pregnant."

Jock raised his hands, palms facing forwards. "Look, I haven't a fucking clue how it happened, or how long, or any of that bullshit. All I know is one minute she looked like all the others, and the next she's like this."

"Have you told anyone else?"

"No."

"We have to. This changes – "

"Everything," Jock cut in. "I know that. But you know what those people will do if they find her. Hell, they're tearing each other apart out there; what will they do to her?" Jock sighed heavily. "Please," he begged. "Don't tell them."

Cole looked again to the Doll. He closed his eyes, tried to flip into her mind. He felt his breathing quicken, his heart swell. And then he was inside her head, searching, feeling.

It was different inside Kirsty Marshall.

He could see her soul, her memories, and many of them felt human.

He could see her with her husband. They were playing with their child in the park. Laughing, calling the child's name. A dog ran across the grass beside them, barking gleefully. The child was throwing a ball. It didn't go very far, but the dog ran dutifully to it each time, scooping it up in its mouth, then running back to the child. Dropping the ball, then waiting, its little tail wagging.

Cole could feel the Doll's love for the child. It filled every part of her. Raced through her blood as if alive in its own right.

He watched as Kirsty relaxed onto the grass, sitting on a blanket and taking a drink. She reached casually for a daisy, started to pluck at its petals, smiling.

Cole reached for another memory, found a more recent one. It felt different, darker.

A small, middle-aged man dragged her body across the grass towards what looked to be the mobile classroom at a school. He opened the doors, looked around, then pulled Kirsty inside. He paused for a moment, catching his breath, before stooping by her body, opening his flies and pulling his trousers and pants down. Cole watched as the odious little bastard massaged his cock, before arching over Kirsty's corpse and entering her.

Cole wanted to look away, but he couldn't. It was like the Doll was stopping him, needing him to see this. He watched through her eyes as the man lay across her, his face red and sweaty, drawing close to her ear. The sound of his panting and groaning filled Cole's mind. His rough hands groped the Doll's motionless body, his pelvis thrusting faster, harder until he began to shake, and the warmth of his cum sprung up within her.

Cole felt a kick in the Doll's swollen belly, causing her to cry out.

The face of her child, little Nicky Marshall, filled his head, blending with a light tapping sound, coming from inside the Doll's body. Cole reached further inside Kirsty's flesh with his mind, past the stillness of her heart, the hollow lungs, the gut, finding her womb. The sound grew stronger, and Cole realised it belonged to whatever grew inside there. He reached further, desperate to find out more, but something pulled him away, and he flipped back out of the creature.

He was in the storage room again, Jock shaking him, trying to bring him back. "Cole, listen to me. We need to leave. Something's happening."

Cole tuned in to the noises filling the airport. Screams, shouting. The all-too-familiar shriek of Dolls. He grabbed Jock by the shoulders, looked into his eyes. "That thing growing inside her. It's alive," he cried. "*Really* alive."

Jock regarded him suspiciously. "You sure about that?"

"I'm sure."

Jock sighed. "Jesus, why are you doing this to me?" he asked no one in particular. Looked back to Cole, said, "We have to get her out of here."

"And go where?" He was still reeling from the memories and feelings of the Doll. The Voices in his own mind were mute, staring at him with open mouths.

Showgirl was the first to speak, wiping a tear from her eye and telling him, "You've got to help her. Nobody should go through what she went through. She needs you, man."

Cole looked back to the door, thought about the other survivors out there.

Thought about Star.

Jock was helping the Doll to her feet. He gently led her to the door of the storage room.

He looked to Cole, the other survivor still dumbfounded. The sounds from the main complex grew stronger. Whatever was coming towards them would be on them in seconds. "For Christ's sake, come on, man!" he said.

NINE

The canteen was in turmoil. Barry Rogan stood over the corpse of a young woman, the nails of his fingers raking into her flesh, scooping out handfuls of her innards. People were screaming, scattering in all directions.

Chef came out of the kitchen, looked at Noel. "What the hell's going on?"

"Those things. I t-think they've broken in!" Noel cried.

Chef raised his shotgun, pulled back the hammer. Everyone looked like a target; he couldn't take a chance with anyone. He fired once, emptying the first barrel, the shot spreading an older woman's face across the canteen wall. His second shot tore through the gut of another woman, this one running for the kitchen.

Chef swore, fought to reload.

Red approached him. "Stop it," he cried. "You're shooting people, for God's sake! Innocent people!"

The doctor noticed Barry Rogan again, now at the side exit of the airport, pulling back the recently erected barricade, wrenching the doors from their welded hinges with inhuman strength.

An endless stream of creatures poured into the airport.

"Oh no," Red lamented.

The creatures attacked without mercy, hunting the survivors with gusto, blood spraying like red mist as they burrowed through the densely populated canteen.

Red fell to his knees, deflated. There was nothing to do but wait, and then die.

A single creature approached him. She had red hair and a t-shirt that read FORGET ME NOT. She stood in front of Red, glaring at him with an almost affectionate smile on her face.

Red looked at her, and his eyes watered. He stood up, touched her face, ran his fingers across her mouth. "Julie?"

Her head twisted to the side, leaning into his caress. Her eyes started shifting between colours, the dark shade of red fading to a melancholic blue. Tears of blood rolled down her cheeks, and Red caught them with his finger.

She stabbed his chest with her fist, piercing his skin and breaking through his ribs. Her fingers tore through his flesh, curling around his still beating heart and ripping it from his body.

Red's eyes swelled, then died.

TEN

The carnage spread throughout the airport like a virus. Star looked through the windows of her studio. Latched the door, then turned to man sitting in her chair.

Dave Phillips smiled sadly at her. "End of the road," he said.

Star nodded, then ran her eyes over the work she'd just done on his arm. "I think we still got time to finish this."

Dave laughed. "You think?"

"Yeah." She stopped to wipe his arm, then looked at it again. "Just a little more colour and we're done."

Dave pulled his glasses off, calmly wiped his eyes. Replaced the glasses, said, "I'm ready."

Star settled herself on the stool and retrieved her needle.

As her machine whirred into action for the last time, bodies continued to fall in the canteen.

Noel fired at will, his shells piercing survivor and dead alike in the messy fury of the fight. Behind him, Chef reloaded once again then opened fire in a similarly cavalier fashion. They moved back towards the kitchen store's door, Archie already inside, calling to them.

The horde drew thick around them, and Noel was caught unawares by a tall, blonde creature wearing a police uniform. He screamed to his boss for help, but there was little that could be done. Chef took aim, putting his final shell through the other man's head.

He spotted Jimmy the Saint under one of the tables in the kitchen, hands over his ears. Called to him, but the younger survivor couldn't hear. Swearing, Chef darted under the table, grabbing Jimmy and pulling him out the other end, as several creatures slithered towards them, slipping on the freshly polished tiles.

Chef and Jimmy made it through the storeroom door, and Archie slammed it closed behind them. They fought to quickly barricade the door, using the heavy gas cylinders as leverage.

Across the way, Star was putting the finishing touches to Dave Phillps' tattoo.

The creatures hammered at the door to her studio, beating the glass with their fists, finally breaking it down.

Star finished one last stroke, dropped the machine, then rammed her trolley at the door, straining to hold it closed.

Dave pulled himself up from the chair, flexed, moved to the mirror at the other side of the shop. Checked his arm.

"You like it?" Star said, still working the trolley.

"Love it," Dave said. He winked at her.

"I'm glad," Star said.

The trolley slid from the door, the creatures bursting in.

They were on Dave in seconds, digging into him with their claws and teeth as the tattooist watched.

Star grabbed the bottle of isopropyl, fumbled in her pockets for her Zippo. She sparked it, placed it to the muzzle of the bottle and squirted furiously. A burst of flame left the end of the bottle, engulfing both Dave and the Dolls. Their screams filled the shop.

Another of them was on her, and Star dropped the empty spray bottle and lifted the autoclave from a nearby bench. She brought the damn thing down heavily on the bitch's head, flooring it, then dropping the autoclave, finishing the job by slamming the heel of her boot down on the creature's neck.

She reached for another of the creatures, slapping her across the face, screaming "What have you done to me?" Grabbed a pack of needles from the trolley, rammed them through the thing's eyes. "WHAT HAVE YOU DONE TO ME?"

More swarmed the shop, but Star was on them, raking her own nails across their flesh, biting into them as they bit into her. In the mirror, she could see her own eyes burning a deep, dark red, her tattoos seeming to take on a life of their own, the Medusa on her neck snarling, its snake hair leaping out from her skin at the surrounding creatures.

And in that moment, Star died. In death, she became something different, something powerful, something with less restrictions, no longer a slave to the skin she'd felt so uncomfortable within for most of her life, no longer enslaved by her mind, her conscience, her past, her mortality.

She pulled away from the others, lifted her hands up. Her eyes slipped back in her head, and she cried out in unison with the other dead things around her.

ELEVEN

A shrill cry rang throughout the corridor.

Cole swung around, nervously. "What was that?"

Jock glared at him. "What do you think it was?"

He cast a glance at Kirsty. The pregnant creature was slow. They'd need to pick up pace, or the creatures would be on top of them.

"Up there," Jock said, pointing towards the ladder dead ahead. "Quickly, go."

"You first," Cole said.

Jock rested Kirsty to the floor, then climbed the ladder.

Cole slung his rifle from his shoulder, waited.

They hadn't much time. The Dolls would be on them in seconds: Cole could hear the clatter of their footsteps echoing throughout the corridor.

Jock opened the hatch, climbed onto the rooftop. Cole helped Kirsty climb the first few rungs of the ladder, and together the other two survivors lifted her up through the hatch.

Cole followed suit, then turned to reseal the hatch, but he was too late. A hand reached through, made a grab for him. Cole fell back as the first of the Dolls clambered up onto the roof. "They're here!" he cried.

Jock was in the helicopter, firing up the engines. The rotors kicked in, spinning slowly at first, before speeding to a frenzy.

Cole reached for Kirsty, tried to help her up, but she wouldn't move. She lay on the ground, arched back, a painful grimace spreading across her face. An unholy shriek broke from her lips as what looked to be blood sprayed out from between her legs.

The Dolls filled the rooftop, surrounding Kirsty and Cole in a wide arc, pacing them.

Cole fired, the hail of bullets from his muzzle tearing through their first line.

He turned back to Kirsty. Watched as her body shook, and her legs spread wide. Her swollen belly pulsated as her offspring spewed out from under her skirt, then slopped onto the rooftop floor.

"Jesus Christ," Cole said.

His eyes were fixed on the child, his rifle raised.

The child started to cry.

Cole closed his eyes, trying to flip inside its head, to read it…

In his mind, Showgirl stood by a cot, dressed in pure white. In the cot was Nicky Marshall, Kirsty's son during life. Showgirl was spinning a mobile fixed above the child, cooing gently. She noticed Cole, smiled.

Cole moved over to the cot, looked in.

The child stared back up at him. Cole reached one shaking hand inside the cot, the child accepting it, curling its own tiny hand around the Derry man's little finger. And in that instant, Cole felt its warmth. The base needs and desires within its tiny little brain. Its innocence. The beat of its heart, the swelling of its lungs.

The child was alive.

Cole opened his eyes, finding himself face to face with a line of Dolls. They stood opposite, Kirsty and the child next to him.

The helicopter was still running, but Jock was out of it, now stooped over Kirsty Marshall. The creature seemed in pain, the baby still crying between her legs. The umbilical cord ran from her womb like a thick vine. Blood slicked across the child's skin like fresh tar.

Cole stared at the child, then at Jock. "Cut it," he yelled. "Cut the fucking cord." He pulled a knife from his belt, threw it to Jock.

Jock grabbed the knife, looked to the cord, then to Kirsty. He stooped to the ground, started cutting. It was like sawing through iron chains. He was making no headway at all. "Can't do it!" he cried.

The rotors on the helicopter continued to gather speed.

Cole dropped one mag, inserted another. The Dolls were lining up to attack again.

He looked to Jock. "Hurry!"

"I can't. This fucking thing's like steel."

Kirsty bent forward, started swiping at the cord herself. Her nails cut through with ease, like she was slicing cheese. The child continued to cry, waving its arms around. It was cold, frightened, confused.

Jock pulled his jacket off, gathered the child up in his arms. Looked to the other survivor. "Come on," he said.

Cole turned to him, a despondent look across his face. "No," he said. "You go without me."

Kirsty struggled to her feet, head tipping to the side.

Jock went to reach for her, but she pulled away. Hissed at him, and then turned back to the gathered Dolls.

"Go," Cole said again to Jock. "Take the child and go."

Reluctantly, Jock retreated across the roof, dipping his head as he approached the chopper. He slowly climbed in, rested the child in the co-pilot's seat, pulled the goggles over his eyes and reached for the stick.

Back on the roof, Cole looked to Kirsty and nodded.

The Dolls thundered forward.

Cole unloaded his fresh mag. Several made it through, one Doll, a small mousey thing with bobbed hair, slicing her nails across his neck. The Derry man fell to his knee, both hands reaching for his throat. His whole face shook as blood gushed through the wound, the world spinning around him as he gasped for air.

But Kirsty moved to him, pulling the Doll away and tearing her own nails across its face. She fought brutally, standing her ground as they rushed her, knowing that the longer she was able to hold the line, the better chance little Nicky stood of surviving.

As his eyes began to cloud over, Cole heard the helicopter's engine roar as it lifted off the ground.

EPILOGUE

Chef watched as the storeroom door bent against the force of the creatures outside. He could hear the roar of their voices by the door, one voice more hoarse than the others, Chef suspecting it to be the voice of Barry Rogan.

Never liked that prick, he mused.

Against the far wall, Archie sat with his bottle cradled to his chest, shivering, one eye swollen and closed over, the other wide and moist.

Jimmy was crying. "I don't want to die," he blubbered, snot and tears shiny on his round face.

"I know, mate." Chef said. "I know…"

He reached for one of the gas cylinders stacked by the door. Carefully, he unscrewed its nozzle, releasing the gas into the stuffy air. He worked on the other cylinders, doing likewise.

He waited for a while, then sat himself back on the floor. Pulled the distraught Jimmy to his side and comforted him. And when it looked like the doors were just about to burst, Chef lit his final cigar, managing to inhale one last puff before the roar of flames ripped through the storeroom like the breath of an angry god, blowing the doors, blowing away Barry Rogan's head and the head of every bitch within a mile's radius.

...

Their helicopter swayed in the blow-out as the airport below them crumbled in the explosion. The runway was littered with flaming debris and torn body parts. From his vantage point, climbing into the sky, Jock watched a line of Dolls streaking across the runway, doused in fire.

"Jesus H. Christ," he breathed.

Several beads of water fell upon the glass windscreen of the chopper. Soon, the rain fell heavier, beating furiously upon the airport grounds. The sky darkened. Lightening flashed, followed by a deep-throated roll of thunder.

Jock looked at the child wrapped in his jacket beside him. He could see it was a little boy. The lad had stopped crying and now just stared up at the rotors, watching them as they spun.

"Where to, mate?" Jock asked him.

The child glanced over at his voice with wide eyes.

Acknowledgements

First and foremost, I would like to thank my readers, past, present and future.

Thanks also to Grant 'Moph' Wastle, Garry Charles, Dave Lightfoot, Jan Moat, Martin Hancox, Sween and Staff Nurse Leigh Adamson for all the tech help.

Huge thanks to all the booksellers who have supported me, in particular: Steven Caunt, Sam Cowling, Trevor Proctor, David Torrans and everyone at FPI Belfast.

To Dave Phillips: thanks for your generosity and patience. Hope you enjoyed the cameo!

Thanks also to my agent, Gina Panettieri, and everyone at Snowbooks.

To anyone I've forgotten: Sorry! And thank you!

And finally, to Rebecca: Thanks for your love, support and belief in what I do.

ABOUT THE AUTHOR

Belfast born, Wayne Simmons has been kicking around the horror scene for years. He penned reviews and interviews for several online zines before publication of his debut novel in 2008. Wayne's work has since been published in the UK, Germany and Spain.

Wayne currently lives in Wales with his ghoulfiend and a Jack Russel terrier called Dita.

Look out for Wayne at various genre and tattoo cons, or visit him online:

http://www.waynesimmons.org